D0969253

SCAPEGOAT

A PATRICK FLINT NOVEL

PAMELA FAGAN HUTCHINS

SKIPJACK PUBLISHING

FREE PFH EBOOKS

AUTHOR'S NOTE

I like to use real settings, but, in *Scapegoat*, I have made up a river and a guard station. They may bear similarities to an actual river and guard station, but they're not the same ones. You won't find them on any map. However, they are as close to authentic as I can make them.

CHAPTER ONE: LOCK

Jackson, Wyoming
Thursday, June 23, 1977, 10:00 a.m.

Patrick

Patrick Flint kept a tight grip on his wallet as the owner of Wyoming Whitewater pulled out a pencil and tallied up the damages, tongue out and eyes squinted. The shop was in a musty log cabin near downtown, close enough to the Jackson Hole Historical Society & Museum to taunt Patrick. He was dying to see their new exhibits—one on the history of bighorn sheep in the area and another on the Mountain Shoshone or "Sheep Eater" Indians who had inhabited the surrounding high country since long before the advent of Yellowstone as a national park.

He glanced over his shoulder. Out the front windows, the green stripes of ski runs crisscrossed the face of the mountains that were crowding the downtown area. It was pretty, but it paled next to the wonders he'd seen in the previous twenty-four hours. During their drive to Jackson that morning after camping near Dubois, Patrick had been amazed by the sharp granite teeth of peaks in the Shoshone National Forest. By the prominence of stately Gannett, the highest peak in the state. By the high sagebrush flats in the Wind River Range. In fact, the whole drive from Buffalo to Jackson had further cemented his belief that Wyoming was the wildest and most beautiful state in the nation. From the bright red cliffs of the Chugwater Foundation, to the range of colors in the palette of the arid western slope of the Bighorns, to the high canyons, gorges, and gulleys carved by wind and water. But by far his greatest moment of wonder was his first glimpse of the iconic skyline of the jagged Cathedral Group peaks. Grand Teton's rocky, snow-topped spire stood above the rest, basking in the mid-morning sun.

His skin actually tingled with anticipation. He couldn't wait to get out into the wilderness, where he felt closest to nature, his true self, and the majesty of the Almighty, but the shop owner's voice drew him back around.

"You want four canoes, eight paddles, and eight life jackets, for three days. Canoeing the backcountry. Like in the movie *Deliverance*. Or, actually, let's hope it's *not* like *Deliverance*." Patrick had never seen *Deliverance,* and he had no idea what the man was talking about. "That comes out to . . ." The owner, whose name was Brock, quoted a number and brushed sun-bleached curls from his eyes with his other hand. Mid-to-late twenties, tall and stooped, looking more California cool than Wyoming rough and ready. He also gave off an odor like he'd poured most of a bottle of cheap cologne down his chest. No self-respecting mountain man left the house smelling like that. "Anything else, man?"

Patrick groaned. Not for the first time, he compared the cost of the extra gas he would have used if he'd borrowed the gear and equipment back in Buffalo, to the rental total. Just when he'd been about to hit up his friend and co-worker Wes Braten to make the trip with them and pull one of the trailers, his wife Susanne had put the kibosh on the plan. She didn't like the idea of caravanning with trailers through multiple mountain ranges, regardless of the savings he'd projected. Patrick had been disappointed and not just because of the expense. Wes and his International Harvester Travelall, "Gussie", were a rugged pair and good to have along.

"Do you offer any kind of volume discount?" Patrick suggested a lower number.

Brock laughed. "It's 1977, not 1957, you know? That's my best price. And you won't find a better deal in the western part of the state." He straightened the shoulders on his t-shirt, light green with short-sleeves and the words LUNCH COUNTER below a graphic of a turbulent river. Identical shirts hung on a carousel rack. Shelves displayed sunscreen, Chapstick, hats, insect repellant, and bumper stickers with the state flag. Elsewhere on racks, the shop offered life jackets, paddles, seat cushions, and much more. In one corner, a cooler contained drinks and snacks for sale. The walls showed off an array of action photos on various local rivers, mostly the famous Snake River. The showpiece of the place was an ancient rowboat that no longer looked like it would stay afloat. A nameplate was affixed to its stern. SNAKE CHARMER.

"All right, then." What Brock said about the price was true. Patrick knew, because he had called all the shops in Jackson. And in Cody. "What's that mean on your shirt, 'Lunch Counter?'"

"It's a super awesome rapid on the Snake River. You wouldn't want to go down that in canoes. Or anything but a nice, big raft. The water is moving at fifteen hundred cubic feet per second, just like you'll find on the Tukudika. But two of my buddies are convinced they can surf it."

"With surf boards?"

"Yeah. But they'll probably die trying." He grinned. "There'd be less competition for guides on the river then."

A bell dinged, and a cool breeze swept through the building. Wyoming could be warm during June in Jackson Hole—the wide, flat 6000-feet elevation valley on the west side of the Continental Divide, between the Tetons and Gros Ventre mountain ranges—but it often wasn't. The paper the owner had been writing on levitated and tumbled through the air. Patrick chased it and stomped on it. He wanted to check the math.

Before he could, the floor creaked and familiar voices reached his ears.

"There's my boy." The tinkle of bells. That's what he thought of when Lana Flint spoke.

He turned and caught sight of her. His mother was dressed as if for an African safari, only jauntier, with a pink and red scarf tied around her neck. *Probably one of her own designs.* She had worked as an inhouse designer for a clothing manufacturer ever since his youngest sister Patty, his daughter Trish's namesake, had left for college.

"Hi, Mom." He continued naming his family members as they filed into the store. "Dad. Pete. Vera." Then his throat dried, and his words stuck. "And the . . . the . . . rest of you."

Patrick had thought his brother Pete and Pete's young wife Vera were traveling without their kids, but he counted all seven of their young brood behind them. The oldest, Annie, scowled at two brown-headed boys. Stan and Danny. The three of them were Pete's birth children. Vera's kids were tow-headed and freckled. Brian was holding the hand of Bunny, the youngest, and Bert and Barry were peeking around their big brother's shoulders.

"Just call them the seven dwarves," Joe Flint didn't crack a smile under his thin mustache. The older Flint—shivering in brown corduroy pants, a green and navy flannel shirt with what looked like a t-shirt underneath, and hiking boots—was a flat-top wearing whipcord. He had a tongue like one, too, which he used anytime he thought people wanted his opinion, usually about whether they carried an excess ounce of flesh, and he'd been known for his heavy hand as well when his kids were young. Patrick had his father's brown hair and blue eyes, but, despite their similarities, something kept them from looking much alike. Maybe it was World War II that had hardened Joe and pinched features that on Patrick were rounded and full.

Patrick didn't laugh. When his father had announced the visit and asked to go fishing, Patrick had planned a few modest day trips into the Bighorn Mountains near the Flint family's home. Then his mother had phoned to ask if Pete and Vera could come and told him how much they all wanted to see Jackson Hole and Yellowstone National Park. Patrick had been dying to visit the area. So, he'd planned this trip on the Tukudika River, excited that his thirteen-year-old son Perry was finally old enough and strong enough, and sixteen-year-old Trish cooperative enough for a canoe and fishing trip to be feasible. He'd read everything he could on the Mountain Shoshone native to the area, and he was really hoping to see some authentic artifacts in the wilderness.

He hadn't counted on Pete and Vera's young family.

Patrick looked toward the line of humanity still filing into the store. Susanne waved Trish and Perry in last, scowling at her offspring. He felt a familiar pride that a woman as vivacious, lovely, and kind as Susanne had chosen to be his wife. She looked so darn cute in cut-off blue jean shorts, a sleeveless t-shirt, hiking boots, and a red bandana scarf holding long brown curls off her face. And was it his imagination, or had Perry grown an inch overnight? Not that his son was tall. He was still six inches behind his grade level buddies. But taller, and his face looked slimmer, too. His body slightly harder than it had been in shorts and a tank top the summer before. He hoped so. Perry hated being small. Trish, on the other hand, had clearly blossomed into young womanhood.

With her long braids and bright blue eyes and a body toned by basketball, running, horsemanship, and youth, she radiated vitality. He felt the shop owner's eyes light on her.

Back off, buddy. She's too young for you.

Just as his eyes traveled from his kids back to his wife, Trish socked Perry in the kidney. Patrick didn't react. He was too numb from shock over the seven youngsters for anything else to faze him.

"Honey, can I talk to you for a second?" he said to Susanne.

As she made her way over to him, all smiles now, he hugged his visiting family members one by one, starting with the children and moving on to his brother, Pete. The two of them had bedeviled scout leaders and teachers for years with their nearly identical looks, although now Pete had long sun-streaked hair while Patrick kept his darker hair fingernail short. The brothers were best friends, partners in crime, and Irish twins, separated by less than a year in age. Vera was next. Her marriage to Pete was recent, and Patrick had only met the tiny woman a few times before, and then she'd been tongue-tied. She was from a large family in a very small town, but that was about all Patrick knew about her.

After Patrick embraced Vera, she pulled Danny forward. The eight-year old had olive skin, a shock of jet-black hair, and dark eyes, just like his mother, who had passed away soon after he was born. But he looked enough like Vera that he could have been her birth child.

"What do you think of this rash?" Vera swiveled Danny around and rolled up the hem of his cut-off jeans. "This one's always into something. He's been scratching like a flea-bitten dog half the day."

Patrick crouched beside Danny and examined the red, irritated skin closely. As a doctor, he was on call twenty-four/seven when it came to family. Heck, who was he kidding? He was on call twenty-four/seven with anyone he encountered. Kneeling to pray at church. Paying the cashier at the hardware store. Throwing out his garbage at the town dump. He turned Danny around and smiled at him. The boy smiled back. The expression gave him a mischievous look.

"Do you feel bad anywhere else, Danny?"

The boy shook his head, sending his hair flying around the crown of his head like he was a human May pole.

Patrick laid the back of his palm across the boy's forehead. No fever. "Say ah."

"Ahh."

Patrick considered the boy's tongue and the back of his throat. *Pink and unremarkable.* He palpated Danny's belly. The boy didn't react.

Patrick stood. "Is he allergic to anything?"

Vera frowned. "I don't know. I don't think so."

"Well, I don't think it's anything serious, but let's give him a Benadryl, since it's probably his skin reacting to something he came into contact with. Do you remember touching anything itchy?" he asked Danny.

"No."

Vera said, "They were playing in the grass when we took a rest stop earlier."

Danny nodded. He sounded solemn. "I fell on my bottom in a bush."

Wyoming bushes that cause irritant dermatitis? Russian thistle. AKA the tumbling tumbleweed, once it dries out.

"All right." Patrick eyeballed Danny, pegging his weight at about fifty-five pounds. "But just one Benadryl. Twenty-five milligrams. Do you have any?"

Vera shook her head. "Not with us, I don't think."

"It's good to travel with some, especially when you're going to be in a remote location. I have some in our Suburban." He called to his daughter. "Trish, can you bring the Benadryl in to your Aunt Vera? It's in my—"

"—Doctor's bag behind the driver's seat. I know," Trish said, in a singsong voice. "Why don't you make Perry get it?"

Patrick glared at her.

She rolled her eyes. "Okay, okay."

He pitched her the car keys, and she headed for the front door.

"Thanks," Vera said. "Gotta love little boys."

"That we do." Patrick riffled Danny's hair. He missed the days he'd been able to do that with Perry, who had decided when he turned thirteen that hair mussing was undignified for a fellow of his advanced age. Vera was already chasing after Bert and Barry, who had knocked over the t-shirt display and run for the hills before it hit the ground.

Patrick walked over to join Susanne beside a bathroom door covered in hand-painted psychedelic peace signs. She tilted her head toward him so he could talk quietly into her ear, and her long brown waves fell over a bare shoulder. After a few cold Wyoming winters, cool June temperatures didn't bother her anymore.

He kept his voice low. "What's going on? Are they planning on bringing the kids on the river trip?"

Facing away from their family, she widened her eyes. "I think so."

"This isn't a trip for little kids."

"Tell them that."

Patrick's lips started moving, but no sound came out.

"I can't understand you when you're talking to yourself."

"Probably best if I don't repeat it."

"It will be okay." She winked at him. "It's our vacation. How bad could it be?"

He snorted. The last family vacation Patrick planned had ended with Trish kidnapped by multiple-murderer Billy Kemecke. Not exactly idyllic. This trip was his do-over. His chance to show his Texas family a wonderful time in his chosen home state.

"It had better be wonderful. We're celebrating Kemecke taking the plea deal for life in prison, and you being off the hook from testifying against him."

"Thank the good Lord for that. But we've still got the Barb Lamkin trial to go."

Lamkin was the most recent criminal the Flints had faced, and Trish's former basketball coach. She'd used Patrick's family to bait her former lover into meeting her in the mountains, fully intending to kill all of them. Luckily, a mountain lion in the road had sent her vehicle plummeting toward a creek bed, where Perry had achieved hero status by rescuing his mom and sister. Patrick arrived just in time to free Lamkin by hacking her trapped wrist off with a hatchet and getting her out before the truck had exploded. Now Lamkin was facing first degree murder charges, but the trial couldn't be held until after her due date, because she was pregnant. The baby's father, a judge, had been charged with fraud in a slam-dunk, decades-old case the county prosecutor had just uncovered.

The thought of the baby made Patrick queasy. An infant born in jail, with both parents behind bars—it would be tough going for the child unless someone came forward to foster or adopt.

Yes. We need a vacation. It's been a tough year, and it's not over yet.

Trish tapped him on the shoulder and held out his keys.

"You gave Aunt Vera some Benadryl?" he asked.

"Yes, sir."

"And you put it back in my bag and the bag . . ."

". . . Back where I found it. Yes, Dad."

He nodded. "Thanks." Then he turned back toward the extended group of Flints. They had scattered like a covey of quail around the store and out onto the sidewalk. "Pete, a word?"

His brother sauntered over, an arm around Vera's curvy waist. The two of them looked like half the Mamas and the Papas. Pete with his rock-star hair and bell bottoms, Vera with her yellow-lensed John Lennon sunglasses, a headband over her straight hair, and a gypsy-sleeved top. The comparison wasn't far from reality. Pete was eking out a living as a musician—guitarist, singer, songwriter—gigging in bars, opening for the openers at Austin-area concerts, and playing for tips when he couldn't get a booking. Vera had met him at one of his shows. She was his roadie and number one groupie, in addition to being the main herder of cats in their large household.

Pete slung his arm sideways to grab Patrick's, in a combo low-five/handshake. "So good to be here, bro."

"I can't believe you're *all* here. I thought it was going to just be you guys and Mom and Dad."

"Isn't it great? Vera said we should just bring everybody, so we stuffed them all in the station wagon, and here we are."

Vera beamed. "The kids are going to remember this their whole lives. Gotta love a family trip."

From outside, Patrick heard a shriek, then clattering hooves. *Uh oh.* He shot forward like a sprinter out of the blocks. But before he could make it to the sidewalk, Brian hustled a wailing Bert back inside and to their mother. The rest of the kids followed, eyes huge. Bert wasn't limping or bleeding, which were both good signs.

Vera wrapped Bert in her arms. He seemed a little small for his age, like Perry had been "What happened?"

"A big animal attacked him," Brian said. "Well, it tried to, but I scared it away before it got him. Good thing, because he fell down running away from it."

Patrick raised an eyebrow. "Was it tall and dark brown with hooves?"

"Yes. And really long legs. I think it was a baby, though, because it ran down the street to an even bigger one. Then they ran off."

"Moose," Patrick said. "You'll want to leave them alone in the future. Especially the ones with babies. Very dangerous." He smoothed Bert's blond hair, which stood straight up like a cockatiel's feathers.

"Wild animals in the middle of town?" Vera said.

Patrick smiled. "Sometimes. It's Wyoming. You okay, Bert?"

The boy had stopped crying. He nodded.

"Where does it hurt?"

Bert shrugged. Another good sign. It looked like the worst injury was to his pride and feelings.

"Does your head hurt?"

This time Vera prodded him. "Use your manners and answer your uncle. He's a doctor."

"No. I mean, no sir, Dr. Uncle Patrick. It didn't get me."

"Just Uncle Patrick. You'll have a good story to tell your friends."

Bert nodded. Vera released him, and Brian took him by the arm. The kids headed straight back outside. Apparently, they weren't all that worried about moose.

"It's always something when you have seven," Pete said, shaking his head, but smiling.

Patrick had thought it was always something with two. He couldn't imagine seven kids. "So, let's talk about the trip. You know we've booked canoes so we can camp and fish on the Tukudika River?"

Pete nodded. "Sounds awesome."

"I'm trying to work out the logistics. We've got six adults, three of whom are women. And nine kids. Or, seven kids since we're counting Perry and Trish as adults for purposes of canoeing. I'd booked four canoes and eight life jackets. I had planned on Dad, you, me, and Perry each taking responsibility for a canoe. My worry is, how are we going to fit everyone in?"

Vera bit her lip. "We'll need more life jackets."

Patrick clenched his teeth. *Obviously.* "I'm also worried about room in the canoes." Pete and Vera's kids ranged from five to ten years old. None of them were old enough to reliably paddle an additional canoe.

Pete rubbed his chin. "I guess we can put two of them in each."

"That was where we were going to stash our gear and supplies. Food, tents, sleeping bags, and the rest of it take up a lot of space."

Susanne had joined them. She added, "And gold panning equipment."

Patrick had been reading up on the area, and there was a not-insignificant amount of gold in and along the Tukudika and its tributaries. Most of it was too fine to interest prospectors or miners, but he'd thought it would be fun to try their hand at panning anyway.

Pete stood taller. "There's gold up there?"

Patrick shrugged. "Some. Maybe."

"Sign me up."

"If we can fit the panning gear in the canoes." He lowered his voice to a mutter. "Or any of our gear and supplies."

"Can we get another canoe?"

"Who would man it?"

Brock cleared his throat. "I don't mean to eavesdrop, but you could ferry a gear canoe. You know, by a rope."

Patrick rubbed his forehead. *Which wouldn't come free.* "Yes, I suppose we could."

"Your bigger problem is the water. We've had a really dry year, but it's still early in the season. You might run across some Class III rapids. In a wet year, you'd maybe even encounter some Class IV."

Vera's brow furrowed. "Is that bad?"

Brock waffled his hand. "Depends on your level of experience."

Susanne harrumphed. "We didn't survive Kemecke, Riley Pearson, and Lamkin in the last year only to die in a river."

She had a point. Patrick hadn't even tallied crazy Riley when he'd been thinking about the Flints' tough year. Riley had been obsessed with an Eastern Shoshone nurse and poisoned Patrick out of a misguided sense of loyalty to her. It had happened not too far down the road, in Fort Washakie on the Wind River Reservation. No, they hadn't survived them all only to die now. He'd studied up on the river, too, and on canoeing in general.

He shook his head. "Nothing over Class II for this group. Even then, I think we'll want to put the kids ashore to walk whenever we get to *any* rapids."

Brock shrugged. "Where you can. Some areas, the shoreline is as dangerous as the water. Or impassable."

"What would you suggest we do, given our group's . . . sudden growth?"

Brock motioned for them to follow him back to the counter. He pulled out a map of the Tukudika and a red pen. He circled three areas. "These are the spots where the water gets sort of aggressive, you know?" He drew lines across the river before each circle. "If you get out where I've marked, there are trails you can hike to bypass the whitewater. They're not easy, but they're doable. If you, like, go any further, then you may not be able to get off the water in time."

"Can you portage on those trails?" Patrick asked.

Vera slipped her hand in Pete's. "What does portage mean?"

"Carry canoes overland."

Brock said, "Yeah, I guess you could, but it wouldn't be fun. Honestly, I'd just offload your gear into backpacks and send your ladies and kids along. You can solo the canoes through the rapids." He dropped his voice to barely above a whisper. "And I can't make any guarantees, but it's likely the water is down to a high Class II or a low Class III by now. In most places."

No guarantees. Meaning he couldn't guarantee they wouldn't get their you-know-whats handed to them. "Maybe we should talk it over. It's important to me we always keep the group together. For safety."

Pete pulled out a fifty-dollar bill. "Nah, it sounds like a great adventure, man. I'll pay for the extra canoe."

Brock tapped his pen on the counter. "And seven more life jackets, some more paddles just in case you need them for the extra canoe, and some line to ferry it with?"

"Yeah, sure."

"Are you sure we need more paddles for a canoe we'll be ferrying?" Patrick asked.

"I'd highly recommend it." Brock quoted a number.

Pete blanched. "I'm a little short of that. Can I pay you back later, Patrick? We're trying not to carry too much cash on us, you know?"

Without comment, Patrick pulled out his wallet and started counting bills. At the same time, he said, "We'll need more of everything. Groceries. Water. Sleeping gear. Tent space."

Their patriarch wandered up. "What's the problem, boys?" His voice sounded accusatory. He was holding one hand in the other.

Even though he and Susanne weren't touching, Patrick could feel her stiffen beside him. No one could understand how Lana had put up with his father since the two of them had eloped as teens, but love defies logic.

Patrick decided that if his father was going to criticize someone, he'd let it be him. "We just added a gear canoe. Dad, did you do something to your hand?"

Lana was listening, and she raised her voice to answer for Joe. "He slammed his thumb in the door a minute ago when he went back to the car for a jacket."

Joe Flint was the most accident-prone person Patrick knew. Falling off ladders. Shocking himself in electrical outlets. Hammering his fingers, which he'd done too many times to count.

"Let me see it, Dad."

Joe held it up. Blood dripped from under the nail, and it looked flattened. "It's nothing."

Brock smiled at Joe, wasting the effort of twelve muscles to do so. "Funny coincidence. We're about ready for safety instructions for the group."

Joe crossed his arms, not smiling back.

"Dad, could you help us get everyone together?"

Joe's lack of smile deepened.

Vera continued beaming and holding Pete's hand.

"They're your kids," Joe finally said, to no one in particular.

Patrick sighed. If he didn't need his father to paddle a canoe, he'd be tempted to leave him in Jackson.

Susanne walked around the store, clapping her hands and raising her voice. "Everybody. Everyone. All of you. That means you, too, Perry." He quit talking to Brian and grinned at her. "Time to get our canoe safety lesson. Come on." The younger kids pretty much ignored her. "Trish, starting now, you're in charge of Bunny, Barry, Bert, and Danny. Perry, you've got Annie, Brian, and Stan. When I ask for something, you guys make it happen with your troops. So, by the counter, line them up, *now*."

Trish put her hands on her hips. "Mom, no."

"No arguments."

Trish sighed dramatically. "Do I at least get paid?"

"No, but you get to continue living." Then she softened. "If you do a good job, we'll discuss it."

Trish made a sound deep in her chest that didn't sound like enthusiasm, but she turned back to the kids and started barking orders like her mom had just done to her. Perry stood up taller and his chest seemed to puff out as he rounded up his charges. Lana led Bunny by the hand from a table where they'd been studying a diorama of the Gros Ventre Wilderness. Within seconds, the kids were assembling in a line that was about as straight as a dog's hind leg.

Brock picked up a blue pen. "Mr. Flint, here are a few more things you should know about the river." He drew arrows toward it. "This is where you'll start. You can put in here, or you can portage upriver and extend the length of your float." He drew another arrow. "You'll need to get out before the falls. Here."

"Falls? Like waterfalls?" Pete sounded hesitant about the river for the first time.

"The same, but different. They're not as high as the falls in Yellowstone, but you still don't want to go over them, man. We'll pick you up Sunday at three, here." He drew a third arrow near the second. "If you beat us there, the fishing is dynamite."

Now Pete moved in closer to look at the map.

"Thanks," Patrick said. "We're really interested in any suggestions you have for good fishing, hiking, camping, or gold panning spots."

"Gold panning? Far out." Brock drew a couple of fish on the map, then added what Patrick assumed were either skulls and crossbones or campfires, and then triangles. "Fishing, camping, and hiking. The hiking trails should be marked by signs." Then he waggled his eyebrows. "As for gold panning," he drew several stars along the river, and a few more on tributaries, "here are some good places to try your luck. Let us know if you find anything. We can, like, add you to our wall of fame." He waved toward the wall to his right.

For the first time, Patrick noticed framed photos posted above a display of gold panning equipment for sale. They featured people holding panning equipment and what might be tiny gold nuggets.

"We will." Patrick took the map, folded it, and slid it in his shirt pocket.

A shorter, bushier-haired man burst through the back door of the shop. Through the opening, Patrick saw racks of canoes, kayaks, rafts, paddles, and used life vests.

"Brock, the Tomson party just got back." His voice held a shrill note, and Patrick noted that his breathing was rapid and shallow, pupils dilated, face flushed, and nostrils distended.

A look of annoyance showed in the sudden lines around Brock's eyes. "Cool, man. But I'm with some customers."

The man rushed on. "They found a dead body on the Tukudika. No life jacket, no fishing or hiking gear, not one of our customers."

"They found *what?*"

"A dead body. They canoed him back. They were freaking out about leaving him, so we loaded him on the trailer and brought him back here."

Brock's eyes bugged. "The dead guy is here?"

"Well, he's on the trailer outside, but, yeah."

Brock stabbed the air with his finger. "You're not supposed to move a dead body. Evidence, you know? Call the sheriff. Now."

"Uh, yes, sir."

As the shorter man hurried to the phone, Brock muttered, "I'd better not get my license pulled over this."

Patrick felt a burst of adrenaline. He had to check on the man. Administer CPR, if it appeared it would do any good. But as he rushed through the back room, a thought started looping through his head. *Please Lord, not a murder on my do-over vacation.*

CHAPTER TWO: SHOCK

Trish

"Watch out for Bunny!" Trish shouted at the rest of the kids. Perry had organized them into a game of freeze tag on the grassy town square. All around it, the wooden buildings were designed to make the place look like a spiffed up Old West town. Tourists streamed in and out of the doors and milled on the sidewalks. Trish would have rather browsed the fancy shops and galleries than play tag, but she knew better than to take the kids inside the stores. "You break it, you buy it" was a phrase she was very familiar with from her parents, and, as the one in charge, she was afraid she would be responsible for any damage by the seven dwarves.

At first, tag had been a good way to distract the little ones from the thought of the dead man at the canoe shop. She didn't have such an easy time forgetting him, though. When some freaked out short guy had run in and shouted out that he'd brought a corpse in on a trailer, she'd been curious and snuck out back to see for herself. The dead guy had looked a lot like a puffer fish she'd seen in her Aunt Patty's aquarium. Vampire-white, water-logged, eyes wide open, with funny black whisker spots on his face like her dad's at night when he hadn't shaved since morning. He was missing one shoe, and his hands were wrinkly. Trish's got the same way when she stayed in the bathtub a long time. He'd smelled funky, too. Bad in a way that was hard to describe, but that she'd smelled once when she'd ridden her horse Goldie past a dead, rotting deer. *Yeah, that will be in my nightmares tonight.*

She'd only had a brief look at the body, though. Her parents had been furious when they realized she was out there. Before they could get her back inside, the sheriff's deputies had come and shooed the grown-ups out of the way, too. Her mom, Aunt Vera, and Gramma Lana had huddled, then left Trish with a ten-dollar bill for snacks and strict instructions to keep all the little ones distracted and out of trouble, while they went to buy more supplies. Trish had hustled back in the shop and done just that.

She had a lot of experience babysitting, especially in the last two months. Trish was saving up for a down payment on a used car. But she'd never kept this many kids at once, and the freeze tag competition had gotten out of hand, for everyone except Danny, who was pretty much swaying and staring into space. The Benadryl really seemed to have hit him hard.

Bunny, who was on the base of one of the four enormous antler arches at each corner of the square, was doing what she called her "pwincess dance." It consisted of twirling on her tiptoes with her hands to the sky. Suddenly, Bert rammed into her, and she tumbled sideways. Her head thudded into pointy antlers.

"Bunny!" Brian screamed. He raced over to her, just ahead of Trish, as the little girl crumpled to her knees.

"Are you okay?" Trish was afraid to look at her, expecting blood. A lot of it. And a gored eyeball hanging from its socket.

But Bunny popped up and shook her finger at the arch. "Bad antwers," she said through missing front teeth. Then she rubbed her head. "Ouch."

Brian exhaled.

Trish laughed. "Bad elk. That's what the antlers are from." Since the nearby National Elk Refuge was one of the subjects her dad had lectured the family on—and on and on and on—during the drive-across-the-state-that-had-seemed-like-it-would-never-end, Trish knew the antlers came from there.

"Bad eh-welk."

Perry sprinted up. "Is she all right?"

Trish nodded. "I think it's time we go back to the canoe store, though, squirt." She knew he hated it when she made fun of his size. But he needed to face facts. He was a *serious* shrimp.

Perry glared at her.

She said, "Come on, everybody."

They all ran toward her, except Danny. The kid looked like he was going to fall over asleep on the grass. Brian prodded him up. Then Perry helped her marshal their charges into a line from youngest to oldest. He led the way back with Trish bringing up the rear. She hoped when they got to the shop, the dead guy was gone.

"I'm hungry," Stan said.

Six voices echoed his.

Trish raised her voice so everyone would hear, all the way to the front of the line. "We already had ice cream on the way to the square."

"That was a long time ago," Barry whined.

"I'm sure we'll get lunch soon." *How does Aunt Vera deal with this every single day?* Trish was never going to have kids. Or maybe one. Two at the very, very most. She kept them marching.

Five minutes later, they arrived at the back of Wyoming Whitewater. Trish's mom was standing beside her dad. Grandpa Joe and Gramma Lana were in their station wagon, windows up, with her aunt and uncle. The kids hopped in the car with them. Gramma Lana was reapplying lipstick, but she waved to Trish. Everyone in the family said Trish looked just like her. Trish hoped so. She knew they had the same big, blue eyes, blond hair, height, and high cheekbones.

Perry walked over to their family's Suburban and leaned against it. Trish moved closer to her dad so she could hear her parents' conversation, keeping one eye on "her" kids to make sure none made a break from the station wagon.

"Are the deputies done?" Trish's mom asked.

He nodded. "They just loaded up and left."

Her mom said, "Good. We bought more of everything, and we found some kids' sleeping bags and river gear."

"How much?" her dad said.

She smiled. "Let's talk about that later, honey."

He groaned.

"You're just going to have to forget about the cost and enjoy your family."

"I'm going to enjoy them. You know how much I've looked forward to Pete being here."

"I know you have. So, do the deputies have any idea how the guy died on the river?"

"They didn't, but I do."

She raised her brows. "Do tell."

"Head trauma."

"Like from a fall?"

"Impossible to say for sure, but more than likely."

She lowered her voice. "So, not murder?"

"Can't rule it out, but a rock is the most likely culprit."

"He still could have been pushed."

"You see murder everywhere." He smiled at her. "Have you ever thought about becoming a cop? You could work with Ronnie at the Johnson County Sheriff's Department."

Deputy Ronnie Harcourt was their former next-door neighbor, a beautiful woman who could have been a model instead of a cop. She was one of Trish's mom's best friends. She teased Susanne all the time that she'd make a real Wyoming woman out of her yet. From what Trish could tell, this meant her mom would ride horses, shoot whiskey and big game, and camp outside in the dead of winter. Ronnie was going to be sorely disappointed if she counted on any of these things happening.

"Pass." Her mom laughed. "You're okay taking everyone out there after this?"

"The deputies didn't seem concerned, and there was no evidence of foul play. It will be okay, Susanne."

She shuddered. "I don't feel good about it. Not after this last year."

Trish shuddered, too. *This last year.* She knew exactly what her mom meant. Trish had been kidnapped, not once but twice. First, by her ex-boyfriend Brandon's insane family. They'd lugged her up into Cloud Peak Wilderness in the Bighorns, where they had planned to leave her to die. The second time was by her own high school basketball coach, who'd taken Perry and her mom, too. Coach Lamkin would have killed them, if she'd gotten the chance. The funny thing was, Trish had loved Brandon, and she had really liked her coach. She'd trusted them, until she'd figured out how wrong she'd been about them. Learning the truth had hurt more than anything she'd ever experienced. She'd been so humiliated. Now she could never trust her own judgment about people again.

The person she hadn't trusted, Brandon's cousin Ben, turned out to have been the truthful one. Even though he'd lived with Brandon and Brandon's mom, Donna Lewis, Ben had testified against his Aunt Donna, for conspiracy and murder, because it was the right and truthful thing to do. Even though it had meant he no longer had a home with the Lewises. But her parents' friends Henry and Vangie Sibley had taken him in. Now Ben was living and working out at their place—Piney Bottom Ranch.

Trish had been babysitting the Sibley's infant son Hank this summer. Ben and Trish had been around each other a lot more. They'd become friends. Good friends. But she was having second thoughts about their relationship. Her parents weren't in favor of it. They'd been right before, about Brandon, and she'd been wrong. Maybe she just needed a break. Because, honestly, she didn't know who to trust. So, yeah, a break from all guys. A break from her best friend Marcy, who'd been acting really weird since the ordeal with Coach Lamkin. Marcy had been on Lamkin's 1976 state champion girls basketball team. She and some of the other girls were upset that Coach Lamkin was in jail. Trish couldn't understand it. Lamkin was a *murderer*. How could a winning basketball team be more important than that? Than Trish and her family?

Basketball had been Trish's passion, too, until the coach had betrayed her. She'd decided to give it up altogether. Instead, she'd started running more and was going to try out for the cross-country team. Make a fresh start.

Her dad said to her mom, "It's going to be fine, Susanne. We'll have a great time."

Her mom hugged herself around the middle. "I think we should reconsider this trip. Cancel the rentals. Just camp out for the night by the river close to town. We can still fish and pan for gold without all of us having to go so far up into the mountains."

Trish found herself nodding along with her mom. It sounded like a great idea to her.

"That wouldn't be fair to everyone else. They've traveled a long way for this."

"They traveled a long way to see us. And they're counting on us not to endanger them."

Her dad's voice grew testy. "Who said anything about endangering anyone? Have a little faith in me, Susanne."

The owner guy came out. Trish didn't like him. He'd been staring at her earlier, in a way that more grown-up men did lately. It made her uncomfortable.

He slapped her dad on the back. "Sorry for the delay, my man. Couldn't be avoided. Why don't you grab some lunch while we load your gear?"

Trish raised her eyebrows, knowing full well what her dad's response to that would be. Lunch out for fifteen people, when they had coolers full of food? That would never happen.

"If you don't mind, we'd just like to load up and go," her dad said.

Trish squeezed her lips to keep from laughing. Her dad was so predictable.

"Fine by me. But I need to let you know we have one little problem."

Her dad's lips twitched. "Just one. Okay, let's hear it."

"The deputies took our six-boat trailer. In case there's evidence on it, you know? All I have available is two four-boaters. I'll need to bring an extra employee along to haul the second trailer, and, like, it's going to cost another twenty bucks."

Trish held her breath.

After a few tense seconds, her dad said, "We'll just carry it ourselves."

"Are you sure?"

"Completely." Her dad turned to Trish. "You know where I stashed all the tow rope?"

"In your emergency supplies box?" she said.

"Yes. Bring it out, please."

Not for the first time, she wondered why he always made her do everything instead of Perry, but this time she kept it to herself. "But we don't have a trailer."

Her dad grinned at her. "But we do have a roof."

He is such a weirdo. Trish opened the back end of the Suburban and dug in the big tub of emergency supplies her dad carried with them everywhere. She thought it was overkill, mostly, but he did use things from it, like his hatchet and now the rope. His buddy Wes had an even bigger stash of emergency supplies in his Travelall. Wes was like her dad's coach on all things Wyoming. She got the rope out and set it on the ground.

Her dad said, "And some sleeping bags."

"How many?"

"Two should do it."

"Use some from the shopping bags," her mom added. "They're closest."

Trish set two army green sleeping bags beside the rope. She put her hands on her hips and turned to face the shop. "Now what?"

The owner turned over a canoe that was propped against the wall below the racks. Something let loose a high-pitched whistle. "Son of a . . ." He jumped back, flapping his hand. Then he sucked the back of it. Trish heard the scurrying of little feet.

"Everything okay?" her dad said.

The owner dropped his hand from his mouth. Blood trickled down his wrist. "There was a marmot hiding under there. Too many tourists feeding them. The yellow-bellied stinkers think they own the town. He's still under there, too." He kicked the canoe, and a fat marmot waddled at top speed through the racks of gear, around a corner, and out of sight.

Trish was glad Buffalo was six hours away from Jackson. They got some tourists in Buffalo, but nothing like Yellowstone and Jackson Hole. She'd seen more out-of-staters today, in Jackson, than she'd seen in the Bighorns the entire time she'd lived in Wyoming. Tourists were loud, left trash in the mountains, and did dumb things, like feed marmots by hand. If she were in charge, she'd make them pay to cross the state line. Or she'd set a limit on the number of people that could visit. Someday, she hoped to work as a wildlife biologist, after she got her degree from the University of Wyoming. She'd be able to study how people affected the environment and wildlife. She couldn't wait.

The store owner grabbed the canoe and balanced it over his head.

Her dad said, "You should really get a tetanus shot and a rabies test."

"Later, man." The owner walked the canoe to the Suburban. "Ready to get this show on the road?"

Her dad frowned. "Yeah. Sure."

Trish frowned, too. She wished her dad sounded a little more optimistic. Oh, well. Things would be better once they were up on the mountain.

CHAPTER THREE: TRANSPORT

Perry

Belting out the words to "50 Ways to Leave Your Lover," Perry's dad drummed the ceiling with his palm as he followed the trailer full of canoes up the mountain road. He stopped. "Why is no one back there singing along with me?"

"We're singing!" Barry said.

Bert shouted. "Yeah. Loud!"

Perry said, "Yay, singalongs." Last year, when he wasn't a teenager, he'd done singalongs with his dad. But he knew now how uncool he'd been. A dork, actually. He'd leave the singing to his younger cousins.

He stared out the window with his nose nearly on the glass. Perry was usually the one stuck in the middle of the backseat, but, this time, that honor went to the little boys. He wasn't so sure he would have avoided the dreaded middle if Brian had been along. The kid was four years younger than him, but he was a beast. Tall, thick, and strong. If Perry hadn't been lifting weights all year for football and then for skiing, he definitely would have been smaller than Brian. Come to think of it, he needed to figure out a way to continue his weights up here. *Logs, maybe?* If he quit lifting, Brian would probably catch up with him, size-wise, by the time the trip was over.

He liked Brian, but he was glad he was in the other car.

Trish rolled the opposite window down and stuck her head out. She moaned. "Da-ad, can't you drive any straighter? I'm going to throw up."

It smelled good outside. A little dusty from the road, but good. Perry liked the smell of the pines. Like the stuff his mom used when she cleaned the house, only real.

"Look at something stationary, in front of us," Perry's dad said.

"It's a steep winding road in a forest. There is nothing stationary in front of us," his mom said.

One of the Suburban's front wheels slammed into a rock, then the hood dropped and the frame jolted as the vehicle dove into a huge pothole.

"Ow!" Trish screamed. She pressed her hand to her ear.

His dad yelled, "Hold on to your . . . your you-know-what, Fred."

Perry giggled before he could help it. His dad was obsessed with *Smokey and the Bandit*, which they'd seen a few weeks before, right when it came out. His dad never usually went to movies, so it had been kind of a big deal, and his mom even let his dad get away with saying the *real* word from the movie line occasionally because of it.

A back wheel hit the same rock and pothole.

"Great aim." His mom's voice sounded sarcastic.

As the Suburban lurched out of the hole, his dad accelerated. "Steep incline ahead. Everybody lean forward!"

Bert and Barry took him seriously, not realizing this was another one of the silly games Patrick played. Trish and Perry sighed in unison. The Suburban bucked and bounced. The engine whined. Patrick shifted to a lower gear as they made a switchback turn.

"Almost to the top," he said.

Trish said, "Top of what? We have like a bajillion miles to go."

His dad ignored her. A few jolting seconds later, the Suburban turned back to the right. Now they were parallel to the river far below. It was dark and looked browner than Perry had expected. Wasn't water supposed to be blue? Then he saw something completely cool. White water tumbled over a cliff.

"Wow, is that a waterfall?" Perry rolled his window down. In the distance, he could hear the roar of the water.

"It is." His dad sounded as happy as if he'd created it himself.

Bert said, "In Texas, we live by the Colorado River, but we had to drive through Colorado to get here and there wasn't a Texas river there."

"What's this river called?" Barry added.

Trish flopped her head against the seat back. "Don't get him started again."

"The Tukudika," his dad crowed. "Do you know why they call it that?"

Perry flopped his head back, too. "No. Just no. Eight hours of driving to get here. He talked about it the whole way. I can't take it anymore." His dad was obsessed with American Indians. He lectured all the time about the tribes local to north central Wyoming, where the Flints lived. The Crow and the Cheyenne, with a little Sioux thrown in occasionally. Back in Texas, he used to tell them about the Apache, the Comanche, and the Karankawa. But once they'd left the Bighorns, it had been all Mountain Shoshone, all the time.

"No, why?" Barry said.

"Because the last Indians to live here were called the Tukudika."

"What does Toocoodeecoo mean?" Bert asked.

"No, silly, he said 'Toocoo dookie.'" Barry giggled.

"He said dookie." Bert pointed at his brother.

"You smell like dookie."

Both boys dissolved in laughter.

Perry's dad went on in a serious tone, like his young audience wasn't talking about feces. "Tukudika. It means Sheep Eater. The Shoshone liked to name groups of people by what they ate. That's how the Mountain Shoshone got the name Tukudika. Because they ate bighorn sheep."

Bert laughed. "That's a weird name."

"Not if bighorn sheep were a major part of your diet."

"Hey, Dad, it's a good thing you aren't a Tukudika, then, or you would have starved." Perry covered a smile. His dad had been unsuccessful on a previous hunt for bighorn sheep. They were his second favorite thing to talk about, after American Indians.

"Very funny."

"Have you ever even seen one in the wild, Dad?"

"You'd know I had if you hadn't been asleep on your horse when it happened. But mark my words, we won't be able to beat them away with a stick out here."

"My Shoshone name is macaroni and cheese," Bert said.

Barry cackled. "Mine is Cap'n Crunch cereal."

His dad laughed, too. He accelerated some more as the road flattened out, with less rocks. "Now, those boys are funny."

"Do the Dookietikas still live here?" Barry said.

The boys laughed again.

"Tukudika. Some of them do. Down south, mostly, on the Wind River Reservation. Not up in the mountains anymore. But if we're very lucky, we'll see things they left behind."

"What things?" Bert almost chirped with excitement.

"Arrowheads. Wickiups. Vision sites." Patrick goosed the Suburban up another incline.

"Wicky yucks?"

"Watch out," Susanne shouted.

Perry's dad swerved to the left to avoid a thick tree branch hanging over the road. Pine needles swept over the windshield like the brushes in a drive-through car wash. Then there was a scraping noise all along the top of the Suburban.

"Oh, no." Susanne winced.

His dad slammed on the brakes.

CRUNCH.

The noise behind them was loud. Perry, Bert, Barry, and Trish swiveled around to see what had happened.

"Uh, Dad, we lost our canoe," Perry said. Which was like the world's biggest understatement. Their canoe had flown off the top of the Suburban like it was a ski jump, landed on top of Grandpa Joe and Gramma Lana's station wagon, and slid off the back of it, where it had disappeared. Grandpa Joe was shouting and shaking his fist.

His dad wasn't going to be happy. But probably not as unhappy as Grandpa Joe looked.

CHAPTER FOUR: INPUT

Susanne

"You guys can put in here, or, if you're feeling super adventurous, head upriver a ways. Prettiest place you'll ever see. I proposed to my girlfriend on a rock ledge above the river back there." Brock lifted the last set of paddles out of the back of the van and set them on the ground.

"What a lovely story." Susanne buttoned up her overshirt. It was far chillier up here than in town. She was changing into her jeans before they got going, too.

She didn't give a rat's hind foot where they put the canoes in the water. Today had gone from bad to worse to downright crummy with the damage to Joe and Lana's car. The hood was creased and scratched, and their windshield had a starburst of cracks in it. Joe had been apoplectic. His eyes were still bugging out, and his voice was hoarse from shouting. Patrick was pretty upset, too. She was worried that the vein in his temple would rupture from the pounding his blood pressure was giving it.

She readjusted her bandana. "Thank you, Brock. We'll see you Sunday afternoon."

"Be safe out there, cats and kittens." He saluted the group and slapped some sideways fives with the younger kids on his way back to his van. Once in it, he made a U-turn and took off down the mountain.

Susanne shook her arms, then rolled her neck. Then she did a slow three-sixty, trying for a mental re-set. As hostess, of sorts, to this outing, she felt gravely responsible for everyone having a good time. Yes, she understood that Patrick intended to give them his version of the ultimate mountain experience that he thought they *should* want. But it was her job to make sure no one was left out. That everyone from Bunny to Joe had fun.

She snorted. To the extent Joe ever had fun. Her smile widened. Maybe that was the secret—to give him plenty to complain about. Thank goodness Patrick had learned from his father not how to be, but how not to be. She'd married an intense fellow, no doubt, and his high expectations were hard to measure up to at times, but he was kind, loving, and flexible, and his intentions were good. They were just lucky it wasn't her family up here, because this would not be the kind of trip they were up for. At least with the Flints, this outing had a chance of success.

Around her, birds chirped. The river gurgled. Children squealed, with the exception of Danny, who was asleep underneath a tree. Across the river, an enormous red cliff rose from the river. She inhaled, all the way to her belly button, and drew in the fresh scent of pine, flowers, clean water, and good old Vitamin Dirt, as Patrick liked to call the earth. The river itself rushed by, a dark grayish green, looking swift but fairly calm through the break in the forest. Aspens, birches, firs, Ponderosa pines, and willows fought for space with the boulders on the riverbank. At the edge of the clearing at the end of the road, a weathered cabin with a plaque beside its door nestled in a field of purple and white lupine. The front end of a Jeep poked out from behind the building. On the far side of the water upriver, cliff faces with trees on top like crew cuts looked down on them. Ever-taller peaks rose behind them. One mountain in particular drew her interest, since it looked like a fat sleeping Indian in profile. *Maybe one of Patrick's Tukudika.* A hint of a smile made its way over her lips. *Okay, this place is magnificent.*

"Mom?" Trish's voice drew her around. "Can we talk about the babysitting thing?"

Susanne turned to her daughter. "You mean helping out with your cousins?"

"Yes. They're, um, a lot of work."

Susanne walked toward the Suburban where her husband was unloading their gear. Pete was doing the same thing at the station wagon. Trish kept pace with her. Patrick seemed less tense than he had in the Suburban after the canoe debacle, but his movements were still jerky, and he wasn't smiling yet.

"Your efforts will be remembered when it comes time for you to make a down payment on a car. Is that what you wanted to hear?"

Trish whooped. "Thank you. How much, do you think? We're going to be out here three whole days."

Susanne couldn't help it. She laughed. Her daughter might look like a woman these days—willowy, blonde, and rosy-cheeked, with disturbing curves—but she still acted like the girl she didn't want to be but still was. "The more you help, the more we help. The better your attitude is, the better mine will be. Now, let's see what your father has in mind."

But before Susanne could check in with Patrick, a gray-haired couple approached from the cabin. They were dressed identically in button-front shirts with U.S. Forest Service patches. Their shirts were tucked into Bermuda style shorts, belted, and they wore hiking boots and round-brimmed hats. Besides their gender, the main differences were their height, and the petite woman's very knobby knees.

The woman spoke first, her voice sounding slightly Bostonian, and her eyes sharp behind horn-rimmed glasses and a long fringe of white bangs. She was looking out over the river. "Good afternoon, folks. Looks like you're planning for a big time."

The man's gaze followed hers. "Welcome to Bridger-Teton National Forest and the Gros Ventre Wilderness." He pronounced it Grow Vaunt, just like Patrick did, but with a Boston accent thicker than the woman's. He leaned on his walking stick, looked back at Susanne and Trish, and winked. "Seen any Yeti out and about today?"

Susanne laughed. "No Yeti or Abominable Snowmen. I'm Susanne Flint. This is my daughter Trish, and all of those many, many people are our family."

Trish's voice was shy. She tended to warm slowly around adults. "Hi."

The man thumped his chest. "I'm Klaus, and this is my better half,

Sylvie. We ranger in these parts in the summer. If we're not out making our rounds, you can find us here at the Yellowjacket Guard Station, right along Yellowjacket creek." He pointed upriver. "It feeds into the Tukudika just beyond the cabin."

Patrick walked up to the group. "Patrick Flint."

The men shook hands.

"Where are you guys heading with all those little ones?" Sylvie asked.

Patrick launched into his plan. "We thought we'd put in for the night upriver from here, maybe spend some time this afternoon letting the kids fish and play. Do a little gold panning, cook some dinner, camp out. Hit the river tomorrow until we find another great spot to do more of the same." Patrick pulled the map Brock had marked-up from his pocket. "Any particular spots you'd recommend? These are the suggestions we got from Wyoming Whitewater. We're looking for adventure and solitude."

Susanne bit the inside of her lip. By the time they got seven small children to hike upriver while the men portaged canoes and ferried supplies, it would be dark, and play time would be a pipedream. She caught Sylvie's gaze. The older woman raised her eyebrows. Susanne wasn't one to talk out of school, so she merely smiled in reply.

Klaus peered at the map. "Don't know how far you'll make it with those troops of yours. No, sir. And keeping a group like that happy and together. Good luck. Good luck to you."

"We got a late start, unfortunately. A dead man washed up down river." Patrick lowered his voice, although Susanne wasn't sure why, since all of their family knew about the body.

Sylvie shook her head. "We just heard about that on the radio. It's such a shame. There's a death or two every season. That's why safety is job one out here."

Klaus tapped his walking stick on the ground. "Couldn't have said it better myself, Sweetheart. Speaking of safety, this is bear country. Be warned and be ready."

"We are," Patrick said. "I'll be hoisting our food into trees away from camp. We plan to make lots of noise."

While Patrick didn't mention it, she knew he was also armed with his favorite pistol, his .357 Magnum revolver. She was glad of it, and glad he practiced regularly.

"Good. Now, if you cross the foot bridge here," Klaus pointed at the map, "my favorite camping spot is just an easy mile hike upriver."

"Oh, Klaus, don't send them there. It's so remote. We haven't even been up that way to check on things yet this year. And there's no good trail."

"The man said they're looking for adventure."

Susanne was about to shake her head and say, "Not that much," when Patrick said, "That we are!"

Klaus beamed. "Outstanding. So, here's how to find my spot. Mind you, there'll be two wet-foot crossings. The Yellowjacket, which I was just telling you about, and on the other side of the river, Trout Creek. Might have to do some piggy-backing." He winked again. "After you cross Trout Creek, hike, oh, a quarter-mile or so to where you'll find a nice rock cliff looking over the river. Then walk north, on the near side of the cliff. Give it another half-mile more or less—"

"More," Sylvie said.

"—and you'll find it. A nice flat area with good-enough access to water from Trout Creek, a big fire ring I put together myself, and views worth the hike. Plus, if you're panning, the Trout is one of the best creeks for it."

"A foot bridge over the river." Patrick rubbed his thumb and fore-finger over his upper lip. Susanne realized he hadn't shaved. She'd just gotten him to hack off his winter growth a few months ago. He was chal-lenged in the facial hair department, but determined—he couldn't grow anything more substantial than the fur on a mangy dog. She wasn't ready for it again so soon. "That's great. It will get us a little further from the road and civilization."

Sylvie rocked up on her tiptoes. "Be careful out there. The wilder-ness can be wicked unforgiving. Just ask that fellow who floated down the river this morning."

Klaus put a hand on his wife's shoulder. "They don't seem like a bunch of chowderheads to me, Syl. Just remember, we're usually here if you need us, and there's a radio in the guard station for the times we're not. It will reach you all the way back to Jackson."

"Thank you," Susanne said. "We're going to do our best not to need any help while we're up here." As soon as she said it, she looked around for wood to knock on. No use in conjuring up trouble.

CHAPTER FIVE: SETUP

East of Trout Creek, Bridger-Teton National Forest,
Wyoming
Thursday, June 23, 1977, 6:00 p.m.

Patrick

P atrick eyed the fire, which had burned down to the nice hot coals
they needed for roasting hot dogs and marshmallows for s'mores.
In his mind's eye, though, the picture was different. It was filled
with the vista along the river. The cliffs hundreds of feet high. The rocks
at their apex jutting out over the granite below—ramparts at the top of a
crumbling fortress. The paths of thousands of years of drainage from
snow melt, like the tracks of Tukudika tears. Downriver, the smaller red
cliffs, where the tears turned to blood. For a moment, he felt melodra-
matic and foolish. But then he remembered the dense stone sculpted by
an unseen hand in rows at the bases of the cliffs. Statues, busts, shoulders, *faces*. Uncovered by erosion, exposing the heart of the mountain,
those who long ago were vanquished and heart-broken here, but could
never be forgotten. Not as long as the mountains stood. *The Sheep
Eaters*, he thought. *The Tukudika. They're here.* He'd been to Mount
Rushmore once as a child. It had been unsettling. Unnatural, even if
imposing and impressive. *This. This is the real thing.*

The river was aptly named, in his opinion.

He cleared his throat and his mind. "The fire's ready."

His mother and father were huddled on a log beside him, swathed in layers of sweaters and jackets. His father was sharpening sticks for skewers. Patrick would be disinfecting and bandaging a cut before the evening was through, he was sure.

Joe's face was pinched. "It's not giving off any heat."

"This is as good as it's going to get, Dad. We can't build a bonfire up here. It may not be the dry season yet, but forest fire is always a risk. If you're cold, put on more clothes."

He knew his father wouldn't do it. And that his mother would do whatever his father did. They say that boys marry women like their mothers. If so, he would have picked a soft-spoken lady. But, somehow, he'd married a feisty woman who wasn't afraid to throw coffee cups when she was mad, something his mother would never have done.

He wouldn't trade Susanne and her feisty spirit for anyone or anything.

From all the way down by the creek, his brother's laugh carried over the sound of kids laughing and hollering. Patrick stacked a few more pieces of wood by the fire. Pete had always been the more exuberant of the Flint brothers, and Patrick envied Pete's creativity and risk-taking "life without a net" nature. Patrick lived within the structure he built around his own world. But as much as he admired Pete's free spirit and sense of fun, he could do without the noise in the wilderness. No self-respecting animal would stick around within five miles of it, so their chances of seeing elk or moose were out the window. On the other hand, it would keep the grizzly bears away. Which reminded him, he needed to have the bear talk with everyone, and soon.

He straightened to survey the dinner-making activity. Susanne and Vera were arranging wieners, buns, ketchup, Frito's, graham crackers, marshmallows, and Hershey's bars on a "table" they'd made with a tarp on the ground. Susanne emptied three cans of Wolf Brand chili—no beans—into a large saucepan, the only cooking vessel they'd brought with them, since they planned to rely heavily on sandwiches, fruit, and a few snackable veggies for most of the short trip. She stood and settled the pan carefully on the edge of the coals.

Patrick said, "Careful or it's going to stick on the side of the pan closest to the coals. We'll end up with burned chili."

She dipped her chin and looked up at him. "I've got it. Can you go tell Pete and the kids it's time to eat?"

He nodded. "Yes, ma'am."

She swatted him on the backside as he struck out for the creek.

He'd been on the scouting hike to the creek earlier, and it wasn't a long walk. Downhill most of the way, too. He exhaled and attuned himself to his environment. The sun was still peeking over the Tetons to the west, but that wouldn't last long in the shadow of the mountains, even in the week of the longest days of the year.

Soon he'd relaxed enough that his mind wandered over the day, stopping and processing when it encountered troublesome bits, of which there were plenty. Honestly, it had been a challenge. A big one. If today was any indication, this trip was going to test his leadership capabilities. Forget the drama of the dead guy at Wyoming Whitewater. The surprise of the seven dwarves' arrival. The canoe to the station wagon. No, even without all that, just starting at the guard station and hiking upriver with the kids had been like pushing overcooked spaghetti.

Each of the men had been carrying a canoe overhead and a pack on their backs, with Trish and Perry carrying the fifth canoe, and arguing about it the entire way. Susanne and Vera were carrying heavy packs as well. That had left only his mother for serious child wrangling. She'd been raised a country girl, and she was no shrinking violet, but seven small children running wild on slippery rocks and in and out of the forest had been too much for her, especially with Danny still recovering from the two Benadryl Patrick had discovered he'd taken instead of the one Patrick had recommended. When they'd stashed the canoes riverside at a giant rock that the kids thought looked like a Teddy Bear, right at the head of the trail to the camping site, he'd thought they'd go out of their minds. They were cute, but they were a handful.

A few times, his father had tripped and nearly gone down. Patrick had pretended not to notice it, or the foul language accompanying it each time. Joe Flint learned to cuss like a sailor in the Navy, and he resisted all of Lana's efforts to convince him it wasn't appropriate for genteel conversation. Patrick was surprised his father was having trouble. He'd been an intelligence agent behind enemy lines in World War II. Endured harsh conditions. Won a Silver Star he wouldn't talk about. Terrorized two strapping teenage boys with ease. Still looked tough enough to take on Robert Blake in a fist fight. But his dad was showing his age, and it worried Patrick.

Notwithstanding his father's issues, Patrick figured the adults alone could have made it from the guard station to the camp site in an hour, uphill and carrying canoes. But it had taken them three with the kids. *Three.* How could two miles, more or less, take *three* hours? So much for an afternoon of fishing and panning. It had been all they could do to put together dinner, and when that was over, they would barely have enough daylight left to set up tents.

Patrick rounded a curve in the narrow path—little more than a wildlife trail, really—and came upon a sight that banished his negative thoughts and brought a smile to his face. Seven kids, naked to their skivvies and t-shirts, were splashing in the stream, despite the cool air and cooler snow melt water. Danny was still a little sluggish, but he was whooping it up, too. Perry and Trish, with their shoes off and jeans rolled up, had joined in, although they were keeping their distance and staying a little drier than their younger cousins. Pete was shirtless and the center of it all, his hair plastered against his forehead and his pants sopping wet. He was leading the kids in a singalong. One of Perry's favorites. "Rockin' Robin," by The Jackson Five. They were all so into it that they didn't even notice Patrick watching them.

To his surprise, tears welled in his eyes. Yes, today had been a trial. Every moment of it. But this . . . this made it worth it. To see his kids enjoying their cousins and his brother so happy—he couldn't have scripted a better moment, especially since he'd had no idea the "seven dwarves" would be here.

Right now, I'd have to call them Splashy, Slippery, Shouty, Laughy, Squealy, Streaky, and Sleepy. Thank you, God, for my family and Your wilderness.

"Hot dog time, everyone," he shouted. He hated to break it up, but the light had started fading fast.

Ten heads turned toward him.

Bunny splashed water in the air, then held her arms up. "We're gold minders, Uncle Patrick!"

"That's great, Bunny. But do gold *miners* ever cook hot dogs and s'mores over a fire in the woods?"

"Yes!" she screamed.

"Then you'd better get moving, very carefully, or Gramma Lana might eat them all before you get any."

Everyone started laughing and scrambling out of the water, but, when six of the dwarves got to the shore, the seventh hollered from back in the creek.

"Wait!" It was Annie. Her big dark eyes looked panicked, her face stricken.

"Come on, Annie Oakley," Pete said. "You're holding up the gang."

"I can't. I'm stuck. My foot is stuck."

"What?"

Tears started streaming down her cheeks. "Help me, Daddy! My foot is trapped in a hole."

On the bank, the rest of the kids had stopped chattering and were watching open-mouthed.

Pete waded back out to his daughter. He reached under water, a look of concentration creasing his face. Then he smiled. "Got it. Your foot had slipped between some rocks."

Annie broke free, wiping away her tears. She hugged Pete, then picked her way to dry land.

Patrick held up a hand. "And that is why you never, never, never get out of a canoe until it is all the way to shore. If that water had been over Annie's head, what would have happened?"

"She'd have drownded," Stan said, his expression aghast.

"Yes. Or gotten hypothermia."

"What's hippo . . . hippo whatever you said?" Bert asked.

"It's when you're in the cold so long that it makes you really sick. It can even kill you, like drowning."

"Could we have gotten it in the creek?" Barry said.

"Only if most of your body had been under and you'd stayed there without moving a really, really long time. So, when we start canoeing, can you all promise to stay in them until we get all the way to the shore and tell you it's time to unload?"

"Yes, sir," Brian said.

"Yes, Dr. Uncle Patrick," Danny said.

"Just Uncle Patrick." Patrick grinned. "Okay, troops. Let's go get some dinner."

Pete pointed the way, and the kids took off up the trail at a run. Fifteen minutes later, the group finally made it back to camp, with Pete whistling and the kids again shouting at the top of their lungs. *Dusk. Prime wildlife spotting time.* Patrick felt a twinge of disappointment at the missed opportunity, but he was having fun anyway. They found Vera and Susanne tending the fire.

"Where are Mom and the old man?" Pete asked, as he grabbed

sweatshirts from a backpack and started pulling them over kids' shivering bodies.

Vera put a finger over her lips. "Shh, everyone. Grandpa Joe and Gramma Lana have gone to bed. It's nearly eight o'clock back in Texas. Gotta love quiet time."

"And your dad has a cut the size of the Grand Canyon on his hand," Susanne said.

Patrick remembered the whittling. *Figures.* He put his hands on his hips and looked around him. A two-man tent had been erected in the center of the cleared area, and he'd beelined for the fire without even noticing it. He raised his eyebrows at Susanne, and she shook her head, but with an amused look on her face. Perry made a comical zipping motion over his lips. The kids did their best to be less loud, but from the grumbling sounds emanating from the tent, his father didn't think it was quite good enough. The adults hustled the kids through wiener roasting, and, afterwards, s'mores.

When everyone was gathered around the fire, sticky and quiet, Patrick decided it was time for the bear talk. "I need you guys to help me out with something. We're going to gather up all our trash and put it away, then I'm going to walk to a tree far away and hang it high on a branch. Do you know why?"

Head shakes and round mouths were the only answer he got from the younger kids. Trish and Perry probably knew the talk by heart, but they kept quiet.

Patrick tried for solemn but not scary. "Because bears like to steal people food, and we don't want them visiting our campsite."

"And we don't want them to steal our food," Stan said, nodding. "I like Frito's."

"And s'mores," Danny added.

"Right. So, can everyone be sure not to leave any food out tonight? It needs to go in the trash bag or in the backpack. No food on the ground or in the tents or your pockets."

Vigorous nods and even bigger eyes answered him.

"Good. Then your Uncle Pete and I will put the tents up while you guys gather up food and trash. Then you can get ready to go to sleep. Perry, can you help us with tents?"

Perry stood. "Yes, sir."

"Okay, then, troops. Let's do it. Aunt Susanne will lead trash duty and clean up. We've got an early day of fun tomorrow."

"Yes, sir, Uncle Patrick," Brian said, parroting Perry.

Patrick had noticed Brian had a growing case of hero worship going with Perry. Perry seemed to notice, too, and he was eating it up. The two had never spent any time together before this trip. It made Patrick smile, remembering himself and his brother as kids so close in age.

Brian's siblings repeated after him in singsong. Trish and Perry looked amused but joined in, a little sarcastically.

"Follow me, guys," Susanne said, raising a hand over her head and walking a few steps away from the fire.

Patrick, Pete, and Perry tackled erecting the tents. By then it was nearly dark, and they had a four-man and a seven-man to put up. Patrick laid them out while Pete and Perry hammered stakes.

After a few moments of pounding, Pete rocked back on his heels. "This ground. Man alive."

"They don't call these the Rocky Mountains for nothing," Patrick replied.

Perry groaned. "He always says that."

Pete laughed. He stood and arched his back to stretch it. "Sounds like a smart answer to me."

"Me and Burt Reynolds. Smart *and* good-looking," Patrick said.

"Together, you've got 'em both covered, anyway." Pete socked Patrick's arm.

Perry just rolled his eyes, but Patrick saw the lift at the corners of his mouth.

Patrick gestured at the seven-man. "You guys are going to be packed in this tent like sardines. Nine people. Better you than me."

"It'll be seven. Vera and I are going to sleep under the stars."

Patrick's eyebrows lifted. "Bold move."

Pete grinned. "Self-preservation."

It was pitch black out when they finished with the tents, except for the brilliant stars overhead. Patrick didn't know much about them, but he was a big fan of looking at them. An owl hooted. A chill in the air was nipping at his nose. The air smelled fresher somehow. He loved camping. The cares of the day started slipping away. He drew in a deep breath, then called for the kids. He led them to watch him hang the food backpacks in a tree. Afterward, he added logs to the fire. Susanne emerged from a tent where she'd been arranging bedding. Smiling, she handed Patrick his worn paperback copy of Larry McMurtry's *Horseman, Pass By,* which she knew he would read if he was the last man standing at the end of the evening. The whole group, except for his parents, settled around the flames. The kids were close but not touching, laying around the fire like a pack of hound dogs under a porch. Eyes were starting to close, except for Brian's. Vera and Trish sat on a log on either side of the kids. Perry perched on a stump close to where Patrick and Susanne were holding hands, Patrick seated on the ground cross-legged, his book by his knee.

"I wish Pete had his guitar so he could play for us. We could sing campfire songs." Vera rubbed her hands together like they were cold. "Gotta love singalongs."

Susanne said, "That's a great idea."

In the distance, something howled. The hair on Patrick's neck stood up. He had a healthy respect for predators. He'd prepared the camp as best he could, though, and he felt reasonably sure they were safe. Safer than camping in a city park with human predators, he'd bet.

"Maybe tomorrow night. The kids look like they're beat." Pete stood with his hands over the flames. He turned his head to speak to Patrick. "Were those wolves?"

"Coyotes. The last wolves were hunted out of this area fifty years ago. Or so they say."

"What else is out here that could eat us?"

"Well, the bears of course."

"Grizzlies?"

"Yep. And black bears, although they don't attack humans unless provoked, usually over cubs. Also, mountain lions."

Patrick had a complicated relationship with cougars, especially after an ambush by one on Dome Mountain in Cloud Peak Wilderness had nearly killed his horse Reno. The poor animal was only just now fit to carry riders again, more than six months later. But he admired the lions, and he related to them. When Barb Lamkin had murdered the county judge's wife a few months before and then come after the Flints, Patrick had repeated lion encounters, which he believed with all his heart were visits to warn him about the danger. To him, they were a sort of spirit animal.

He wondered whether the Sheep Eaters believed in spirit animals. A helpful librarian in Buffalo had found articles about the Tukudika for him in back issues of *The Annals of Wyoming*. From his reading, he'd learned that the Shoshone believed all matter, animate or not, had a spirit, and that the greatest power resided with those they considered "sky people." Like eagles, or the greatest of the sky people—the sun. Because the Sheep Eaters had lived high in the mountains, some of the other Shoshone believed they had great medicine themselves, because they resided closer to the most powerful spirits. Here in these mountains now himself, the thought gave Patrick goose flesh. The articles hadn't mentioned spirit animals, but Patrick liked to think they believed in them like he did.

Pete bared his teeth like he was scared. "Cougars are the ones I don't like."

Perry nodded. "Me or dad either."

Patrick grinned. "Are you sure you and Vera want to sleep outside?"

"We'll be fine. Predators are better than seven kids. Especially when a few are bound to wet the sleeping bags." Pete shrugged. "But, just in case, what does a mountain lion sound like?"

"Most of the time, you don't hear them at all. But sometimes they make a sound like a child screaming."

"That's disturbing, all the way around."

Patrick grinned. "Isn't it? Just one of the many reasons to keep our group together, for safety. So, don't go wandering off too far when you answer the call of nature in the dark."

"I'm thinking about two steps will be as far as I go."

Perry yawned. Brian's eyes had closed, as had Vera's. A silence settled over them, until, clear as if whoever was speaking was just across the campsite from them, Patrick heard a man's voice.

"Andale, Hector. Andale!"

Susanne put a hand on her chest. "Who was that? Where are they?"

Pete's thin, blond eyebrows shot up. "Am I dreaming, or did we just teleport back to Texas? I could have sworn I just heard Spanish."

Trish jumped to her feet. "A man was telling someone named Hector to hurry up."

"Don't worry." Patrick smiled. "Sound carries out here. They're probably miles away."

There was a loud splash, then laughter.

Susanne wrapped her arms around her torso. "But Sylvie said no one had been up here yet this year."

"She said *she and Klaus* hadn't been up here. It's just some campers, like us." Patrick stood, trying to project complete confidence, but even he found himself staring into the darkness, looking for human shapes that weren't there.

CHAPTER SIX: ABSTAIN

Susanne

"Get out of here. Shoo!" Susanne flung her arms up to scare the gray jays away, but the birds, better known as "camp robbers" in Wyoming, didn't budge. Flapjacks for fifteen people in the wilderness attracted plenty of hungry animals. Chipmunks, squirrels, and, on the fringe of the camping area in the rocks, a marmot. They had plenty to feast on, too, thanks to the children who had ignored instructions not to feed the critters and tossed pancakes far and wide. Dollars to doughnuts, the kids would all be starving by mid-morning, too, now. Susanne just hoped the small animals did a good job cleaning up, so the scraps didn't attract something bigger.

"Who's up for some fishing and panning for gold this morning?" Patrick's voice boomed. He'd woken with the sunrise before five a.m. and scouted up Trout Creek for promising spots.

An excited cacophony of "me's" rang out.

Patrick laughed. "Well then, I guess that means I'll have a lot of help getting us ready." He walked over to the backpacks, a pied piper to a devoted following of short people. Trish, Pete, and Joe came close behind the kids with Perry in the rear of the procession.

Vera and Lana appeared on the trail from the creek, each carrying a web bag of washed dishes. Everyone was wearing the same clothes as the day before, but Lana still managed a total change-up in her look. She'd put a t-shirt under her safari blouse and left it unbuttoned like a jacket. A leopard print scarf hanging loose around her neck completed her transformation. Vera looked rumpled. And tired.

Susanne was tired herself. She'd been awakened over and over by the voices of children crying to be taken to the bathroom. And by Pete and Vera moving into the tent in the wee hours. She couldn't imagine Vera had gotten any sleep at all. Susanne had tried to talk Patrick into more kids. Four would have been the perfect number in her mind. Busy but still manageable. Seven was . . . well, seven was just almost too much for her to comprehend.

"Just set them by the fire. The rinsing water is about to boil." Susanne pushed her bandana back from where it had slipped down on her forehead. It was three times as hard to manage a camp of fifteen with seven kids than it would have been to manage a camp of only eight adults. With a morning of hard work added to her lack of sleep, she was already wiped out.

Perry turned back from following his dad. "Aren't you coming, Mom?"

Susanne imagined an hour—two if she was lucky—of peace and quiet. Everyone else but Lana was going on the excursion. No one would be needing food, a drink, dry socks, or a scolding. Just Lana and her with the blanket of wildflowers, the breeze, the sunshine, and the distant burbling creek. "I think I'm going to sit this one out with Gramma Lana."

Lana smiled. "Good. I get you all to myself. Have fun, Perry-winkle."

Perry laughed, but he looked at the other kids, like he was hoping they didn't hear the nickname his grandmother had used on him back when he was a little kid in Texas.

Susanne said, "And be careful, Perry. You know you can be reckless at times. Be a good example for the younger kids."

He blew her a kiss. She caught it against her cheek, then blew one back at him.

CHAPTER SEVEN: PILE

North of the campsite, Trout Creek, Bridger-Teton
National Forest, Wyoming
Friday, June 24, 1977, 8:00 a.m.

Trish

The day had started out fun enough, but that hadn't lasted long with four kids to watch. Perry's charges, too, whenever he wasn't paying attention, which was most of the time. They were constantly picking on each other, throwing sticks and rocks and pinecones into the water, shouting, and falling behind. Then, Bunny got tired of hiking after only half an hour of not going very fast to begin with. Trish had held her hand and pulled her along, but the little girl started whining. When that wasn't enough to get Patrick and her parents to stop, she had escalated it to crying, then wailing, and finally, after throwing herself to the ground on her tummy, a full-blown flailing, screaming tantrum.

It gave Trish a headache. She gritted her teeth and closed her eyes for a second.

Her dad halted the group and marched back to them. His lips were moving with no sound coming out long before he reached them. "What's the matter, Bunny?"

Bunny didn't answer. She didn't even take a breath.

Trish crossed her arms. "She's tired of hiking."

"We've barely started."

Vera joined them. "Do you want to go back to camp, my Bunny honey?"

Bunny nodded, then rolled to her side and stuck her thumb in her mouth, right in the opening where she had no teeth. From her years of babysitting experience, Trish thought she was a little old for thumb sucking and a little young to have lost her front teeth, but she'd never been a mom, so what did she know, really?

Her dad's jaw bulged. After a few seconds of silence, he said, "Are you going to take her back to camp, Vera?"

"I was really hoping to pan for gold." Aunt Vera widened her big brown eyes. They were her best feature, in Trish's opinion. "Trish, would you mind walking her back? She really loves her big cousin." She bit her lip and half-shook her head. "Gotta love little girls."

Trish's heart sank. She'd hoped to find some gold to help pay for a car. She sent a silent plea to her dad. He always had her back. She was his girl. He'd understand. He had to. Besides, Bunny wasn't hers. She was Aunt Vera's. It should be Aunt Vera's job to take her to camp.

His eyes looked sympathetic, but his words dashed her hopes. "I think that's probably for the best."

"But, Dad—"

"We'll make sure you get to pan and fish tomorrow, Trish. Thank you for helping with the kids."

This isn't fair. Perry was watching, but when she caught his eyes, he turned and trotted up the trail.

She frowned, felt her forehead bunching up. "I thought you said we should always stay together?"

"You know the way back, right?"

Does he think I'm a baby? "Of course. Walk back along the stream. Turn left on the trail. The camp is up the hill."

"Good. Be careful. Make noise."

If he's worried about bears, he shouldn't make me hike alone. Trish reached down for her cousin's small hand, which was now muddy from dust and tears. "Come on, Bunny."

Bunny got up. Her cries had long since stopped. After a few steps, she was skipping alongside Trish. "See me do my pwincess dance, Twish?" She held up her arms and twirled.

Trish groaned. *Not fair at all.*

CHAPTER EIGHT: FREE

North of the campsite, Trout Creek, Bridger-Teton
National Forest, Wyoming
Friday, June 24, 1977, 9:00 a.m.

Perry

"Howdy!" a man's voice called from behind Perry.

Perry jumped. He hadn't known anyone was back there. He turned from the trail toward the voice.

A man was walking up the center of the frothy creek. Where had he come from? This section of the creek didn't even have very many trees around it. Just rolling hills, sort of like what they called tundra in his class at school. Barren, unless you counted the sagebrush that was taller than him in some places, which he didn't. And only a hundred yards back, the trees had been so thick the sun nearly couldn't get through. Without the trees, there was nothing to stop the wind, and dirt stung his eyes. He didn't understand how things could change so fast out here. But, anyway, Perry thought he would have seen the man if he'd hiked over to the creek.

But, no, he had to have come up the stream, fishing. He was wearing rubber wading pants that looked like the kind with boot covers built right into them. Perry desperately wanted a pair. July was the height of fly-fishing season at higher elevations, and if he just had a pair of waders —that, and a ride into the mountains—he could catch enough fish to feed the family every day. The waders would pay for themselves in no time. He could even sell some of his catch. He'd been watching Trish try to save for a car, and he'd decided he'd better start earlier than she had.

"Uh, hi." Perry half-lifted his hand.

The man, who was nearly as short as Perry—which was to say, only a few inches over five feet—was casting a fly rod quick as a whip over the surface of the water. The fly would barely touch before the man would jerk it back and toss it again. Two teenage boys were working either side of the creek with fly rods, just downstream from him. They both had on the fancy waders, too. All three of them wore the equivalent contents of a tackle box of flies pinned to fishing vests. Knives and nets hung from clips on their torsos, plus one flopping bag of fish on the man's hip. The older teenage boy was wearing a John Deere ball cap, but the younger one and the man had on battered cowboy hats with splash marks on the brims. Their pockets bulged with items Perry couldn't see.

"That your group ahead there?" the man asked.

"Yeah. I mean, yes, sir."

"You're a big bunch." The man grinned, stopping his legs but not his casting. "Scaring off all the fish."

"Sorry."

"Not to worry, son. I think we'll just pass right around you, if you don't mind."

"I don't mind. We're hoping to do some fishing, too. And gold panning."

"You with those fellas downstream from here?"

Perry hadn't seen another group downstream. "No, sir. This is all of us. Except my mom, grandmother, sister, and baby cousin."

"Didn't think so. They were a rough looking crowd."

"Did you see a girl older than me with a little girl about five?"

"No. But we just came from making a fish breakfast on the far side of the creek. My name's Ethan Hilliard. These are my boys. The older one is Buzz. The young'un is Cliff."

The "young'un" said, "Dad, I'm eighteen."

Mr. Hilliard winked at Perry.

"I'm Perry Flint. That's my family. The guy with the funny hat is my dad. Patrick Flint."

"That's a fedora. A fine looking one. The kids all swimmers?"

"I'm not sure. We've got canoes and life jackets for the river."

Mr. Hilliard nodded and kept casting. He hadn't had any bites yet, but he didn't let that break his rhythm. "You from around here?"

"Buffalo. But most of the rest of the group is up from Texas. That's where I was born."

"I see. I thought I heard a 'yee ha' a while back there. We're from Riverton. Been fishing on the Tukudika every summer since these boys were little punks. Trying to get them in touch with their roots, since their ancestors are from around here."

The little punks didn't look so little to Perry. In fact, they looked old enough to be in college. In good shape too. Muscular, even if they weren't very tall.

"Cool," he said.

Mr. Hilliard adjusted his hat to shield his eyes. "We're close to a little waterfall where there's usually good cutthroat trout in the plunge pool." He reeled in his line as he spoke over his shoulder to his sons. "Best hurry, boys." Then, to Perry, "Well, I'll pay my respects to your father. Be seeing you on up the river, I expect."

"Yes, sir. You, too."

Perry watched with longing as the fishermen hustled up the side of the creek, stopping to talk to his dad before moving past the Flints. Perry now noticed a waterfall in the distance. It looked so cool. He hoped there'd be fish left in the plunge pool when he got there. If not, he was going to climb up the rocks beside the waterfall. It wasn't very high. How cool would that be?

CHAPTER NINE: IRRITATE

North of the campsite, Trout Creek, Bridger-Teton
National Forest, Wyoming
Friday, June 24, 1977, 10:00 a.m.

Patrick

P atrick envied lucky Ethan Hilliard and his two sons. Far up
Trout Creek, catching one trout after another, most likely.
They'd be getting ready to build a campfire soon and have fresh
fish for lunch. Not so for Patrick. His group would be lucky if they
caught a fish the entire week, at the rate they were going. He glanced
back at the creek bank from his perch on the hill, where he'd walked to
get a look upstream from the waterfall.

Bert had snagged his line in a tree, and Perry was helping him
untangle it. Or trying to. Barry had dropped his line and was throwing
rocks into the stream, scaring off all the fish. Vera was sitting on a boulder, shouting at him to stop. Danny—his rash far better than the day
before—was standing under the waterfall, screaming as it doused his
hair. Stan was napping under a tree. Brian was climbing out of the creek,
where he had fallen in wearing the backpack with their lunch sandwiches in it. Water ran off of it like it was an extension of the falls.

Annie was screaming as Pete tried to get her to put a worm onto her hook. Joe was fishing downstream, ignoring them all.

The seven dwarves' names from last night didn't apply anymore. Now, he'd call them Screechy, Clumsy, Sleepy, Trouble, Hurly, Oopsy, and Pushy. Not that he'd say any of those names out loud. He loved his nieces and nephews, and he didn't want to hurt anyone's feelings. But his frustration was rising. The trip wasn't turning out how he'd envisioned it, at all, and it was wearing on him. He'd planned for six adults and two teenagers to be eating fish for dinner by sundown a few miles down the Tukudika, after a day of adventure and camaraderie with his brother. But there was none of that with so many kids along.

To top it all off, they'd encountered bighorn sheep on the rocky expanse above the stream earlier, closer than he'd ever imagined being to one, and his dad had said they looked and smelled like goats. Goats! One of God's most majestic creatures, goats? A flock of ewes with bouncing kids. A ram with a three-quarter curl horn. All of them leaping nimbly on the face of a rocky slope that no human could have survived.

The kids had started calling them bighorn goats after that.

The animals deserved some reverence. They used to number in the thousands in these mountains and had sustained a way of life for the Sheep Eaters. Then, when domestic sheep had been introduced to the area, disease had decimated their numbers, driving them nearly to extinction, not unlike the plight of the American Indians when settlers and gold rushers had flooded across the West. It had taken decades to build and stabilize the bighorn sheep population to a fraction of its earlier numbers. Yet here they still were. Strong and wily, persevering. They were nobody's goat.

He rubbed his forehead so hard he knew he was leaving a blotchy red spot. *Okay, maybe that shouldn't be a big deal to me, but it is. It just is. It's enough to drive a man to drink, if a man had thought to bring a Pabst with him.* He hadn't, of course. All he had was a canteen of water still warm from a purification boil that morning. Last time he'd camped, he'd gotten a wicked case of giardia, and he wasn't ever going to let that happen to anyone else on his watch. He took a deep cleansing breath. This trip was supposed to be fun, and he needed to control his blood pressure and try to enjoy it. He gulped another breath. And another. They didn't seem to do him much good. He shook his head. He had two more days on the river with his family. He'd have to figure out a way to improve his attitude, or it was going to be a really, really long two days.

Patrick decided it was time to pan for gold, then get the kids back to camp, since the food for their picnic lunch had no doubt been ruined in its dunking. They'd have to make more sandwiches before they got on the river for their next camp site down the Tukudika. A further delay. He ground his teeth, then walked back to his family and got the gold panning equipment from his dry backpack.

He pasted on a big smile. "Okay, prospectors, let's put up that fishing equipment and find us some gold nuggets."

His announcement was met by a chorus of complaints ranging from one kid being hungry, one cold, one wet, one not having caught anything yet, and one not wanting to pan for gold. Only Brian and Perry abstained from the grousing.

Brian started gathering up the rods. He brought them to Patrick. "I want to pan, Uncle Patrick."

"Count us in." Pete ignored the protests of the children and put an arm on Vera's shoulders.

Perry brought the tackle box. "How do we pan, Dad?"

Patrick rubbed Brian's hair, and was just about to do the same to Perry, but he stopped when his son ducked. That, finally, brought a sincere grin from Patrick.

"First, we ignore the naysayers."

He passed out the pans, which attracted Danny and Stan. He scooped up sediment and water, then shook his pan, demonstrating how to slowly drain away the water, dirt, and rocks, leaving—if they were lucky—only gold behind. The kids scooped and shook their pans. Danny slung the contents of his pan at Stan, who screamed and ran, then fell face first into the stream. He got up swinging. Danny laughed, threw his pan on the bank, and sprinted away from his brother. Stan went after him. The kid was fast and caught his younger brother, flattening him from the back. The tussling from the two of them could have woken the spirits of the Tukudika dead.

"I think I see gold," Brian shouted.

Patrick squinted into the boy's pan. Something shiny gleamed from the sand. *Flakes?* His heart sped up.

"It's small, but you may be right. Let's put it in the bag." Patrick motioned toward a muslin bag he'd brought along for just this happy purpose.

Perry ran to get it and brought it to him. Patrick dabbed at the gold fleck with his index finger and carefully transferred it into the bag.

"Can I try again?" Brian said.

"Sure."

Brian started scooping and sloshing again with infectious enthusiasm, as did Perry, Pete, and Vera. Patrick lost himself in the rhythm of panning. The clear water at the edge of the stream seemed to work magic on his murky mind. His tension eased. Time passed. He wasn't sure how much. He became aware that Pete and Vera had given up on panning. Brian and Perry hadn't. The parents had corralled their other children and were drying them off.

"I want to go hunting for arrowheads," Stan announced.

This impressed but didn't surprise Patrick. Stan was easily the most cerebral of his siblings. Patrick wanted to look for artifacts, too. As a young boy in Texas, he'd found many arrow points. With every year that passed, though, they became harder and harder to find.

A cranky voice intruded on the peace. "Somebody needs to get control of these kids." It was his father. Joe shouted a few unprintable words, threw his fishing rod down, and stomped downstream, still spouting unhappy words like a poison fountain. "Don't even treat me like I'm part of this family. No food. Been out too long. Cold. Didn't want to go on this river trip in the first place. Heading back to camp. Just go on without me like you've been doing." His voice faded as he drew further away.

It was the last straw for Patrick. If he didn't remove himself from this situation, he was going to act as badly as his own father. Or worse.

"Excuse me, boys," he said to Perry and Brian.

Then he darted up the trail beside the waterfall, trying to put distance between himself and the group before he blew his cool. An enormous growling scream burbled in his throat. He reached into his pocket, grasping, for what he didn't know, and found a sock. He didn't even care whose foot it had been on. It would work to muzzle the sounds he didn't want the others to hear him making, because he couldn't stand the thought of them thinking he was acting like his father. He stuffed a corner in his mouth, bit down, and chewed madly, like a frenzied cow with its cud, taking his frustration out on the sock instead of his family.

He wasn't sure how far he'd gone—a hundred yards, maybe a quarter mile?—when he stopped. The exertion of the climb and his frantic chewing had leeched some of his irritation away. High to his left on the mountain face, he saw the herd of bighorn sheep again.

"Bighorn goats." Patrick laughed. *Okay, it is kind of funny.*

From downstream, he heard the sound of Perry's voice. "Watch this, Brian."

Across the creek, a flash of movement drew his eye. A man. Ethan Hilliard or one of his sons? But this man had shoulder-length black hair, straight and parted in the center, with feathers tied in it. He was clean shaven, with red paint decorating his cheeks. And he wasn't dressed like a fisherman. Or like anyone of the modern era. He wore loose buckskin pants with—wait, was that a loin cloth over it? And tall moccasins?

The man chinned toward downstream, then walked away, into a stand of trees.

Was he a Tukudika? Patrick thought of the stone figures carved and exposed by erosion. The Tukudika, an immortal guard over their wilderness. They'd believed that all matter had a spirit. Was this man the embodiment of the spirit of one of those rock figures, could he be . . .? But no. Patrick had to be imagining things, no matter how badly he wanted to believe it. There was no way he just saw an Indian, garbed in clothes of a century and a half ago. They were long gone to the reservations. And the embodiment of the spirit from a rock he'd only dreamed up as an immortal Tukudika guard? He knew better, and he also decided he'd better not tell anyone this thought had even crossed his mind.

He shook his head, gaze locked on the stand of trees in case the man reappeared. He didn't. *Because he isn't real.* Unless . . . unless it was someone dressed like a Sheep Eater . . . someone creating an experience . . . reconnecting with ancestors. It was unlikely, but it was possible. What was more likely was that Patrick had Tukudika on the brain, something his kids had accused him of on the drive to Jackson. *No.* There hadn't been anyone there.

There was a medical term for this. *Hallucinations.* They were a good sign that it was time to pull himself together and go back. The family could pan another day.

In a minute, he decided. The peace he had found here was a balm to his inflamed emotions. He'd just soak it in a little longer. And watch the stand of trees.

But then the peace was shattered when he heard someone scream, followed by Vera's wails in the deathly silence following it.

CHAPTER TEN: DISRUPT

Susanne

"Should I make more coffee?" Susanne brandished the empty pan. She'd just poured the last of the coffee into her tin cup.

Lana put a hand over her own cup. She was sitting on a log next to the fire ring. "I've had plenty." She smiled. "But isn't this nice? Peace and quiet. Just us girls."

Susanne dumped the grounds into the grass and set the pot upside down on a rock. She'd have to wash it later and rinse it with sterilized water. Then she tilted her face up toward the sun. "Heavenly. Not that I don't enjoy all the family, but they're . . . a lot."

Lana shook her head. "Yes, they are. I don't know how Pete and Vera do it. I'm glad they have each other. Most of my years as a mother, I just had two kids. The boys were nearly out of high school when Patricia was born."

Susanne copped a seat on a stump near her mother-in-law. "But Patrick and Pete were so close in age and so rambunctious."

"They did get into some mischief. But they were always such sweet boys. And best friends."

Susanne smiled. "Yes, they are. Patrick has been so excited for Pete to visit."

"Pete has, too."

Susanne sipped her coffee, then touched a finger to her lips to lift some grounds off. She wiped her finger on the stump. "I'll bet they're all having a ball."

Lana raised delicate brows. Usually, she created a Joan Crawford look with tweezing and eyebrow pencil. Without makeup, her blonde brows were practically invisible. Like Pete's, Susanne realized. She'd never made the connection between the features before. "Oh, I'm sure Joe has found something to complain about by now."

"More than one thing I'm sure."

"He's been perfecting his role as the grumpy old man since we were teenagers. He's gotten very good at it."

They laughed together, Susanne with some surprise. Lana didn't often acknowledge what a curmudgeon Joe was.

Susanne drank the last of her coffee, then stood. "Well, I have a few more things to finish up before the horde returns."

Lana started to rise. "I'll help you."

Susanne held up a hand. "I've got it. You relax. You're on vacation."

"So are you."

"Well, you're my mother-in-law, and I want to take care of you, so I win."

Lana settled back onto her stump. "Just a few more minutes won't hurt, I guess. I can't imagine a more beautiful spot than this. I'm really enjoying the birds."

Susanne paused to watch the tuxedo-clad magpies hop around the campsite. Suddenly, the birds took wing. The shadow of a larger bird crossed the ground. She looked skyward and saw a shiny white head, yellow beak, and rich chocolate feathers across a broad wingspan.

She pointed. "Bald eagle, Lana."

Lana gasped, then put her hand over her heart. "I pledge allegiance, to the bird, the national bird of America." She giggled. "I don't know why I said that. It's just so majestic, it doesn't feel right not to honor it somehow."

Susanne knew exactly what Lana meant. She felt it, too, in a heart-swelling way.

The eagle emitted a high-pitched shriek and circled out of view. Moments later, something large and heavy crashed through the underbrush. Susanne's heart jumpstarted from relaxation to a sprint. She moved closer to Lana. How quickly beauty could turn to terror out in the wilderness. She looked around for something to use as a weapon. Patrick stayed ready 24/7 in the wilderness, carrying his knife and .357 Magnum revolver, but she had nothing. He'd been trying to get Trish and her to carry knives. He'd even suggested Susanne get a handgun. She'd argued that it was pointless, since she was always with him.

She now saw the error of her ways.

Snatching a rock nearly the size of her palm from the ground, she motioned behind her. "Stay back, Lana."

On the edge of the clearing, the branches of a small pine shook. She flexed her knees and shook her arms, trying to stay loose. She expected a grizzly to burst through any second. Her mind raced through all the instruction she'd had on bears. If it's a black bear, wave your arms. If it's a grizzly, play dead. *Please don't be a cub. Cubs have mamas. Mamas get protective.* But what emerged from the forest was far crankier and less lethal than any bear.

It was Joe.

He let a few choice cuss words fly. "Missed the damn trail. Only way I found the camp was your voices."

Lana bustled forward, exclaiming over scrapes on his arms and face.

He shrugged off her attentions. "Haven't eaten a thing since breakfast."

"We haven't either," Susanne said. She glanced at her watch. "But it's only ten-thirty."

"Doesn't mean I'm not hungry. Not after all that hiking and fishing."

Lana's face was completely devoid of expression. "I'll make you a bite." She crouched by the backpack and started pulling out food.

"Where is everyone else?" Susanne asked.

Joe waved an arm vaguely upstream. "Out there. Impossible. Kids are too loud. No one's making them mind. Scared off all the fish. No one was listening to me, and I was wet and cold. Couldn't take it anymore." He slapped at his arm. "And mosquitos. Mosquitos the size of a Buick eating me alive."

Susanne bit the inside of her lip. Joe didn't like it when he wasn't the center of negative attention. But she imagined the rest of the group was a lot happier without his stormy personality in their midst.

So much for peaceful girl time. Now she wished she was with the kids.

CHAPTER ELEVEN: MISSTEP

Trish

"I'm tie-yud." Bunny plopped her little fanny down on a rock beside the trail. It was just the right height to make her a seat. She immediately started picking tiny flowers. Little daisies. What looked like miniature wedding bouquets. Exquisitely small fuchsia blossoms. She gathered them in her hand and pressed her nose into them.

"Me, too. Hold on, Buns. I'm just going to peek over this ridge and see if we're almost there." Trish jogged up a short but steep hill. She knew she wasn't going to see the camp. Nothing around them looked familiar. But she wasn't going to say that out loud, partly because she didn't want to scare Bunny, and partly because she didn't even want to admit it to herself.

It was inescapable, though. She was lost. Lost in a giant wilderness with a tired little girl and no food or water. When they'd first started walking back to camp, Trish supposed she'd been distracted. Consumed by her feelings of being mistreated by the adults. Why was Bunny her responsibility? Why was it just okay to ruin Trish's good time? Why didn't Aunt Vera or Uncle Pete take Bunny? By the time she'd gotten her emotions under control, she'd realized she might have walked too far along the creek and missed the path back to their campsite. Then she'd come upon a trail, heading in what looked like the right direction. Away from the creek.

She'd convinced herself it looked familiar and took it, hoping against hope that it was the right one. She just wanted to get back to camp. But it wasn't the right trail. It had quickly wandered off to the right—which was the wrong direction. It had grown more and more narrow, with branches crisscrossing overhead and blocking out the sun. Bunny was walking upright, but Trish was hunched over. The trees were so close around them and to each other that it made her feel claustrophobic. And jumpy. Squirrels had chittered at them. She nearly came unglued when something hit her in the head, until she saw it was a small branch of pinecones—just the doings of a squirrel.

She should have backtracked when she was still on the creek. Even gone all the way back to her dad and the rest of the group, whether Bunny liked it or not. *The wilderness is not a place for guesswork*, she thought. She was sounding like her dad.

Trish crested the ridge, and her heart sank. No camp. Not even the river. All she could see was a dark ocean of tall, skinny evergreens clustered tightly together, broken up every so often by pools of bright green leaves of aspen. A sob rose in her throat, but she choked it back. She had to be strong. For Bunny's sake. Like it or not, she was responsible for her. She sucked a deep, long breath through her nose, then paused, holding it.

She heard water. A lot more water than little old Trout Creek. More like a river. *It has to be the Tukudika*, she decided. She knew she had a choice.

Option A, she could take Bunny back the way they'd come, through the scary forest, all the way to Trout Creek, then walk upstream and look for her dad. But what if her family had already gone back to camp? She might end up walking back and forth for hours, just as lost there as here.

Option B was to follow this path to the Tukudika, where she'd be able to see the rock cliff and trail to their campsite. The Tukudika sounded close. She could just follow the trail and her ears. She could get her bearings at the river. Just imagining it made her feel slightly less bad.

She walked back to her cousin, giving her a bright smile that hurt her face. "Okay, Buns. We're almost to the river. We can rest there, then we'll be nearly back to camp."

Bunny locked big, trusting brown eyes on her, and Trish almost lost it. There were tear tracks through the dust on the little girl's cheeks.

"Okay." She dropped her flowers, stood, and held out her hand to Trish.

Trish clasped it. Then she said, "Would you like to ride piggyback for a little while?"

Bunny nodded solemnly. Trish crouched, and Bunny climbed on. Trish wrapped her arms around the girl's skinny legs and stood. Bunny was heavier than she'd expected. But Trish had been running more hills lately, and she had confidence in her thighs. She strode off at a brisk pace. Within minutes, Bunny went limp and her head fell forward onto Trish's shoulder. She was asleep. At first Trish was relieved. But, sleeping, Bunny released her grip on Trish, which made the girl's body heavier and more unwieldy. Plus, it made Trish feel even more alone.

The forest grew eerily silent. Trish's footsteps were muffled by the pine needles padding the trail. *There might be bears or mountain lions out here, and I wouldn't even hear them.* If she rounded a bend and came upon a predator, she'd have to drop Bunny and fight—with her bare hands. Trish knew she needed to make noise, to scare them off, but she didn't want to wake up Bunny. Tears pricked the corners of her eyes, and she willed them to stop. *No being a cry baby.* She couldn't even swipe them away with her hands.

She picked up her pace. Her only consolations were that the sound of the water was growing louder and the trail was now mostly downhill. She gritted her teeth. *You can do this, Patricia Kay Flint. You can do this.*

She could do it, and she would, because she had no choice.

CHAPTER TWELVE: CARE

North of the campsite, Trout Creek, Bridger-Teton
National Forest, Wyoming
Friday, June 24, 1977, 10:30 a.m.

Patrick

From the top of the falls, Patrick saw a blond head, wet with blood, a body— unmoving—draped over a boulder mid-stream. His stomach clenched.

It was *his son's* blond crew cut. His son's unmoving body. Perry. *What happened, what happened, what happened?* That refrain was quickly replaced by *Dear God, please let my son be all right. Please, please, please, God.*

He took off at a run down the steep, rocky trail beside the waterfall. It was slippery, and he fell on his rear, sliding most of the way. He landed on his feet beside the hat that tumbled from his head. Then he ran, splashing through the creek. It was only a few steps to Perry, but he was blocked by the six small children and two adults who had crowded around his son.

"Let me through," he said, his voice terse.

Pete had his hands on Perry's temples. He used his dad voice.

"Move. Everyone. Now." He stayed put, though, still holding Perry's head.

Brian shooed Bert and Barry away. Stan and Annie scooted to one side. Danny jumped back and fell on his behind in the creek. Patrick barreled over rocks and through the water toward his son. Vera leaned over and dragged Danny out of Patrick's way.

"What happened?" Patrick knelt in the cold water by Perry. He willed himself to slow down, to be calm. *Think. Be a physician, not a father.* He had to treat Perry like any other patient right now. Any other unconscious patient with a head injury. Any other unconscious patient with a head injury in the middle of a huge, remote wilderness area. *Don't go down that road. You can do this. Check his vitals. Breathing, first.* Blocking out everything else around him, he checked the rise and fall of Perry's chest. He was breathing. And from the regular rhythm, he didn't appear to be in respiratory distress.

"He was playing on the rocks in the waterfall," Pete said. "Climbing them. He slipped and fell backwards. Hit his head."

Patrick was only dimly aware of his brother's words. *Check the wound site.* He probed gently in Perry's hair, careful not to twist Perry's neck, his fingers searching for the source of the blood. It was hard to determine where the injury was. Perry's entire head was wet from water and blood.

Pete kept explaining what had happened. "He hadn't climbed far. Maybe a foot or two. Then he just slipped and fell over backwards. I didn't see him land."

Vera said, "I saw it happen. His behind hit first. Then his head."

Patrick digested their information. Perry's body had broken the velocity of his fall before his head struck the rock. That was good, although the whiplash could have injured his neck, too. But head injuries were dangerous. Patrick had a patient who died from a slip and fall in his own kitchen. On the other hand, he'd also treated mountain climbers who'd tumbled the equivalent of two stories and lived to tell the story. The fact that Perry was unconscious wasn't a positive sign, though.

He asked, "The back of his head?"

"Yes," Vera said.

Patrick slid his hands carefully up Perry's neck and around the back of his head. He breathed a sigh of relief when he didn't find the injury until he'd crossed the unprotected area at the base of the skull. Not that it meant Perry was out of the woods. Just that paralysis was less likely. The wound site was already swelling, which intensified the churning in Patrick's stomach. It could be swelling as much or more on the inside of the skull than on the outside of it. Even bleeding inside it. And the hard skull didn't flex with fluid buildup like skin did—it held it in and compressed the brain with it. The gash itself wasn't long, though—maybe an inch. The blood flow was impressive, but head wounds produced a lot of bleeding. The external bleeding wasn't the problem. The swelling was.

Patrick chewed the inside of his lip. "We need to get him out of the water or he'll get hypothermia pretty quickly, but we have to be very careful. He could have a neck or spine injury."

"What do you want me to do?" Pete asked.

First, he needed to finish his examination. Just to be on the safe side. *Check his pulse.* Patrick put his fingers on the inside of Perry's wrist, found his pulse. "Count to ten seconds."

Pete nodded. "One one thousand, two one thousand, three one thousand," he began counting.

As his brother timed him, Patrick counted his son's heart beats.

"Ten one thousand."

Patrick multiplied his result times six. Sixty beats per minute. A little slow, but Perry was young and in good physical condition.

Check for response to sound. "Perry. Can you hear me?" Patrick raised his voice and leaned toward his son. "Wake up. Perry, wake up."

The boy didn't respond.

Check for parasympathetic nervous system response. Patrick lifted Perry's eyelids. The pupils contracted smoothly and rapidly at the sudden influx of sunlight. That was good. He positioned his thumb and fingers on either side of the trapezius on Perry's left shoulder and squeezed hard, then harder still. Perry flinched. His hand twitched and his feet kicked. That was even better. Patrick exhaled. He realized he was feeling lightheaded. That he'd been holding in his breath. He breathed deeply and exhaled again. *In with the good air, out with the bad.*

He nodded. "We've got to be very, very careful moving him, so we don't cause further damage. It's going to take all three of us. You, me, and Vera." Patrick wished he had a trauma team and a litter, but six arms would have to do.

"I can help, too." Brian's voice squeaked, but it was strong.

"Four of us, then. Thank you, Brian. Come on over, now."

Vera and Brian joined Patrick and Pete, and the group of children surged closer again.

Patrick squatted on his haunches. His butt was in the water, but he didn't care. "We need to keep his back and neck immobilized as much as we can. It's not going to be easy. Here's what we're going to do. We'll need to get on one side of him, then we'll slide our arms under him and lift him with our arms all at the same height. We'll walk him to the shore, and then I want us to lower him to the ground under that tree—" he pointed to a flat grassy area— "very, very gently. I'll take his head and neck. Pete, you take his shoulders and upper back. Vera, you'll have his hips, and Brian, you'll take his knees." Patrick was worried about the weight Vera would bear, but he didn't dare entrust Perry's injured head to anyone but himself. "We'll move on my count."

"Got it, son?" Vera asked.

Brian nodded.

When everyone was standing in position, Patrick said, "Okay, then. Let's slide our arms under him." He knelt and slid his arms through the icy water and under Perry without jostling him. The others did the same. "Now, get in a low stance where you can lift him using your thigh muscles." The others adjusted their bodies. Patrick checked his footing. "On three, lift slowly. Stay together. One, two, three." Patrick gently lifted his son's head, keeping pace with his brother as Pete lifted Perry's back. Vera grunted, but she got Perry's hips in the air, and Brian did the same with his knees. Patrick waited a second until everyone was stable. "Now, a little higher." Perry seemed to levitate in the air. "Walk, slowly, on my count. You absolutely can't trip. Lift your feet out of the water and lower them carefully. Don't move until all your weight is down, and don't anyone get ahead of each other. Ready?"

"Ready." Pete said.

"Ready," Vera and Brian said.

"Step." Patrick paused for everyone to secure their feet. "Step." He paused again. "Step. Step."

Inch by inch, the group strode through the water and over to the edge of the stream. On dry land, the going was easier, and they moved faster. When they reached the tree, they lowered Perry to the ground in unison. Patrick held his breath until his son was settled securely against the earth.

"Now what?" Pete clasped Patrick's shoulder.

The simple gesture sent Patrick tumbling back in time through all the moments his brother had stood by him. When Patrick had gotten up after a beating from a neighborhood kid who had bullied Pete. When Pete had gone down hard blocking for Patrick on the football field, and Patrick had run the ball he'd caught for the touchdown back to his little brother and helped him stand. After Patrick had taken a licking with a belt from Joe for sneaking out and drinking beer, without ratting out Pete, who'd been in on the entire escapade. And, when Patrick had been cut off financially by his father for eloping with Susanne, Pete had followed him out to his car, shook his hand, and clapped him on the back. If there was anyone he'd want by his side right now, it was Pete.

He swallowed back the lump in his throat. "I've got to transport him out of here safely. And the best possible way to do that is to get help. We're only an hour away from that guard station radio and our vehicles. But I need to stay with Perry. Can you get there and call for help?" It crossed his mind that he was split up from Susanne and Lana, that Trish and Bunny had gone back to camp, and that his father had stomped off. What had happened to his plan to keep everyone together? Now he was breaking the group up further, but it couldn't be helped.

Pete nodded, hands on his hips. "I'll run the whole way. Do you agree that I should follow the creek to the Tukudika, then head downstream and cross at the bridge?"

"That's what I would do."

"I don't have the keys. But I have hotwiring skills."

"Hopefully you'll be able to call for help by radio."

Pete was dancing from foot to foot. "We're on the east side of Trout Creek off the Tukudika River, just past Yellowjacket Guard Station and the footbridge. Right?"

"Right."

The brothers embraced. Then Pete kissed Vera on the cheek and took off at a dead run.

CHAPTER THIRTEEN: HURT

Perry

The ringing in his ears was so loud that it vibrated his brain inside his skull. *Ow. Make it stop.* Perry tried to clap his hands over his ears, but he felt like he was up to his neck in mud, and the effort to move them was just too much. He tried to ignore the piercing sound and return to oblivion, but it didn't work.

He groaned. "Stop," he said. Or tried to. The ringing was too loud to hear his own voice.

A hand gripped his shoulder.

He struggled to open his eyes. It wasn't much easier to move the lids than his hands. He felt them twitch, then flutter.

"Perry. Come on, Perry. Wake up." The voice belonged to his dad, although it seemed a million miles away.

"Dad?" His words came out as a soft croak.

"It's me, son. I'm right here."

Perry's eyes opened. The light felt like an explosion in his head, and he closed his eyes again. His dad's face was an afterimage in his mind. "What happened to me?"

His dad squeezed his shoulder, but not hard. "You fell and hit your head."

"You were showing me how to climb the waterfall. It's my fault." Brian. Brian was there, too. His voice at least. Perry couldn't see him.

"It's not your fault, Brian." To Perry, Patrick said, "Does your head hurt?"

Perry tensed his face, then relaxed it. "Yeah. I think so." He opened his eyes again. The light wasn't as bad the second time. His dad was smiling at him. Behind him, Perry saw other faces, but they were blurry. He blinked. They came into focus. Aunt Vera and his cousins. "Where are we?"

"Still out on Trout Creek. Your Uncle Pete has gone down to get help."

"Help for what?" Perry started becoming more aware of the pain in his head. It seemed like his head was in a vise that was being cranked tighter and tighter. But that wasn't possible. *Why does it hurt so much?*

"You."

Perry rocked his head from side to side. *Mistake.* It made him feel like puking. "Am I going to be okay?"

"Yes. But we need to be careful. Can you move your hands and feet?"

Perry tried again with his hands. His arms lifted, and his fingers made fists. He bent his knees, waggled his feet, wiggled his toes.

"Great. How does the rest of you feel?"

Perry wasn't sure, so he decided to check it out. He rolled up onto an elbow.

"Careful, now."

The world tilted, swayed, then righted itself. The nausea got worse. A lot worse. He pushed to a sitting position and groaned. Pressing one hand to his head and supporting himself with the other, he slowly rotated his neck. "Feels like I got tackled by a bull, and I wasn't wearing a helmet."

His dad laughed. "Pretty much." He walked a few steps, picked up the hat Mr. Hilliard had called a fedora, and crammed it on his head.

"Was I unconscious?"

"You were.

"How long?"

"Not too long."

"And everyone has just been sitting here?"

His dad nodded. "Worrying about you."

"Without lunch," Stan said.

"Stan!" Vera frowned at him.

"It's true. Because our food got ruined when Brian dropped it in the water."

Perry said, "I'm good enough to go back to camp."

Patrick put a hand on Perry's arm. "Don't be in a rush."

Perry tried to stand. When that didn't go well, he rotated to his hands and knees, then climbed to his feet. His stomach floated up and down, like he was on a boat. "I don't feel so hot." Then he bent over his knees and vomited up breakfast.

Annie screamed. "Ew."

"Sorry," Perry groaned. He heaved for a minute until the barfy feeling passed. Then he wiped his mouth with the back of his hand, straightened, and tried to grin. "Now I'm hungry, too. Let's get out of here."

CHAPTER FOURTEEN: CHANGEUP

Trout Creek near the Tukudika River, Bridger-Teton National Forest, Wyoming
Friday, June 24, 1977, 11:05 a.m.

Patrick

Patrick hiked behind his son so he could monitor his condition. Within minutes, Perry was hiking as well as the rest of the group, and Patrick felt encouraged. He still wanted to get him back to Jackson and to the hospital. He needed to have Perry checked out. Just because a patient was up and about and speaking normally didn't mean there wasn't something going on in the brain that could cause death from a head injury. Perry would need to remain under close observation. But Patrick felt confident the kid could get back to the Suburban under his own power, and that was a huge plus. Patrick thought about Pete's mission to the guard station to call for help. If Pete was successful, it would trigger a massive waste of resources. As a physician, Patrick was sensitive to this, since that meant the resources would be unavailable to anyone else who might need them at the same time. It wasn't outside the realm of possibility that it could cost someone's life.

He had to stop Pete.

Patrick was in the best cardiovascular shape of his life, since he'd been training for a half marathon since March. Pete, on the other hand, lived a musician's lifestyle. Sleep all day, gig all night, with very little exercise, plenty of alcohol, and God knew what else. He didn't have that long of a head start on Patrick. Patrick could catch him. Vera could keep an eye on Perry and walk the kids back. Yes, he'd be splitting the group up even further, but it was the ethical thing to do. They could hike to the Tukudika together. He and Pete could meet them at the canoes.

But the clock was ticking, and with every second, Pete pulled further ahead of him. If Patrick was going to do this, he had to leave ASAP. There was no more time to mull things over.

He jogged past Perry and up to Vera, who was at the head of the line. "Can you handle things with the kids? I need to catch up to Pete and bring him back." He pointed ahead to a rock formation. It was hiding the mouth of the trail back to camp. "That's the turn. From there it's a straight shot back to camp."

Vera was already nodding. "Of course. Should we wait for you there?"

"Let's meet back up at the canoes, on the river. It'll save some hiking and time."

"Sounds good."

He leaned closer to her. "Just tell Susanne that I said you guys need to hurry. I want to get Perry out of here. He needs to be examined at the hospital in Jackson."

She grasped his hand. "Absolutely. You can count on me, Patrick. I'm just glad he's awake and doing better."

"Me, too." He turned back to the others. "Perry, your Aunt Vera is in charge. You and Brian are going to have to carry the packs. I've got to bring Pete back, since we don't need help getting you out of here." He gave them a crisp, military-style salute. "See you soon."

The kids giggled at his gesture. The younger ones saluted him. Brian and Annie looked at each other, and when they saw that neither had saluted their uncle, they trained their eyes on the ground, nodding without being goofballs like the little ones.

Perry waved. "Be careful, Dad. The rocks are slick."

Patrick laughed and took off running. He gave the creek a wide berth. Perry might be kidding, but the last thing this group needed was for him to get injured, too.

CHAPTER FIFTEEN: INTERCEPT

Patrick

To Patrick's ears, his own breathing sounded like a foghorn. His lungs burned as if he'd swallowed a blowtorch. And this was after only a mile, running *downhill*. The combination of nearly 7500 feet in elevation, uneven terrain, heavy footwear, and a punishing pace were adding up. But he really wanted to catch Pete while his brother was still on Trout Creek, before he turned down the Tukudika. And it was only pain, after all, from effort and not injury. He should really be more worried about the livid bruise he was going to have from the nearly five pounds of revolver pummeling his hip. *Mind over matter, Flint,* he told himself. He kicked it up another notch.

After roughly another quarter mile, he heard men's voices ahead of him. *Pete. Good.* He accelerated yet again, relieved to be nearing the end of the effort. They sounded nearly close enough for Patrick to call out to his brother. Just another ten yards or so. He rounded a bend. About one hundred yards ahead on the edge of the creek, he caught sight of Pete with several other men. His attention was diverted momentarily from his footing on the challenging terrain. He tripped and went down, catching himself on his hands, but not before twisting his ankle and banging a knee on a rock.

The pain of the knee injury hit him first, sharp and precise, like a blow from a pickax. He winced and groaned, rolling onto his non-gun hip. But as he pushed off his ankle, it gave him an unwelcome surprise. The ankle hurt a lot more than the knee. The knee pain, in fact, had already started to abate. He caught his ankle with both hands, moving it and pressing into it to check for a break. He didn't see evidence of one, but that was only mild consolation. The pain mushroomed. Before his eyes, his ankle seemed to discolor. Was it his imagination, or was a bruise already blossoming? He held on to it, and he was almost positive that in addition to a pulsing throb, he felt it swelling. Literally *felt* the fluid accumulate and the ankle enlarge.

A sprain. Just what I need.

From his prone position, he'd lost sight of Pete and the other men, but he could hear them. Since Pete wasn't heading anywhere fast, Patrick decided to ice his ankle in the creek for a minute. He could shout out to his brother at any time if it appeared Pete was leaving. An ankle dunking would help with the pain and clear his head, which was muddled from the fall. He untied his hiking boot, slid it and his sock off, and scooted to the stream. He lowered his foot into the stream, which was just deep enough to submerge his ankle. The icy water was shockingly cold, and he jerked his foot back. *Cold enough to stop a heart.* It was especially jarring with his ankle and foot overheated from running in wool socks and hiking boots. He closed his eyes, gritted his teeth, and forced himself to submerge the ankle and foot and hold them there. He started counting. Sixty seconds was his goal.

Pete's voice rose. It was strained and pitched higher than normal. He suddenly sounded as loud and clear as if he were standing next to Patrick. "I'm not going to tell anyone about the gold and the cave. I swear."

A man with a nasally voice snarled an answer. "You're damn right you're not. Winthropp, take him back to camp and tie him up."

Patrick forgot about the cold water. He shook his head, certain he had misunderstood the man. Tie him up? Who would want to tie Pete up, and why? It didn't make sense.

An accented voice came next. Mexican. Like the voice the Flints had heard from their camp the night before. "Les, come on, man. Just let him go."

The snarly voice replied. The man's name was Les, Patrick surmised. "Let him go? You may not care about your share of the money, but I care about mine. I'm not going to lose a fortune to a bunch of weekend warriors with picks and pans. Peak tourist season starts next week. No one, and I mean no one, gets to see what we've found until we've emptied the cave."

"But how are you going to keep him quiet—hold him hostage the whole time?"

"Don't be an idiot, Diego. I'm not wasting our food supply on him."

"So, what, you're going to kill him?"

The silence was deafening, and Patrick forgot all about the pain in his ankle. He drew his foot out of the water and scrambled backwards to his sock and boot. His brother was in trouble. Serious trouble. He had to get to him.

The man repeated himself. "Les, are you planning on killing him, too?"

"No. I'm planning on you doing it. You and Hector. It's about time you pulled your weight. Winthropp handled the job with Jimbo all by himself."

"Les, you're crazy." It was a third man's voice. Scratchy. Wheezy. "He's not the only person we're going to see out here. Heck, he's not the only person we've seen out here today."

The pain was blinding as Patrick pulled on his sock. *Mind over matter.*

Diego, the accented one, said, "And people will come looking for him, man."

"We only need a few more days," Les said. "From now on, full time lookout. Although you were supposed to be our lookout today, Hector, and you can see how much good that did us."

"How was I to know this guy would be jogging the wrong way down the creek? He was on us before I ever saw him. Moving too fast."

Patrick shoved his foot in the hiking boot. It was almost as bad as the sock. He bit his lip to keep from making a sound.

"Well, he's not moving that fast now, is he? You two find a place to take care of him." Patrick heard a slapping noise and a splash. "And don't do it too near the camp. I don't want to attract any grizzlies."

Pete's voice sounded like a wire about to snap. "Man, you do *not* have to do this. Seriously. I've got zero interest in your gold. I just want to get back to my family."

"Family? Who all is with you?" Les asked.

An icy sensation prickled Patrick's face. *Oh, no. No, no, no.*

"Uh, no one. I meant back out of the wilderness *to* my family."

"Where are they?" Les asked.

"Uh, down in Jackson."

Patrick was relieved at his brother's quick thinking.

But Les didn't seem to be buying Pete's story. "You told us earlier you were running to the guard station to get help for your kid."

"Not *my* kid. A kid. One with another group. I ran into them, and because I was, uh, running this direction, they asked me to go for help."

"And they're upstream?"

"Yeah. Way upstream. Way, way upstream."

Les sneered. "I didn't see any groups with kids go by. Did any of you?"

Diego and Hector both said no.

A fourth voice, deep and slow, said, "Not me, boss."

Boot tied, Patrick crawled forward, ignoring the pain and keeping low to the ground, until he could see his brother. A man was holding Pete by the neck with the crook of one arm. He'd pinned Pete's arms behind his back with the other. The man towered over Pete by a good head in height, and Pete wasn't short at a hair under six feet. Pete and his captor were facing upstream, and the other men were looking downstream. *Winthropp*, Patrick thought. *The big man is Winthropp.* One—half the height of Winthropp—was olive-skinned with short black hair and a stocky build. *Diego.* He wasn't sure about the other two. Patrick wanted Pete to see him, but he didn't see how he could reveal himself without the other men catching sight of him, too. He had to get Pete away from these guys, but so far, he had no idea how to do it. There were too many of them for Patrick to confront them directly. He had his .357 Magnum, but if they were armed, that was four guns to one. And all it took was one gun to end Pete's life. Or Patrick's.

Diego said, "Great. Then we should expect more people, then, coming downstream with the kid, no matter what we do with him."

"We'll be prepared. Or were you not listening, dipshit?" It was the man with the nasally, sneering tone.

Now Patrick had a face to the voice and name. Les. He was a pasty, short white guy with a shaved head and crazy eyes, who looked like he needed to eat a bag of Big Macs if he wanted to keep his pants up. That meant Hector had to be the very normal-looking man with dark blond hair. Average height and weight, no noticeable deformities or unusual features. Just a man in a red plaid shirt like any of the thousands of others in Wyoming.

In a deep, slow voice, Winthropp said, "Want me to take him to camp, boss?"

"I've changed my mind. Hector and Diego will handle him from the get-go. You be my lookout. I've got to keep working. We *are* here to unload that cave of gold, after all."

Diego and Hector took Pete's arms. Winthropp released him.

Diego shook his head. "You're crazy, Les. And you're going to get us killed."

Les laughed. Now that Patrick could see him, his voice was chilling. "That means more gold for me. Don't tempt me."

Diego and Hector pulled Pete along between them. They crossed to the west side of Trout Creek, holding Pete up when he slipped and nearly went down in the water.

Les shouted, "And no guns. Make it look natural, and don't leave any evidence. Just in case a person finds him before the grizzlies do."

To Patrick's horror, Diego and Hector veered north and headed straight for him.

CHAPTER SIXTEEN: RECONVENE

Susanne

Susanne and Lana had just finished cleaning the campsite and repacking after Joe's lunch when Vera and the kids traipsed in.

"We're starving," Bert announced.

Susanne surveyed the kids. "Bert, your seven dwarves name is going to be Hungry."

Barry shouted, "I want to be Hungry, because I *am* hungry."

She laughed. "No, you're Shouty."

"Who am I, Aunt Susanne?" Danny said.

"Itchy." She didn't even hesitate.

Bert and Barry howled with laughter.

Susanne turned to Brian. "You're Teacher. Because you're always helping your brothers and sisters." To Stan, she said, "You're Hidey, since you're so quiet I can never even find you." And to Annie, she said, "You're Sweetie, because you're the nicest niece I could ever imagine." Looking around, she frowned. "And Bunny is Bunny, because she keeps us hopping. Where is she now, though? Bunny?"

Vera said, "Susanne, can I talk to you for a second?"

Susanne, still looking for Bunny, caught sight of Perry. His hair and shirt were covered in something reddish brown. It took her a moment to register that it was blood. "Perry! What happened to you?" She ran to him. "Are you okay?"

She probed his face, his noggin, and his shirt, and he only winced a little bit when she grazed the lump and cut on the back of his head. "I'm fine, Mom."

Vera said, "That's what I need to talk to you about."

Susanne pulled Perry to her in a fierce hug.

Perry's voice was muffled against her. "I fell and hit my head on a rock. Dad said I was unconscious for fifteen minutes."

"Oh, my God!" Susanne squished him so tightly that he squirmed.

"Mom, you're hurting me."

She released him. "Sorry."

Vera tugged on Susanne's sleeve. "It's important. I have a message from Patrick." Then she looked around. "Where are Bunny and Trish?"

Susanne frowned. "Where is *Patrick*?"

Vera led Susanne a few steps away from the others. "He went after Pete, who Patrick sent to the guard station to call for medical assistance for Perry."

"What?!"

"That was when Perry was unconscious. But when he woke up and was doing well, Patrick asked me to come get you guys. He wants us to meet them at the canoes, so he can get Perry to the hospital quickly."

Susanne's heart fluttered in her chest. "Hospital?" Her panic was building quickly, and her voice came out a little bit shrill. "I don't understand. I thought he was fine."

"I think he is. Patrick said we don't need to get emergency help. But the plan is to go back to the cars so you can drive Perry to town for tests and stuff. And Patrick said to tell you we need to leave right away." She adjusted her headband. "Gotta love men telling you what to do."

"Okay. Okay." Susanne put her hand to her chest and closed her eyes. She had to calm down. "But he's going to be all right? Perry is?"

"That's what Patrick said."

I can trust Patrick. Sometimes being married to a doctor was a trial. On call, long hours, high stress, and, well, a wee bit of a superiority complex. Patrick did think he knew best. About everything. Other times, it was a gift from God. Now was the latter.

She nodded. "Then let's get moving."

Vera grimaced. "Will you tell Joe?"

"Tell him we're leaving?"

"Yes. I don't think he likes me."

"I'm sure that's not true."

"I'm, um, younger than Pete. And I have all the kids. I don't think he approves. It's taking me a while to fit in."

"You'll get there."

Vera looked embarrassed. "He, uh, he doesn't always listen to me."

Susanne snorted. "Or me either. But this time he doesn't have a choice." She turned to the group, but she didn't see her in-laws. "Joe? Lana?" When they didn't answer she raised her voice. "Joe? Lana? Where are you?"

She walked the perimeter of the camp, calling to them. On the far side, the sound of a male voice cursing told her she'd found them, or him at least. She followed it to a rocky overlook with a view of the river beyond. The river wound a twisting path slowly downward toward Jackson Hole, as far as her eyes could see. Trees clustered against its edges like green fringe. From this height, though, it was more like a painting than the loud, powerful body of water she'd seen up close the day before. Her in-laws were sitting on a boulder. Lana was gazing outward, serene and peaceful. Joe's eyes were down as he whittled another stick. His thumb was bleeding. Again. The man was a bit reckless.

"Hi, guys." Susanne stepped in front of them. "We need to get on the trail. Perry fell and hurt his head, and Patrick and Pete are meeting us at the canoes. Patrick wants to get him to the hospital."

Joe looked up at her, his lips pinched. But for once, he didn't say a single negative word. He just stood, folded up his knife, and put it in his pocket. He started walking toward the backpacks, then stopped and turned back to them. "Aren't you coming?"

Lana and Susanne shared a look. Susanne arched her brows. *Will wonders never cease.* Lana took her hand and winked.

"After you," Susanne said to her father-in-law and followed him, still holding Lana's hand.

CHAPTER SEVENTEEN: RESCUE

Trout Creek, Bridger-Teton National Forest, Wyoming
Friday, June 24, 1977, 12:30 p.m.

Patrick

Diego and Hector turned Pete ninety degrees and frog-marched him into the thick lodgepole pines on the other side of the creek. Downstream, Les was pointing Winthropp toward something in the opposite direction.

Now. The time to act is now.

Patrick pushed himself to his feet. The pain was excruciating. He sucked in a deep breath, clenched his teeth, and hobbled upstream twenty yards, until he was out of sight of the men. He crossed the creek there, arms out for balance, all his focus on not twisting his ankle further. Then, channeling what he had learned in his studies of American Indians, he started working his way through the woods back downstream, mindful of the way sound carried in the dry mountain air. He opened his mouth to breathe. He tested the wind. It was moving toward him. *Good. Sound—and smell—will carry better from them to me than from me to them.* Then he used what he had read described as the fox-walking technique. He moved toe to heel, with his weight on the outside of his feet. His steps were slow and soft, his knees flexed and back erect, and he kept his weight on his back leg until his front foot found a quiet place to land. It wasn't fast going, but he was more concerned about stealth than speed, and the forest floor was a minefield of pinecones, rocks of all sizes, twigs and branches, and slippery, crisp pine needles.

For ten yards, he was a ghost in the forest. He sped up as his confidence grew. A long stretch of flat, mostly underground boulders gave him the chance to speed up even more. On its far edge, he lost traction on a patch of damp moss. One hundred and seventy-five pounds of Patrick slid forward, then came down on a dry twig. It snapped, the sound like a rifle shot to his ears. He froze, eyes closed, heart pounding, adrenaline surging. He turned an ear toward the men, listening for any sign that they'd heard him.

If they'd been alerted to another presence, they didn't show any sign of it in their voices. He felt weak with relief.

"I say let's just tie him up. We'll give Les a chance to cool down and come up with a different plan. We're not murderers." It was Diego's voice. And it sounded closer than Patrick had expected, although he couldn't see them.

Patrick looked around. Most of the trees had skinny trunks. None were thick enough to provide cover. But a few yards away there was a fat rock outcropping tall enough to make a good hiding place. He moved to it and squatted behind it, one hand on its rough surface to steady himself as his ankle protested. He sucked air in through his nose, getting a strong dose of the loamy scent of soil and decay. *Time to get ready.* He didn't want a confrontation, would do almost anything to avoid one, but he had to be prepared in case the men discovered him, or if it became his only option to save his brother. He unsheathed his knife from its belt holster. Not for the first time, Patrick thanked his lucky stars for a friend like the one he had in Wes, his co-worker at the hospital in Buffalo. Wes had given Patrick the six-inch knife with SAWBONES engraved in the handle to replace the sissy pocketknife Patrick used to carry. *Wes.* What he wouldn't give to have his buddy by his side right now. Wes would give Patrick strength in numbers, experience, and sheer Wyoming toughness. No use thinking about it now, though. Patrick was on his own, and he'd have to make do with the knife Wes had armed him with instead. He always had his revolver, but the sound of gunshots would bring Les and Winthropp running, and Patrick didn't want that. The gun would have to be as a last resort only.

He flipped the knife open and strained to hear.

Hector said, "Agreed. We've got to stall."

"Let's just walk upstream and stay out of his way. Come back in half an hour."

Pete's voice was pleading but firm. He didn't sound cowed. *Good.* "You don't have to do this at all. You can let me go. I won't tell anyone what I saw."

Diego said, "I'm sorry, man. Les is crazy. If we let you go and he finds out, it's us he'll kill."

"You can say I escaped. That I told you I was Special Forces in Vietnam."

Hector laughed, but it didn't sound like he thought anything was funny. "Same result."

Diego said, "There. I think he's secure. Test the rope, amigo. What do you think?"

After a few seconds of silence, Hector said, "Good enough that he won't be going anywhere until we want him to."

"What'd you say your name was again, man?" Diego said.

"Pete. Pete Stone."

"Where you from Pete?"

"Texas."

"Big state."

"Austin."

"Hector and I are from San Antonio. Just down I-35. If things don't go the way we want, we can send something to your wife. Like, some money, you know? We've got all this gold. How do we find her?"

"You don't. She doesn't need your money. She needs me."

"Well, you can't say I didn't offer. We'll try to change Les's mind, but no promises, man."

Pine needles crunched under footsteps. They were heading toward Patrick and his hiding place. He tried to make himself as small as possible by turning to the side. *His hat.* The fedora made him taller than the rocks. He slipped it off and held it to his stomach. As the men drew near, he moved around the rocks in a circle, keeping the outcropping between them and himself, and setting his feet down as silently as he could. He held his breath. They walked by no more than twenty feet away from him.

When they were well past him, he exhaled. Three times he counted out a minute, waiting to be sure they were really gone. *Fifty-nine. Sixty.*

He put his hat back on. Then he stole a deep breath for courage, fought to ignore the pain in his ankle, and ran on his lightest possible feet toward his brother.

CHAPTER EIGHTEEN: ESCAPE

Patrick

Pete's eyes were fixed on the ground as he struggled against the rope binding his hands behind a tree trunk.

Patrick whispered, "Pete."

His brother's eyes flew up, then widened. Patrick held a finger to his lips and raised his knife in his other hand. Pete nodded. Patrick moved to the back of the tree and made quick work of sawing through the rope right between his brother's wrists. It was his routine to sharpen his knife on Sunday nights, and he was grateful he hadn't skipped it the previous weekend.

Pete dropped his arms, shook them out, then rubbed his wrists. Patrick folded and re-sheathed his knife while Pete untangled himself from the rope.

Pete's voice was low. "Man, it's great to see you. I felt like I'd fallen into a remake of *Deliverance*." Patrick almost asked him about the reference, since it was the second time he'd heard it, but he didn't want to waste the precious seconds. "How did you find me?"

"Perry woke up, so I came after you as fast as I could. I saw them take you at the creek. Overheard most of the discussion before and after, too. Then I just followed. But now, we've got to get out of here."

Pete snorted. "Don't let me hold us back. Which way? I've gotten a little turned around."

"That's the problem. Upstream, we may run into Diego and Hector. Downstream, Les and Winthropp. And we need to get to the canoes. The rest of the group is meeting us there, since I still need to get Perry to the hospital."

Pete pursed his lips. "We could go cross country."

"The terrain can be intense." Patrick shook his head. "It's too easy to get disoriented."

"Then what do you think we should do?"

"Do you still have enough energy to run?"

"Heck, yeah."

Patrick patted his gun. "Then I say we cross the creek and strike out upstream. We can take the trail through the camp back to the canoes. I'd rather face Diego and Hector than Les and Winthropp."

"Agreed."

"We've just got to keep a sharp lookout and not make a sound."

"And hope they stay on this side of the creek."

"That, too." Patrick pointed toward it. "After you, little brother. When your feet are dry, take a left, then a right after a mile uphill."

Pete nodded and set out like a gazelle. Patrick knew this was going to hurt. He took off after his brother. *Yep. Feels like someone's driving a stake through my ankle.* He was immediately distracted from the pain by how noisily Pete ran, though. When they got to the creek, Patrick sped up, grabbed Pete's arm, and stopped him.

"I think we should cross a little further upstream. We're too close to Les and Winthropp here, and completely exposed when we're in the middle of the creek. But when you get to the other side, try to put your feet down like this." Patrick described the silent fox-walking technique, then demonstrated it. "It's much quieter. The Indians used it when they didn't want prey or their enemies to hear them coming."

Pete nodded. "Okay. I'll try."

The two ran upstream along the west side of the creek, dodging branches, bushes, and rocks. Pete slowly got the hang of fox-walking and his running grew quieter. Patrick barely noticed the scenery around him. All of his focus was on watching and listening for Diego and Hector, and on staying quiet so the men didn't find the brothers first. After about thirty yards, they rounded a bend. Pete turned to the water and looked back at Patrick with a shrug. Patrick nodded. Pete forded the creek, seeming to forget all about quiet during the crossing. Patrick cringed at the splashing.

When they were both on the east side of the creek, Pete whispered, "I'll race you."

Patrick snorted, thinking about the noise. "The winner is the one who doesn't get us caught."

Pete winked and took off at a sprint. *Too fast. He won't last.* Patrick fell in behind him. He was getting used to the pain, but there was no trail, and he struggled over the rough, uneven ground. The going was harder than the downhill had been by a long shot, too, and he fought to keep his breathing quiet. But going downhill, Patrick hadn't felt a sense of urgency, other than to catch Pete. Now, their lives were on the line, and he knew it. So, despite the pain and strain, he ran like his feet had wings.

Pete soon faltered, as Patrick had expected, and Patrick gained ground on him quickly. As boys, Pete had been the faster of the two of them, from long before he caught Patrick in height. Patrick filled out more than Pete when they matured. Never stocky, Patrick was the burlier and tougher brother. Now the two were identical in height, and, since Patrick had taken up training for distance running, his build had become more like his brother's lean stature. After a half-mile, Patrick was only six feet behind Pete.

Movement ahead of them across the stream caught Patrick's eye. With a Herculean effort, he closed the gap between him his brother. He touched Pete's arm.

"Stop," he whispered. He tried to swallow the sound of his gasps for air.

Pete quit running. His breathing was loud, too.

Patrick leaned close to Pete's ear. "I think they're just ahead. Moving downstream. Other side."

Pete nodded.

"Let's cut into the trees. The noise of the creek will cover us some but keep your feet more quiet than ever. Shouldn't be far until we reach our turn."

Pete gestured Patrick ahead with his chin. Patrick eased into the forest, concentrating on his foot placement. Just a few feet in and the trees would make them nearly impossible to spot. But the footing would be far noisier. By the stream, at least the vegetation had been beaten down by the feet of fishermen and animals coming to drink. In the forest, it was completely untamed. He stepped over a fallen tree, careful to avoid the maze of its skinny branches, then skirted a patch of woody bush that snatched off his hat. As he bent to retrieve it, he snuck a look across the creek. For a split second, Diego was in clear view. Patrick held his breath and tensed. Then the forest hid the man again. Patrick turned to Pete, pointed to his eyes, then toward where he'd seen the man. He raised his hand to indicate they should remain in place. He waited, counting to thirty, not seeing the man or his companion again. Then he resumed walking, heading back to the easier passage along the creek and cramming his hat back on as he went. There, he ran faster than ever. Pete's footfalls were close behind him. Each step felt lighter as Patrick lengthened the distance from where they'd last seen Diego and Hector. Within less than five minutes, Patrick found the rock that he knew marked the trail—such that it was. He made the turn just as he heard a shout.

His stomach knotted up. He turned to his brother. "I think they just figured out you're gone."

Pete nodded, his pupils dilated.

Things are getting real now. As if they weren't real enough before.

The two of them sprinted up the trail, away from Trout Creek.

CHAPTER NINETEEN: REALIZE

North of the Tukudika River, Bridger-Teton National
Forest, Wyoming
Friday, June 24, 1977, 1:15 p.m.

Perry

As he hiked behind his cousin Brian, Perry stumbled and nearly fell. His dad's backpack was heavy. He pressed his hand against the bump on the back of his head and winced. It hurt. And he was feeling nauseous again. Dizzy, too, like his head was spinning. He didn't say anything, though. If there's one thing his parents didn't like, it was complaining. Well, that and lying. But right now, as much as Perry wanted to talk about how bad he was feeling, he didn't.

He could already imagine his mother's response, because he'd heard her say it all his life. "No one wants to hear about how you feel, Perry Flint. Your dad sees people at the hospital who feel worse than you, all the time."

And if his dad was there, he'd try to make it into a joke. "You think that feels bad? I can give you something to feel bad about, if you really want it." He'd sock his fist in his hand.

Like he'd ever hit Perry. Or hurt anybody, unless he had to. He'd stabbed a guy in the throat one time, but that had been to rescue Trish from kidnappers. It made his dad really upset when the guy died. His dad was tough, but he was nice. Usually. Once, he'd overheard his mom talking with her best friend Vangie about the times their husbands had drank too much. She hadn't realized Perry was in the next room, and she'd told Vangie that Perry's dad had had too much beer with his brother and his cousin when they were in high school. He'd gotten into a fist fight after a football game with a kid from a rival school and been suspended. It was hard for Perry to believe, and he fully intended to ask his dad about it some time. Even if it was true, his dad had never hit him, except for spankings, and that didn't count, because all parents spanked their kids. Plus, he'd kind of deserved it. Every time.

He stumbled again and had to catch himself on a tree trunk beside the trail.

His mom was in front of the line, but his Gramma Lana was behind him and saw him almost fall. "Are you okay, Perry-winkle?" She stopped beside him.

He cleared his throat. His mouth watered with the need to throw-up. "Uh, yes, ma'am. I was just, um, resting."

She eyed him like she didn't believe him. He wasn't a very good liar, even for a decent reason like not complaining about how he felt. "Do you want me to stop everyone?"

"No, ma'am. I'm fine now." *Sort of.* He started walking again.

She fell into step with him. "Your mom told me that you got really good at football this year."

He straightened up. She was still taller than him, but he had nearly caught up to her. Only a few inches to go. "Yes, ma'am."

"But you broke your ankle. That must have hurt."

"It wasn't so bad. Missing games was the worst part. It hurt more the second time I broke it." Which he'd done when he'd tried to take his cast off before he was supposed to. But who could blame him? He'd had to wear it a really long time. It made things boring, and it itched.

She smiled at him. "Are you playing football again this year?"

"I am. But Dad is also teaching me golf, so I can try out for that when I get to high school."

"Like your Grandpa Joe."

"Yes, ma'am. Trish is learning, too. But I like it more than she does."

His Grandpa Joe had played golf professionally for a few years, then he'd designed golf courses and even coached the Texas Aggies men's golf team. They'd won the Southwest Conference title twice during his time as a coach. When he'd started giving him lessons, Perry's dad had told him it was important to carry on the family tradition. That, and that golf was a game you could play all your life, even after football was over. Perry had said snow skiing was the sport he planned to do all his life, and his dad had laughed and said he'd better learn to golf, too, just in case.

It was fine. Perry liked all sports, and golf came easy to him.

His Gramma Lana said, "Where is Trish? I haven't seen her since you guys came back."

"Oh, she wasn't with us. She and Bunny turned around and came back a long time before we did. Bunny didn't want to hike." Perry gave a goofy grin. Bunny had been a little beastly. The girl could scream big for someone that little.

Gramma Lana frowned. "What do you mean? Came back where?"

"To camp. With you and Mom."

Gramma Lana put a hand over her chest. Her words came out in a fast whisper. "We were all so busy. And then your injury. We were distracted. And needing to meet Patrick and Pete. But how could we have not noticed?" She raised her voice. "Vera. Vera."

Aunt Vera was halfway up the line of hikers. She stepped off the trail and turned around, hands on her hips. "Yes?"

"Where is . . . Trish?"

Aunt Vera frowned. "What do you mean?"

"I haven't seen Trish. Or Bunny."

"What do you mean? Since when?"

"Since the group left for the creek this morning."

Aunt Vera's eyes grew wild. She turned in a circle. "Bunny," she cried. "Bunny? Where are you?"

Perry's nauseous stomach did a somersault. This was bad. Worse than falling and hitting his head on the rock.

"Mom," he shouted. "Mom, Trish and Bunny aren't with us."

CHAPTER TWENTY: ENCOUNTER

Trish

"**B**unny, I need a rest." Trish had stopped to catch her breath, but she wasn't sure she could start back up again. Not with forty pounds of sweaty little girl hanging from her shoulders like a floppy backpack. She shook the girl's ankle. "Wake up, Bunny. It's time for you to walk."

Against her back, Bunny's body stiffened, then arched away from her. "What?" Her voice sounded groggy, and she yawned.

"I need to set you down so you can walk. You've gotten so big that I need a rest from carrying you. Your mom must be feeding you super growing potions or something."

Bunny straightened her legs, and Trish crouched to ease her down gently.

"Where are we?" Bunny said.

Good question. Trish scanned the area around them. Trees, trees, and more trees. Hills that led to more hills. Rocks on piles of other rocks. But no water. Nothing familiar. She'd been sure they'd be at the river by now. It could be that this trail was going upriver instead of across the forest and *to* the river. She'd passed over a little trail about five minutes before. Maybe that had been the one they should have been on. But she was scared of getting even more lost, so she hadn't taken it. They could always go back to it. If they didn't reach the water in five more minutes, she'd turn around.

Trish said, "Remember when we left our canoes by the river?"

"Uh huh."

"We're close to there."

"Is that where we're eating lunch?"

"Um, no. We'll eat at the camp, I think."

"I'm hungry." Bunny pouted.

"Me, too." Trish's stomach growled. She made a silly O with her mouth and clutched her stomach. "Did you hear that?"

Bunny giggled. "Your tummy is loud." Then hers growled and the little girl grabbed it. "Mine, too."

"I don't know. I think yours might be even louder than mine. Maybe they're having a growling contest." Trish's rumbled again.

"Yours wins!"

Trish smiled. It felt fake, but she needed to be confident for Bunny's sake. "Yay, I win. We'd better start walking so we can feed these noisy tummies."

"Yeah," Bunny said, nodding. Then she knelt on the ground. "Oh, flowers."

The girl *really* liked flowers. It was cute.

Bunny stuck her little fingers between two rocks. "Ouch."

"Did something bite you?" Trish's heart jumped like it was coming out of starting blocks. She didn't know what she would do if a snake bit one of them. She'd seen movies where people sucked venom out of a rattlesnake bite. She didn't know if she could do that.

Bunny thrust her hand in the air. "Ta da." She was holding a pink mountain rose, its delicate petals surrounding a sunny yellow center.

Thorns. It was just thorns. Trish laughed, and her heartbeat returned to a normal rhythm. "Follow me."

"Can I hold your hand?"

Trish's throat felt tight. "Yeah, of course."

The two set off, Bunny holding her rose in one hand and Trish's hand in the other. Trish was glad they were holding hands, because the trail suddenly took a steep, rocky dive. Bunny tripped over an exposed tree root, and Trish kept her on her feet by her little paw. If she'd fallen, she would have scraped up her hands and knees, or worse.

"How much further?"

"Not far at all now. Let's sing. It will make time go faster." And alert any bears to their presence. Trish launched into "Twinkle, Twinkle, Little Star."

Bunny joined her, singing sweet and high.

They rounded a bend in the trail, and, ahead of them, Trish saw the river. Only it was a part of the river she didn't recognize from the day before. No cliff. No Teddy Bear rock. No footbridge downstream. She fought back tears.

Then a man's voice said, "What are you girls doing out here all by yourself?"

CHAPTER TWENTY-ONE: CHOOSE

Susanne

"Nobody panic." Susanne grabbed both of Vera's arms, trying not to let her sister-in-law see the absolute panic she felt herself. Free-falling, mind-erasing, soul-destroying panic.

Her daughter was a mature, strong, sensible girl, but the wilderness was dangerous and remote. Wild animals. Rock cliffs as tall as skyscrapers. Fast-moving water. Stinging insects. And, if they were out there long enough, dehydration. Sunburn. Starvation. There were so many ways to get hurt. To *die*. The most important thing for Susanne now was to stay calm. To get information. Think. Make good choices.

She swallowed. Her throat was so dry she nearly choked. "How long ago should they have been back?"

Tears ran down Vera's face. She mumbled Bunny's name but didn't look at Susanne.

Susanne shook her, once, hard. Then again when it didn't work. "How long, Vera?"

Vera didn't answer. Susanne looked to her in-laws. Lana had one arm around Bert and the other around Annie. Joe was pacing back and forth, and his lips were moving. She'd never seen him talk to himself before, but she should have guessed. *Like father, like son.*

Susanne gave up on Vera and tried him instead. "Joe? How long ago should the girls have been back to camp?"

"An hour before us. Maybe more," Joe said.

"All right." Susanne's voice had started to shake. She clenched her jaw to stop it. "Trish is experienced with the mountains. She's going to find her way back to the camp."

Joe shook his head. "But we've all left it."

Perry looked at his mom with big, somber eyes. "And Dad and Uncle Pete are going to go to the canoes, but we're not there."

Susanne suddenly wanted everyone to hush. It was too much. Too much. She wished Patrick was with them. They were partners. He liked to think he was in charge, but the truth was, they discussed the important things and made better decisions together. An insidious thought crept into her brain. Why had he let Trish and Bunny split off from the group? This whole problem had started then. If she'd been with him, she wouldn't have let them go. Maybe none of the rest would have happened. Perry getting hurt. Pete running to the guard station. Patrick going after him. Trish and Bunny . . . lost. They needed to get the group back together.

But somebody had to find Trish and Bunny. *Had to.*

She took a step closer to her son. "Perry, what would you do if you were by yourself, went back to the camp, and no one was there?"

His forehead wrinkled up. "I think Dad would tell us to stay put and wait for someone to find us. That's what I would do. But, um, if I were Trish, I'd be pissed because you'd left me, and I'd go after you."

"Don't say pissed," she said, mothering on autopilot. "But she wouldn't know where we'd gone."

He smiled. "Sure she would. The plan was to go downriver in the canoes after lunch."

"So, she'd head for the canoes?"

"Yeah."

Susanne's brain spun. She couldn't be sure of anything. Not that Trish would get herself and Bunny back to the camp or that Trish would then leave the empty camp for the river.

Joe's voice was testy. "We're closer to the river than the camp."

"And?"

"Just get the group there. Then I'll go back for Trish and Bunny."

Ten minutes. That's how long it would take for the group to reach the river and Joe to be back on the trail. Susanne closed her eyes. She had to have faith in Trish. Surely ten more minutes wouldn't hurt? And maybe Patrick would be waiting at the canoes. She could talk to him. Get his opinion.

Susanne nodded. "Okay."

She heard a heaving sound and turned toward it. Perry was holding on to a tree trunk, leaned over. He stood back up. His face was ashy.

She rushed over to him. "What's the matter, Perry?"

"I've got the dry heaves."

She stared deep into his eyes. How could she tell if something was dangerously wrong with him? She needed Patrick, and she needed him right now. "Do you have a headache?"

He waffled his hand. "I mean, yeah, my head hurts, but I did just hit it on a rock."

That sealed the deal. She had to take Perry to the river and keep the last of the group together, so Patrick could get their son to the hospital. Joe would come back for Bunny and Trish. It would be all right. *It has to be all right.*

"Okay, let's double time march, everyone. To the river." Her words burned her tongue. It might be the right thing to do, but it still hurt. Her daughter was out there.

"No," Vera cried, finally breaking out of her stupor. "I can't leave without Bunny."

"Come on, honey." Lana lifted Vera's hand and gave it a tug. "Joe will bring her to you."

"No," Vera screamed. "No, no, no!"

Joe strode to his daughter-in-law. Without a word or the slightest hesitation, he slapped her across the face. "Enough."

Vera's head snapped away, and she stumbled back. Joe grabbed Stan's and Danny's hands and jerked them along the trail with him. He didn't look back at Vera.

Vera's screams turned to sobs, but the slap had worked. She stumbled after Joe.

Susanne waited for the rest of the group to pass before falling in behind Perry in the rear, where no one could see her tears.

CHAPTER TWENTY-TWO: CATCH

EAST OF TROUT CREEK, BRIDGER-TETON NATIONAL FOREST,
WYOMING
FRIDAY, JUNE 24, 1977, 1:30 P.M.

Patrick

Patrick entered the campsite where his family had spent the previous night, still running. He stopped, hands on his knees, panting and easing weight off his ankle. He glanced down at it. It was swollen and multi-colored—definitely not his imagination—a sickly camouflage of black, gray, and blue. He looked up and around. Susanne and Lana had done a good job breaking camp. Other than pressed grass and ashes in the fire ring, they'd left no trace, and the fire was dead out.

Pete flopped over at the waist, too. "I don't hear anyone behind us."

"Me either."

"But they could be looking for us on the river."

That was exactly what Patrick was afraid of. "Yes. We've got to catch up with our family before they cross paths with them." He groaned as he put his weight back on his ankle.

Pete seemed to notice Patrick's injury for the first time. He frowned. "What the heck happened to you?"

"I fell. Twisted it. Before I found you."

"Can you run on it?"

Patrick nodded grimly. "I have been so far. I have to. Come on."

He took the trail toward the river, doing his best not to favor his ankle. Luckily, this trail, while still a single track, was less overgrown and saw more use than the one they'd been running on for the last twenty minutes. The footing was far less difficult. Unluckily, the terrain was steeper and mostly downhill. Each running stride put seven times his body weight on his ankle, more on the down slopes, and he felt every ounce of it. But each second that passed was more time for Hector, Diego, and their crazy friends Les and Winthropp to find them, or—worse—find their family. So, he didn't slow down. He couldn't. Instead, he forced himself to run even faster. On the run up Trout Creek, he'd been able to distract himself from his burning lungs, his aching thighs, and his protesting ankle by trying to be quiet. Now, he did it by cataloguing his surroundings. It was a mind game that usually worked well for him. The trees—mostly lodgepole pines. The rock—granite. Sandstone. Shale. No obsidian, at least not that he'd seen yet. The Tukudika had used the glasslike volcanic rock to make arrow points, so he'd been looking for it. He went back to cataloguing. The trail, crisscrossed with lesser trails he hadn't noticed on the hike in. Game trails or fishermen trails, he guessed. Scat, from deer, elk, moose, and coyote. Running out of things to list, he did a quick calculation of his run since he'd left Vera and the kids. Four or five miles, maybe? Not the longest, but definitely the hardest run of his fledgling endurance career. After this, the half marathon would be a piece of cake.

In the trees, he caught a glimpse of old, rotting poles leaning together to form a circle at their base. He stopped. He couldn't help it. It was a wickiup.

"What?" Pete said.

Patrick wished he had a camera and time to explain. But he didn't. "I thought I saw something." He started running again, fighting off a creeping sadness at the missed opportunity to explore the artifact. He tried to return to cataloguing, but it didn't work for him anymore, so he just ran.

Less than ten minutes later, he spied water through the trees, looking greenish and smooth edged, like clay. Then he saw the distinctive shape of the fat teddy bear rock. As he broke from the forest and onto the rocky shore, his eyes cut to his right, where they'd stashed the canoes. His family was milling about there. The relief he felt when he saw Perry nearly buckled his knees. *Thank you, God.*

"Susanne," he shouted.

She turned toward his voice. The expression on her face . . . something was wrong. Even from ten yards away, he could see the tears. *Perry?*

"Oh, Patrick."

When he reached her, she threw herself against him. He threw his arms around her. "We have to get on the water. No time to explain. Can you tell me what's wrong when we're safe?"

She shook her head. "Trish. Bunny. They never came back to camp."

He felt like all the blood in his body drained out of him in that instant. With all that had happened, this was the last thing he expected to hear. "What?"

"And Perry's vomiting. His head hurts."

Patrick's pulse throbbed in his temples. His face felt like he'd stuck his head in an oven. It was hard to comprehend everything that was going wrong, much less figure out the best way to handle it.

Pete reached Vera. She collapsed into his arms, and he nearly buckled at her sudden weight. The sound of her sobbing tore at Patrick's heart. Her little girl was missing. Both of their little girls were missing.

His father's voice grabbed his attention. "I'm going back to camp for the girls."

Patrick's head cleared a little. *Think. You have to think.* "But they weren't there. We just came from there."

Joe hesitated, then strode toward the trail. "Well, they're not here, and someone has to go find them." In seconds, he'd disappeared from view.

Patrick studied the rocky ground in front of him. His thoughts were spinning. He couldn't pin them down. His daughter. His niece. *I have to find them.* His son. *I have to get Perry to the hospital.* Then, something made him lift his gaze.

Down the riverbank, breaking from the trees, he saw a man. A very, very big man. *Winthropp. Maybe he won't recognize Pete.* The group was good camouflage. But, to Patrick's horror, the giant cocked his head, pointed at the Flints, and yelled something behind him into the forest.

Patrick shouted, "Pete, it's them."

Pete released Vera. She stumbled but stayed upright. The brothers looked at each other, then at Winthropp. Les appeared behind him, holding a rifle.

I can't be everywhere at once.

Patrick said, "We've got to get everyone out of here. If we leave, Les and his gang won't know about Joe and the girls. We'll take four of the canoes and leave the fifth up in the trees for them. And we can come back for them. With the authorities."

Pete frowned, but he nodded. They started running for the canoes.

Over his shoulder, Patrick yelled, "This isn't a drill. Get the canoes on the river."

He grabbed one and started dragging it to the water. He glanced out at the river. A tiny island—more like a large sandbar—split the river in two for a little way. The willows and trees on it provided good cover. "Susanne, get in. Take Bert and Barry. Cross the river. Paddle on the other side of the island. Then down to the guard station."

"But—"

"No buts. You can do this."

"Of course I *can*. I taught canoe at summer camp when I was a teenager." Her eyes bore into his. "I just don't understand."

"Do you trust me?"

"You know I do."

"I love you."

"Okay. I love you, too." She loaded the little boys, slipped off her backpack, and grabbed the paddle as she got in.

"Go." Patrick shoved the canoe off the bank as hard as he could, and she shot into the middle of the river.

"Bert, Barry, put on your life jackets," he heard her say.

Patrick whirled and returned for another canoe. Pete was pushing a canoe with Perry, Vera, and Annie after Susanne. Patrick manhandled another canoe to the water. He snuck a glance down river. Les and Winthropp were headed their way, waving, but Hector and Diego were nowhere in sight.

He turned away from the men. "Mom and Danny, you're with me."

They loaded up, Danny sitting in the floor of the boat behind his brother on the front seat, Patrick's mother in the middle. All three of them were wide-eyed. Their grips on the sides were white knuckled as Patrick ran them into the current and vaulted into the canoe. He didn't even waste the time to take off his backpack, just started paddling like mad for the opposite shore. He heard a splash and looked back. Pete was launching the fourth canoe. Brian and Stan were with him. *Good. That's everyone.* At least, everyone except Joe, Trish, and Bunny.

Patrick sent up a prayer. *God, please, help my father find the girls, and let them be all right.* It was all he could do for now, and it didn't feel like nearly enough.

Then a crushing realization settled on Patrick. He hadn't warned his father about the gold prospectors. But maybe it was okay. The men wouldn't know Joe and the girls were with Pete, even if their paths crossed. And, what his father lacked in pleasantness, he made up for in grit and situational awareness. Joe Flint could do this. Patrick had to believe that.

But he couldn't think about it anymore. Not now. Now, he had to get the group away from Les and Winthropp.

"Life jackets," Patrick said.

Lana helped the boys with theirs, then cinched hers on. Ahead of them, Susanne and Vera had their canoes upright and were about to pass behind the little island. The current was fast but not too rough, and there weren't any mid-stream hazards that Patrick could see. Of course, not every hazard was as obvious as a patch of rapids, a drop off, a boulder, or a fallen tree. Sometimes the danger was invisible, beneath the surface. Again, not something he could think about now.

He paddled quickly and was soon covered by the island and only a few yards behind the women. Susanne looked smooth, but Vera was jerky. Her canoe was having trouble maintaining course. His stomach roiled. There was nothing he could do to help her until he caught up with her. He settled into a paddling rhythm, concentrating on quick turnover, and smooth, strong strokes. Behind him, he heard Pete's voice and the sound of his paddle splashing into the water.

The women broke from behind the island. Patrick had almost caught up with them. He passed out from behind cover as well. He glanced at the riverbank and didn't see the prospectors. *Good.* They'd passed them.

But then he heard something else. More voices. Les was shouting after them.

Patrick didn't think it was possible for his stress to rise any higher, but it did. He paddled faster.

CHAPTER TWENTY-THREE: DISCOVER

Patrick

Pete pulled his canoe alongside Patrick's. Patrick was a little surprised his brother had caught up with him, since Patrick thought he had been paddling pretty hard. Could running be robbing his upper body of muscle mass? Maybe he needed to add weights to his workout schedule. Or maybe it was just his ankle injury affecting him without him realizing it. At least paddling was a lot easier on it than running.

Pete said, "Do you think they'll come after us?"

Patrick stroked in an even rhythm on alternating sides of the canoe, trying not to make it obvious that he was putting more effort into it now. "I can't imagine they would, not unless they have watercraft handy. Or steal ours. Plus, you'd think they'd be put off by how many of us there are."

"We're mostly women and kids."

"It's still a lot of humans to deal with. What are they going to do, kill all of us? That would attract some attention. I can't imagine it."

"When I heard voices and crossed the creek to look for the people because I thought maybe they'd have a radio, I walked right up on them. They had a fortune in gold. Plus they'd excavated a cave that they said was filled with Indian artifacts. Some people would kill for that."

For a moment, Patrick's mind conjured up a cave of Tukudika treasures. Never mind the gold. The artifacts would have lasting value. He hoped the gold-hungry men didn't destroy them, carelessly or on purpose.

Patrick's canoe bumped into Pete's, so he ruddered to the left. "But chasing down a group of our size? It doesn't make sense."

"With normal people, I'd agree, but that Les was crazy."

Patrick nodded. "I heard him."

"Crazier even than he sounded, man. You had to see him up close to understand. The guy is scary. And Winthropp didn't seem like he was all there either. He did whatever Les told him to do, like a robot."

Patrick didn't like the sound of this. "What was that they were saying about killing someone already?"

"You heard that, too, huh? Some guy named Jimbo who was their partner and got crossways with Les. That's what has me most worried. They know that I *know* they murdered someone out here."

And now, by extension, they'd think anyone Pete was with would know, too. The odds of them pursuing the Flints might be higher than Patrick had figured.

Patrick suddenly remembered the body that had come to the canoe shop on the trailer. "Jimbo. I'll bet he was the dead guy that floated down the river."

"That would be my guess."

They crossed under the footbridge. Susanne's and Vera's canoes were side by side. Susanne appeared to be coaching Vera on paddling, and Vera's canoe looked more under control. On the riverbank, a big-eared mule deer doe and fawn lifted their heads from the water to watch them. The doe bounded off. The spindly-legged fawn went after her, but with none of her grace or speed.

Susanne turned back toward them, and the nose of her canoe drifted in the same direction as her head. "Patrick, what's going on?" She stuck a paddle in the water as a rudder and corrected her course.

Patrick dug his paddle in harder and increased his rhythm. He eased up when he reached the stern of her canoe and drifted in beside her.

Vera's canoe was on his other side. Sweat dripped down his forehead. He wiped it with his sleeve.

"Hey, guys," he said.

Susanne said, "Who were those men?"

Patrick paused before answering her, eying Perry for a second to assess his condition. His face was pale and pinched. Patrick was worried. He didn't want to think about the damage bleeding and swelling could be doing to his son's brain at that very moment. All the more reason to move downriver as fast as they could.

He turned to his wife and lowered his voice. The kids might still be able to hear him, but they'd have to work harder for it. "They're gold prospectors, and they've had a major discovery. Pete ran into them on Trout Creek. Unfortunately, they're territorial about their find, and they're nuts. When I came up on them, they were going to kill Pete so he wouldn't tell anyone about it."

"What?" Her tone was skeptical. He didn't blame her. It defied logic.

Vera must have had hearing like an owl. "What did they do to you, Pete?" She did *not* choose to keep her voice low.

Pete, who was now right behind the other three canoes, said, "I'm fine."

"It doesn't sound fine. And this was over gold?"

Annie hugged herself. "Why would men want to hurt you because of gold, Daddy?"

"I don't know, Annie Oakley. It doesn't make sense, does it? But all they did was tie me up, and then they left. Uncle Patrick found me and cut me loose. That's all. Really."

Stan's voice was grave and his eyes huge. "Were you scared?"

"A little bit."

"But they're still after you?"

"Maybe. I'm not sure."

Lana said, "They're the ones who murdered the guy that floated downriver, aren't they?"

"Oh, my God," Susanne said. "Trish, Bunny, and Joe are still out there, and so are those men."

Patrick scowled. "The prospectors don't have any reason to feel threatened by Joe and the girls, though, even if their paths do cross. If Pete hadn't seen the gold, he wouldn't have had a problem with them, either."

Bert piped in. "Will Bunny be all right?"

Patrick nodded. "Your cousin Trish is a smart girl. And Joe Flint is one tough hombre. He'll find Trish and Bunny, and he'll keep them safe."

Perry spoke, but his voice was wobbly. "Those guys that were fishing are back on Trout Creek, too. The Hilliards. What if they try to hurt them?"

"I don't think they will. And I don't think they'll hurt us either. We just need to get out of here and get Perry to the hospital."

Vera started to cry again.

Pete reached across the water for her hand, letting his canoe drift for a moment. "Bunny will be all right, love."

"But there are grizzlies out there."

Pete smiled at her. "But lots of people. No bear is going to hang around this river. It's like Grand Central Station."

Patrick wouldn't have gone that far, but there had been a fair number of people on Trout Creek. "Here's our landing."

They'd reached the pebbly beach that led to the guard station. He turned toward the shore and accelerated his paddling until the canoe beached. Then he jumped out and pulled it further up the bank, wincing when he stepped on the foot with the injured ankle, although the cold water did feel numbingly good.

His mother shifted her weight forward in her seat like she was going to stand.

"Just a minute, Mom. I'll come back for you."

Lana shooed him with her hand. "Your father and I canoed in the Ozarks every summer with you kids. I know my way around a canoe." She exited with balance that surprised him. Then his memories surfaced. With chagrin, he pictured his mother—young and strong—paddling him and Pete as they fished the Mulberry River. His father wasn't in the frame. That wasn't unusual. Joe hadn't changed much over the years. So, yes, his mother had always been a lot more capable than he gave her credit for.

Patrick hauled Susanne's canoe in and shot a glance back upriver. He thought he saw movement on the far shore where they'd last seen the prospectors, but they were too far away to be sure what it was.

As some of the kids started to get restless, he said, "Everybody stay put until we get all the canoes in, then Pete and I will help you out."

Pete beached his and Vera's canoes. Then, the brothers lifted the smaller kids and helped them through the shallow, rocky water and to the firm ground. Susanne got out by herself. Vera tried, but she lost her balance and fell backwards. When her tush hit the icy water, she screamed. Not the "having fun, gosh the water's cold" kind of scream, but an "I'm at the end of my rope" kind. Pete hurried over to her. He hauled her up, then in for a hug, even though she was sopping wet. Her scream had ended in a strangled sob.

Patrick joined Susanne. He whispered into her hair. "It's going to be all right. We made it back to the cars. Now we just have to drive down the mountain."

She turned to him and put her arms around his waist. She fit so perfectly, it was like they had been made for each other. Two halves of a whole. Patrick pulled her close. Her heart beat so hard he could feel it against his own chest.

"Patrick, I'm scared about Trish."

"Dad will find her."

"And Perry."

"We'll get him to the hospital."

"And the men."

"I just checked, and I don't see them coming after us." He rocked her from side to side. "But I still think we should get moving." He released her but grabbed her hand. "Come on everyone."

Susanne stopped. "Do we have the keys?"

Patrick's stomach dropped. "I sure hope so. They were in the front pocket of the Army surplus backpack."

"That one was in our canoe," Susanne said.

Patrick went back for the pack, waiting until he had it on the shore to check for the keys. He dug in the pocket and found both sets.

He grinned and held them up. "Got 'em. Now, last one to the cars is a rotten egg."

His teasing fell flat, and no one except Danny ran to the vehicles. The boy was a little speed demon, and he slapped the hood of the station wagon while the others were still twenty yards away. Patrick cocked his head as he looked at it and then the Suburban. Something seemed different about the vehicles. They were lower. Like they'd sunk in the mud.

Only there wasn't any mud.

Like . . .

"Hey, Dad, the station wagon has a flat tire," Danny called. "I can help you change it."

And that was it. That was what Patrick had been noticing. The tires —not just the one Danny had pointed out—were flat, all of them that he could see anyway. He felt the hair rising on his arms. How could the tires on both cars be flat? He broke into a jog. His ankle was stiff from the time in the canoe, and it protested, which kept him slow. Pete pulled ahead of him. Each brother made a circuit of the cars.

Eight flat tires. Patrick checked them twice to be sure. What were the chances? *Nearly zero.* One flat on each they could have handled, but the vehicles only carried a single spare apiece. With eight flats, the cars were completely disabled.

Patrick knelt by the front driver's side of the Suburban, trying to put most of his weight on his good ankle. He gritted his teeth. He was only partially successful. What he saw when he was in position was a kick in the solar plexus.

He pitched his voice so only Pete could hear. "Slashed."

Pete crouched beside him. "Who would do this?"

"Les? But he was still upriver. He couldn't have gotten down here and back to where we saw him. Not in the time he had after Hector and Diego discovered you missing."

Pete rubbed his chin. "Did you see them—Hector and Diego?"

"No."

"Me either. Could it have been them?"

"Possibly. But, it would have been awfully hard for them, too. They'd have to have left immediately and moved quickly after they discovered you missing. But why would they have come here? They didn't know we had cars here."

Pete nodded. "Yeah."

"I didn't see any evidence of any watercraft on the riverbank either. Which they would have had to have to get here in time to do this."

"Hmm."

"What are you thinking?"

"That maybe I'm just paranoid, but it sure feels like we're being watched."

Patrick stood and surveyed the forest around them, fronted by the clearing where the vehicles were parked near the guard station cabin. Behind the brothers was the river and a smattering of trees and rocks. There was a disturbing number of places to hide.

"I don't see anyone," he said. "But if someone's out there with a rifle, we're sitting ducks."

"What next, then?" Pete said. He shoved his longish hair away from his face. His cheekbones seemed sharper than usual, and his eyes were red rimmed and had dark circles underneath them. Patrick wondered if he looked the same.

If there really was someone armed watching them, Patrick had to figure out how to protect the family. But how? If they all clustered together, they made a big, easy target. He patted his hip, finding his revolver and knife. He had weapons, but they wouldn't do any good against someone taking pot shots from a tactically superior hiding place. His brain whirred, processing so hard he could almost imagine a motor. And it generated an idea. *The cabin.* It could provide shelter. And if Klaus and Sylvie were there, they would help. He glanced at the little building. The Jeep wasn't parked behind it. So much for Klaus and Sylvie.

But the cabin had a radio. And he didn't need their help to use that.

He pointed. "The cabin. The radio."

Pete nodded. "Good idea. I'm not sure why I didn't think of that."

"Or me, sooner." Except that Patrick was very familiar with the effects of stress on brain function. He imagined his effective IQ had fallen twenty points since Perry's injury, the interaction with the prospectors, and losing Bunny and Trish. Just another reason he needed to get control of his emotions and keep breathing.

Patrick faced the others. The kids were milling around, a little on edge, but nothing too troubling. They'd hold themselves together if the adults did. The women were huddled, and stress radiated off them so hot and intense they almost glowed.

He raised his voice, trying to imbue it with confidence and positivity. "Hey, everyone, let's take a rest over in the cabin. But no racing this time, Danny. I want to go in first."

"Why, Dr. Uncle Patrick?" Danny asked.

Patrick had given up on erasing the "Dr." in front of Danny's "Uncle Patrick." "In case there's anyone in there. I don't want to scare them."

"Oh. Okay."

Patrick started toward the cabin. The after image of the family in his head didn't include his son. Frowning, he turned back around. "Where's Perry?"

Susanne said, "Sitting in the shade. His headache and nausea are getting worse."

Medical texts were filled with examples of worst-case scenarios. When it came to head injuries, patients who had been walking and talking after an injury, like Perry, could still succumb to bleeding inside the brain hours or even days later. *Epidural hematomas. Subdural hematomas.* Even thinking about the medical names made Patrick shudder. Perry's symptoms—the headache, the nausea—might indicate nothing more than a concussion, or they might be signs that he was facing a very serious issue. But now was not the time to panic. If Perry started to show paralysis or confusion, slurred speech, or a fixed, dilated pupil, or if he lapsed back into unconsciousness again, then panic might be understandable. Unavoidable, even for a doctor. Because there would be nothing Patrick could do to help his son. Not out here. There might not even be much they could do for Perry in Jackson.

Between Perry, Trish, the vehicles, and the prospectors, Patrick's adrenal system was redlining. But he had to stay steady, for everyone's sake. He had to forget this was his son and tear his mind away from all the horrible possibilities. Instead, he needed to focus on what he could do, which was to keep working on getting Perry out of the wilderness. But time was of the essence, and now they had no vehicles. The clearing was big enough to land a helicopter though. He could ask for one to be sent when he radioed for help.

He swallowed and kept his tone casual. "I need Perry inside with the rest of us. He can't be out here alone."

"I'll stay with him."

"The two of you can't be out here alone."

Understanding dawned across her features. "Got it." She turned to Perry. "Come on, honey. We're going into the cabin. It'll be nice and cool in there."

Perry got up, but he moved slowly, like his head was made of glass he was afraid he would break. Patrick didn't see any drooping or jerky movements that screamed the beginning of paralysis to him. *Good.* He shook off his parental urge to run to his son and cradle him. *Focus on getting him out of here.* He headed toward the cabin.

At the door, he stopped. "Pete, could you make sure everyone stays to one side, please."

Pete herded the family back, where the door would be between them and anyone who might answer it. Susanne put a hand under Perry's elbow and led him to join the group. Her eyes looked as worried as Patrick's felt. *Do what you have to do.* He rested his hand on the butt of his revolver. Then he knocked and waited. The cabin was small, and it wouldn't have taken anyone but a moment to get to the door.

When there was no answer, he shouted, "Hello. Is anyone home?" He waited again, longer this time. To the family he said, "I'm going inside. Stay put until I invite you in. Please." He drew the revolver, but kept it pointed down and didn't cock it. Then he eased the door open, keeping as much of himself out of the frame as he could. The hinges creaked as the door swung outward. "If anyone's in there, this is Patrick Flint, and I'm entering the cabin now." He stepped inside and looked around, gun barrel aimed at the ground in front of him.

The cabin was empty of people. It was a one-room structure, with two unmade twin beds on one end. A stone fireplace, a square wooden table, and four rickety chairs were on the other. Light shone through twin windows, and dust danced in its beams, like mist in a spotlight. The floor was made of wide wooden planks. They groaned and sagged as he walked across them. He caught a whiff of chili. *Last night's dinner?* He swung his head around and saw a metal desk against the front wall, in the corner away from the window. A rusty folding chair sat in front of it. On its surface was a radio.

Patrick holstered his revolver. "There's no one here. You guys can come in, but don't mess with anything. People live here, and we're not invited guests."

The cabin had felt small before the rest of the Flints entered, but with twelve people in it, it was a matchbox. Patrick edged over to the radio. He didn't have a lot of experience with them, but his father-in-law was an expert. Patrick had picked up a few pointers from him over the years, enough to operate one, anyway.

He twisted the dial on. Nothing happened.

He leaned in for a closer examination. Nothing he'd learned from Susanne's father was going to help him with what he saw.

"Pete," he said.

His brother didn't have to walk far to join him.

Patrick gestured toward the radio.

Pete's face fell, and they stared at the unit together.

All the wires had been pulled out of the back. But that wasn't the worst part. The misshapen mic looked like it had been crushed with a mallet.

The radio was just as useless to them as their vehicles.

CHAPTER TWENTY-FOUR: MEET

YELLOWJACKET GUARD STATION, BRIDGER-TETON NATIONAL
FOREST, WYOMING
FRIDAY, JUNE 24, 1977, 2:30 P.M.

Perry

Perry's head felt like it was being squeezed between the massive hands of a giant. It made it hard for him to concentrate. To think at all. And the crowded little cabin didn't have enough air. He was suffocating. His dad had said he had a concussion. Perry's best friend John had gotten one in the last football game of the season. John had vomited on the sideline and had a headache for days. But he'd been fine. Perry knew he just needed to toughen up. "No pain, no gain," his dad always said. Of course, that was usually related to workouts, but he also liked to say, "What doesn't kill you makes you stronger." If that was really true, then Perry was going to be a lot stronger after this.

His cousin Brian was standing in front of him now, saying something, and it was like Perry was looking at him through a dark tunnel. ". . . football when I get in junior high . . ."

Perry nodded. Something in his stomach jarred loose, all the way up into his throat. It burned. And it wanted out.

". . . can't fix it . . ." his dad said.

Uncle Pete answered him. ". . . maybe we should walk out . . . not expecting it . . ."

". . . too far for the little ones . . . take too long . . . Perry . . ."

Perry clapped his hand over his mouth. His dad had told them to stay inside together, but he also told them not to mess up the cabin. Puking counted as messing it up, he felt certain. He threw the door open and ran, barely making it outside before the acid came up. He'd already emptied all the food out of his stomach earlier. He held himself up with his hands on his knees while he retched and heaved. His eyes watered and his nose ran. The acid burned his throat, his mouth, his nose. He wanted to lay down in the dirt and put his cheek on a cool rock, but he'd splattered clear yuck all over the ones in front of him. He heard the sounds of a lot of footsteps and chattering kids.

"Are you okay, honey?" His mom laid a hand on his back.

"I don't feel so hot."

"I'm sorry. We're headed to town now."

"How?"

Then his dad said, "Susanne. A word?"

She patted Perry's shoulder and stepped away.

His dad spoke in a low voice, but Perry could still hear him. "No radio. No cars. The fastest way to get to town is on the river."

"I don't like it, Patrick. What about Trish and Bunny? And your dad?"

"We're going to have to trust Dad. I know he doesn't show it very often, but he's a capable and determined guy. And Perry needs a hospital, Susanne."

"He was throwing up again. Do you think it's a concussion?"

"At least."

"What does *that* mean?"

"It means we need him checked out. I can't see inside his head. But the skull is an unforgiving barrier when it comes to bleeding and swelling, which puts a lot of pressure back inward on the brain."

Her voice rose in pitch. "But he's awake. He's walking around. He's talking to us. Aren't those good signs?"

"Probably so."

His dad sounded like he was trying to calm his mom down, and that scared Perry more than his words. Perry closed his eyes. He was going to be fine. Just like John was.

Perry's mom drew in a shaky breath. "Okay."

"So, right now, we've got to get moving. For Perry, and before the prospectors decide to come after us."

"They wouldn't do that, would they?"

"Honestly, I would think they'd stay with their discovery and that load of gold Pete saw. It would be the rational thing to do. But, up until now, they've behaved pretty irrationally, so I don't know. There's no sense in sticking around to find out. We'll just have to pray for Dad's success and the girls' safety."

"Will you?"

"Will I what?"

"Pray with me for them. Now."

Perry's dad cleared his throat. "Of course."

Perry knew this was big. *Dad never even goes to church.* Perry stepped over to them and took his dad's hand. His mom grabbed Perry's other one. The three of them formed a human chain.

Perry's dad said, "Dear Heavenly Father, please watch over Trish and Bunny and keep them safe. Help Dad find them and bring them home. And please Lord be with Perry with his head injury and with all of us as we journey down the river. In Jesus's name I pray. Amen."

"Amen." Perry's mom squeezed his hand.

An unfamiliar man's voice from behind him made Perry jump, which rattled his brain in his head. Perry turned toward the voice, slowly.

"I didn't know it was Sunday—or is everyday church day for you folks?" The man facing them grinned, showing stained teeth. Perry thought he looked like he'd been out in the wilderness a long time. He was thick—his legs, his body, even his head, thanks to a shaggy brown beard—and everything about him was dark, including his skin, but that was probably because of the layer of dirt he was wearing. The only thing that wasn't dark about him was his bright orange hat. Stink didn't usually bother Perry too much, but this guy hadn't had a bath in a long time, he guessed, and it made Perry's queasy stomach do weird things again.

His dad stepped in between Perry and his mom and the strange man. "Hello."

"How are you people doing on this fine afternoon?"

"Fine, but in a bit of a hurry. My son has injured his head, so we're headed to town. If you'll excuse us." Perry's dad gave him a push in the center of his back. Not hard. Just enough to direct him toward the canoes.

"You've got a big mess of kiddos."

His dad didn't break stride as he walked Perry and his mom toward the shore and waved at Pete to do the same with the rest of the family. Aunt Vera's eyes widened, but she kept her lips zipped. Gramma Lana didn't hesitate, marching Bert and Barry ahead of her. Aunt Vera recovered and brought Danny along, while Uncle Pete walked with a hand on Annie and Stan's shoulders, Brian beside him.

The man called out after them. "You folks take care now."

Perry's mom whispered, "He gives me the creeps."

At the river's edge, their canoes were as they had left them. His dad counted and named the items in the canoe.

He grimaced. "Fifteen life jackets. We have them all."

Aunt Vera frowned. "But Bunny needs one."

"And Trish and Joe do. Well, hopefully they'll just wait by the river for us to get back. They have the food in the backpack Joe was carrying. What do we have in these?" Patrick pointed at the ones that had made it with them.

"Bread, chips, peanut butter, and jelly, and a few other odds and ends," Gramma Lana said. "Jackets. Bedding. The tents."

"Good," Perry's dad said.

"I'm hungry," Barry said.

"Me, too," Bert echoed, followed by several other sounds of agreement from the rest of the kids.

Gramma Lana smiled. "When we get going, I'll make sandwiches, and you can canoe over to me and pick them up. Like a drive through window at McDonald's. Sound good?"

That met with everyone's approval.

It only took a few minutes for Uncle Pete and Perry's dad to figure out who was riding with whom, but to Perry it seemed like hours.

"Can we go now? I'm tired," he said.

"Yes. You can rest, but you can't sleep, though." His dad was holding his mom's hand while she climbed in the canoe.

"Now, this just ain't right," a man said. It was the same thick guy from up by the cabin. "You've got women paddling. How about I ride along and help you out?"

"I'm fine," Perry's mom said. "I taught canoeing at summer camp."

"And you, pretty missy?" he was looking at Aunt Vera.

Uncle Pete bristled.

She giggled. "I'm good enough."

"Good enough looking, but I'd be happy to paddle."

"We said we're fine." Perry's dad sounded tense.

The man held up both hands. "Have you canoed the Tukudika before?"

"No."

"It's not as challenging as the Snake or the Gros Ventre, but it has some tricky patches. Do you have a map?"

Perry's dad looked at his mom.

She shook her head. "It's in the backpack Joe's carrying."

Perry's dad's lips started moving. *Uh oh.*

The man followed their exchange. "Listen, you'd be helping me out. And I could help you out. I was hiking into town for provisions today. You'll save me that long walk, and I'll show you where the bad spots on the river are. Keep you from going over a waterfall."

Perry knew his mom didn't like the guy, but his Aunt Vera nodded and smiled. She seemed pretty excited about the idea. She hadn't been close enough to smell him yet, though. Perry was in her canoe. He sure wasn't voting to bring the guy along with them.

"Can we say yes, Pete?" Vera asked. "I really don't know how to canoe."

Perry's dad crossed his arms. "Did you see anyone besides us around the cabin?"

The man narrowed his eyes. "No. Why?"

"Just wondering." Perry wondered why his dad didn't mention their flat tires and the broken radio. But his dad changed the subject. "Where are you camping?"

"South of here. I'm fly fishing the Yellowjacket." The man pointed toward the creek behind the cabin. "Fewer people."

Perry's dad nodded.

The man grinned. "And where are my manners? Been back up in the wilderness too long, I guess. My name's Booger. Booger Stanton."

Perry's mom mouthed *Booger?* Then she shook her head.

But Uncle Pete stuck out his hand and shook Booger's. "I'm Pete Flint. This is my wife Vera. All the kids are mine except for the teenage boy. This is my brother Patrick, his wife Susanne, and my mother, Lana."

"Pleased to make your acquaintance, Flints."

Patrick grumbled something under his breath, but then he sighed and shook Booger's hand, too. "A ride in exchange for a guide. All right then. Let's hit the river."

Perry groaned. Booger was coming with him and Aunt Vera. He and Aunt Vera got in the canoe and Booger waded it into the river. Just as they were all pushing off, Perry looked upriver. Another canoe was paddling toward them, but it was still too far away to see who was in it.

"Um, Dad . . ." Perry pointed.

"Is it Joe and the girls?" Lana said, tenting a hand over her eyes.

Perry's dad squinted into the distance. "I don't think so."

As they were watching, the canoe beached on the far side of the river. Whoever was in it dragged it off the water and into the trees. *Maybe they're going fishing. It even could be the Hilliards. They were nice.*

"Friends of yours?" Booger asked as he hauled himself into the canoe.

Patrick dipped his paddle in the water. "Maybe. Maybe not."

Booger snorted. "I sure hope they are. Guiding is in trade for a ride. Fighting's extra."

Perry saw his dad pat his hip, checking his weapons. He'd been doing it a lot. And Perry knew what it meant—his dad didn't think it was Trish and Bunny with Grandpa Joe in that canoe.

CHAPTER TWENTY-FIVE: SHOOT

Susanne

Susanne rested the paddle over her knees and rolled her shoulders. Gentle waves lapped at the sides of the canoe, and it rocked through the water as it slowed. "Want to paddle for a little while, Brian?" Her arms were already protesting, even though the river had been smooth and swift since they'd left the guard station. She snuck a glance at Vera's canoe. The strange man, Booger, was expertly piloting the canoe and he must have been cracking jokes, too, because Vera was laughing. Perry was staring into the distance and didn't appear to be listening to him. She turned her attention back to Brian.

The smile he flashed her spread ear to ear and dimpled one of his cheeks. *Such a cute kid.* "Sure!"

She handed the paddle up to him in the middle seat. "Do you know how to do it?"

He dug into the water immediately. "Yes, ma'am. Pete taught me."

It caught her off guard that Brian called his stepfather Pete, but she supposed it made sense. To Brian, the name "Dad" was already taken by his birth father. "All right. Let me know if you have questions."

Lana held up two handfuls of sandwiches. Patrick angled his canoe toward Susanne's.

When he had it alongside them, Lana handed them over to Susanne. "PB&Js. Do you have water?"

Susanne held out two sandwiches to Brian. He stopped paddling, took one, and passed the other to Annie, who had switched into Susanne's canoe.

Susanne said, "We have a full canteen. Thanks, Lana."

"Of course. More to make and deliver." She winked. "I need a name for my new business."

"Any of those sandwiches left?" Booger shouted. "We're starving over here." Booger had paddled the canoe carrying Vera and Perry into the lead. It felt wrong not to have Patrick in front. Rattled Susanne for some reason.

"Just a minute," Lana called.

"You should call it Flint's Fast Food," Brian said. "And deliver it to my mom's canoe fast."

They all laughed.

"But are you getting paid?" Susanne asked.

"Time with my family is all the payment I need." Lana waved goodbye.

Patrick smiled at Susanne as he pointed his canoe toward Vera's. Lana was already making more sandwiches in her lap.

Susanne didn't like that they were sharing their food with Booger. The deal had been "guide for a *ride*," not a ride and meals. They were low on supplies after lunch for the whole family had ended up in Trout Creek and one backpack had stayed behind with Joe.

"Ready for me to take that paddle back so you can eat?" Susanne called up to Brian.

"Ladies eat first," he answered.

Annie took a bite of her sandwich. "He called me a lady," she said through a full mouth.

"You're a smooth talker, Brian." Susanne dug into her own sandwich.

She tried to relax and take in the view as she ate. If everything hadn't gone so wrong, she would have enjoyed it. The mountains rising on either side of the undulating dark ribbon of water were breathtaking. Purple lupine and golden balsam root created a haze of color on a meadow. In the far distance, Grand Teton peak and its brethren were carving a black hole in the startling blue sky. And all around them, green. The color of life and renewal. Yet their family was fleeing down the river under threat of life or death, for Perry with his condition, with the girls lost, and with the prospectors that Pete and Patrick thought were after them. She swallowed another bite of sandwich. It stuck in her throat like a hunk of wood. She'd lost her appetite.

"I'll trade you half my sandwich for that paddle, Brian," she said.

"Really?" Brian's voice was enthusiastic. He immediately sent the paddle back toward Susanne. She handed the sandwich forward.

He took it from her and consumed it like a hyena on a gazelle carcass.

Susanne barely noticed. She was hungry for the paddle, remembering her youth and the soothing power of repetitive motion. It had been hypnotic then. Soon, she was on autopilot. Unfortunately, with her mind freed thanks to the task of paddling, her problems seized it until her insides were floating on a current of anxiety far rougher than the river.

She wished she was in the canoe with Patrick. She wanted to tell him how uncomfortable she was with Booger. Why had Patrick let him join their group? Booger had appeared out of nowhere in the wilderness. His timing was odd. The things he had said were disturbing. His appearance and odor were off-putting. If they'd been driving down the interstate and he'd had his thumb out on the side of the road, they wouldn't have stopped to pick him up. Patrick was vehemently against giving rides to hitchhikers. It was one of the things he'd preached about endlessly when he'd taught her and the kids self-defense. He'd even cut articles out of the newspaper about a hitchhiker who murdered a motorist in Colorado the year before. Not to mention that Patrick was supremely confident in his own abilities. To a fault. That trait combined with his experience with strangers in the wilderness the year before, when he'd run into Kemecke, ought to have made him even more leery of Booger.

So why was Booger in the canoe with Vera now?

Then the answer hit her, and she felt dense that she hadn't realized it earlier. *Pete. Pete is why.*

Patrick wasn't a different person, per se, around his brother. But he wasn't the same, either. For one thing, he acted and seemed younger. Like he'd regressed back to his teens, the age he was the last time he and Pete had lived under the same roof. For another, he went out of his way to build Pete up. It went beyond respecting his brother and his feelings. So much further that she'd asked Patrick about it once.

He'd been uncomfortable talking about it at first. But he'd finally told her that, as boys, he'd gotten a lot of positive attention for his type A personality. He was an achiever. An *over*achiever, and book smart, too. Pete was—is—an artist who moves to his own beat. Smart like Patrick, but interested in different things. And schools reward the Patricks of the world.

It had made sense to her. She could even relate. Not for herself, but with her kids. Trish took after Patrick. Perry was more like her. More like *Pete*. While it was athletics instead of art that drove Perry, he didn't care about grades and academic achievement as much as his sister did, and the teachers noticed. He entered their classes under the weight of their high expectations because of his conscientious sister. Except he wasn't her. He was one hundred percent himself. The only time their differences bothered Perry, really, was when the kids brought home report cards, and Trish had all As and glowing remarks, and Perry didn't. Except from the coaches, who talked about his heart, his courage, and his effort. It had gotten to the point where Susanne had asked Trish to downplay report card day. Not because they weren't proud of her. They were very, very proud of her. But to make it sting less for Perry.

Lana, according to Patrick, had the same talk with him as a boy that Susanne had with Trish. And Pete was his best friend. So it was never a problem for Patrick like it was for Trish, who seemed to resent it and remember fondly the days when every grade and first prize was a celebration instead of a secret. Patrick might not completely understand his brother, and he might occasionally get frustrated with him, but he was his biggest fan, most steady supporter, and most loyal champion.

If Pete said they were picking up the river hitcher, then of course Patrick would bow to his wishes, if he possibly could. She got it. But she didn't like it, not when she thought Booger was a problem. But what could she do about it when the brothers were in alignment?

Ahead of them, Booger quit paddling, which wrested her thoughts back to the present.

He turned and raised his voice. "Okay, people. We're almost to some rapids. These ones aren't so bad. But when we're through them, we need to pull off to the right. It gets a lot worse. Too much for this group."

Patrick slowed alongside Susanne. Bert and Barry waved at Brian and Annie like they'd been apart for a decade. Perry turned back toward them from Vera's canoe. He gave Susanne a halfhearted grin. He looked like he could barely hold his head up. Susanne wanted to gather him in her arms and rock him in her lap. It wasn't possible, though, and not just because they were in separate canoes, but also because Perry would never allow it at his age. Her heart ached for the time her children had been little. She wished she and Patrick had had more kids.

"You ready?" Patrick asked Susanne.

"I think so."

"You'll do great, Aunt Susanne," Brian said.

Annie clutched the sides of the canoe. She cast a round-eyed, frightened glance back at her aunt and brother. "Brian, trade seats with me. I don't want to be in front."

"Cool," he said.

The two exchanged seats.

Patrick locked eyes with Susanne. "Ride the water. Don't fight it. If you're heading for an obstacle, paddle on the opposite side to turn from it. Dragging a paddle to rudder only works when you're going faster than the current, and we won't be."

Susanne nodded. His words and tone soothed her. He was repeating information she already knew in theory but hadn't used in real life, so she was glad for the reminder. The closest she'd gotten to white water as a summer camp counselor in Texas was in the hot tub. The camp was west of San Antonio where the rivers were lazy and warm. Nothing like the Tukudika. She stared ahead and saw the white ripples of the rapids.

"I can help paddle," Brian said.

"I need you hanging on so you don't fall out."

"Okay."

"If one of you falls out, do you remember what Brock told us to do in our safety talk back at the canoe shop?" Patrick asked the kids.

Susanne hadn't even thought about the possibility of one of the kids getting thrown from the canoe. She felt short of breath. And what if Perry was thrown out? What if he hit his head again? She couldn't let herself think about it or she wasn't going to be able to do this. She forced the thoughts away, but she still felt short of breath.

"Um, don't drown?" Brian said.

Annie shook her head. "No, dummy. Roll on your back and put your feet downstream, toes to the sky, and arms out."

"You forgot part of it." Brian looked smug.

"No, I didn't."

"Lift your head so you can see where you're going."

"Oh. Yeah. That, too."

"And when you get near the canoe, roll over and swim like mad to catch it."

"Or you can do that to get to the shore," Annie said.

"But what *don't* you do at the shore?" Patrick asked.

Bert and Barry chimed in. "Don't stand up."

"Not until you're all the way out on dry land. So, no standing, no jumping out, keep your hands and feet inside the canoe, and stay still in your seat so you don't knock the canoe over."

"What if Aunt Susanne falls out?" Annie asked. Her olive face had lightened several shades, and her eyes were locked on the rapids ahead again.

Not a pleasant thought.

"Then I'll paddle." Brian looked like he hoped it would happen. "And we'll pick her up."

"What if she drops the paddle?"

Patrick smiled. "You've got an extra, right in the bottom of the canoe. Just ride the canoe, and your dad or I will come get you. It will be all right."

Susanne took a deep breath. The water under them was speeding up and getting louder. "Everyone's life jacket is buckled and tight, right?"

Brian gave her two thumbs up, but Annie checked hers first before nodding.

"Whoever screams first is a rotten egg," Bert crowed.

"I'll bet it will be Annie," Barry said.

Ahead of them, Booger's canoe slipped into the rapids, dipping, and bucking. Vera screamed.

"Mom's a rotten egg!" Bert hollered.

Seconds later, Pete's canoe followed them.

"I'm going last in case you have trouble. See you on the other side." Patrick reverse paddled, and Susanne's canoe drew ahead.

"On the other side," Susanne echoed, but her voice was a whisper.

And then a powerful, rumbling force lifted her canoe ever so slightly and propelled it across burbling water. The rushing, bubbling, tumbling sounds intensified. The nose of the canoe started to move back and forth in the current, finding its way through the rocks as if guided by an unseen hand.

WHAM.

The front right side slammed into a rock. Brian whooped and pumped a fist. This was *nothing* like summer camp canoeing.

WHAM.

The other side crunched into another rock. Susanne had never experienced anything like this before. She thought riding a galloping horse with the ground far below was scary. That was Mickey Mouse compared to canoeing whitewater.

Annie screamed. She clutched the seat on either side of her legs. "We're going to tump over!"

Susanne had her paddle poised and ready, but there was nothing she could do with it. The water was in control. She felt helpless, and, at the same time, exhilarated. *Faith. The water is all-powerful and yielding to it is like faith.* The thought itself made her feel stronger, more courageous. *Thank you, God.*

Pete turned around in his seat and yelled something at her. He shook his paddle, but she couldn't hear him. She glanced further downriver. In the distance, Booger had cleared the white water and pulled to the righthand side. But then she saw the enormous boulder in the middle of the stream between her and Pete, and she realized exactly what he had been trying to tell her.

They were heading straight for the rock.

She knew she needed to paddle to the side of it, but which side? Both looked equally treacherous to her. She pictured Pete's canoe. Which side of the rock had he been on? The left, she decided. She dug her paddle into the water on the right side of the canoe and started pulling the water, but the canoe didn't change course.

It was being drawn straight at the boulder.

"Aunt Susanne!" Annie screamed. "The rock!"

Susanne grunted with effort. She paddled harder than she believed she could, lifting her bottom off the seat an inch as she pushed through the back half of each stroke. "Turn, you stupid canoe. Turn!"

Finally, the bow veered to the left ever so slightly. The rest of the canoe followed. And not a moment too soon, either. They slipped by the boulder so close that she could feel the vortex of water around it sucking at their canoe, pulling it toward a collision, or worse. But the downstream current and their momentum was enough to keep them free of it. She held her paddle to the right, ready to push off, but in the end, she only gave it a "not today, buddy" tap.

Annie was clinging to the seat and bracing her feet on either of the inside edges of the canoe. Brian threw both his arms in the air like he was on the downhill plunge of a roller coaster.

After the boulder, the last twenty yards of white water passed in a blink. Susanne paddled on the left, pushing the canoe toward the others lined up on the shore.

"You did it, Aunt Susanne! That was so cool!" Brian shouted.

Her ears were ringing, but she smiled. "Wow. That was something." With the excitement over, she was lightheaded.

"I wish we could do it again!"

"Not me," Annie said. "It was scary. Get me out of this thing."

"We're almost there, Annie."

The girl rose from her seat. The canoe lurched.

"Wait. You're going to knock us over, and then you'll fall in, too. When we beach, your dad will give you a hand."

Annie sat down with a thump. She still looked ready to eject herself. She waited, just barely, for her dad's hand.

When everyone was ashore, Pete slapped Susanne a high five. Patrick walked up to her.

Something looked different about her husband. "Where's your hat?" she asked him.

He smacked himself on the head. "Darn it. Must have lost it on the rapids." Then he hugged her. "I'm so proud of you."

Even Perry gave her a wan smile, although he looked green at the gills. She ached for him. But more than that, she worried about Trish and Bunny. Even if Joe found them, how would they get through those rapids without life jackets? If one of them fell in, they could hit their head. Get sucked into the hole by the boulder. Drown. Then she caught herself. She was doing it again. Giving in to fatalistic thoughts. She couldn't go there. She had to stay positive. She had to rely on Joe. She had to have faith.

Booger's voice pulled her the rest of the way out of her spiral. "Now we portage for a mile or two."

There were groans all around. Susanne looked up. And up. The path was steep and led up a rocky single track trail through a narrow strip of trees along a rocky cliff.

"Which is it," Pete asked. "A mile or two miles?"

Booger just grinned and shrugged.

"It sounds harder than it will be," Patrick said, smiling. "Vera and

Susanne, can you carry a canoe together? Booger, Pete, and I will each carry a canoe and a pack."

Susanne frowned. Booger hadn't had a pack of his own with him. If he was going to town by foot for supplies, what would he bring them back in? She wanted to ask, but now wasn't the right time.

"I can help them," Brian said.

Vera hugged him to her, but she looked sad. *Bunny*, Susanne suspected. "Gotta love my little man. That would be great, buddy."

"All right, everyone. Time's a-wasting." Patrick lifted his canoe in a smooth motion. "Oh, I almost forgot. Paddles and life jackets. Everybody wears their lifejacket. And if all the kids could take a paddle, and Brian and Perry take two each, we'll be set." His lifejacket was hanging from one shoulder.

"And no using paddles as walking sticks," Vera said.

Bert and Barry looked disappointed.

"Or swords," Pete added.

Danny mouthed, "Rats."

Susanne and Vera each took an end of their canoe.

"How do we flip this thing over?" Susanne said.

Pete grabbed it from the middle. "Here. Step under." He swung it up and over his head in one smooth motion. The women took their ends, letting the weight of the canoe floor rest on their heads.

"How does my hat look?" Vera's voice sounded echoey to Susanne with them both under the canoe.

"About as uncomfortable as mine feels." The smell was worse, though. Mildewy. A little fishy. She wondered if they had been cleaned after their last use. And then her stomach turned. What if this was the canoe that had transported the dead guy down the river? If she hadn't been holding up the canoe, she would have put her hand to her mouth. Definitely a thought she had to banish.

Brian stepped between the two women. He slid the paddles under the center seat support. Then he grasped the sides of the canoe and took some of the weight off his mom and aunt.

"Follow me," Booger said.

Patrick marched off behind Booger, and Susanne, Brian, and Vera filed in after Patrick and before Pete in the rear, with the younger kids, Lana, and Perry spread out in small groups between each of the canoes.

Just as they were leaving the riverbank for the forest, Susanne noticed someone had left a bright orange hat hanging from one of the trees.

"Did someone leave a hat?" she called out.

All she got back was a chorus of nos. It was a nice hat with a wide brim. Dirty, but it looked sturdy and useful. Too bad she didn't have a hand to get it or she would have claimed it for Patrick.

CHAPTER TWENTY-SIX: PORTAGE

Trish

The nice man they'd run into on the trail had insisted on walking Trish and Bunny back to their campsite. Trish hiked behind him. His red plaid shirt and light hair were normal-looking, and it made her feel better. She'd been a little nervous about joining up with him at first, but she was glad she wasn't alone anymore, even though he was a stranger.

Not that she'd been alone completely before. She had Bunny. But she was *responsible* for Bunny, and Bunny was no help. Trish had lost her bearings. She'd been completely turned around. How had she managed to get them *upriver* from the trail that led to the camp? It seemed to her that the trails would have had to cross. The only explanation she could think of was that the other trail just hadn't been big enough for her to notice it. It could have been small, like a path left by wildlife heading for a drink of water. The trails she was used to in the Bighorns were wider. More established. Not that there wasn't plenty of wild places with no trails there, too. The awful night with Kemecke she'd ridden double on her horse Goldie up Dome Mountain, with no trails at all. But her *family* only went to places that were marked on a forest service trail map.

Not like here, where her dad had taken them to a place that some old coot in a ranger's hat described. Totally backwoods. What had her dad been thinking? If he hadn't dragged them out here, she and Bunny wouldn't be lost right now. She was kind of mad at him, actually. She'd still be glad to see him when they got back to camp. Really glad. But she was going to tell him how she felt about everything. Respectfully, of course, because she still wanted the babysitting money for the down payment on a car, and her mom had said that her attitude would factor into how much they paid her.

The nice man—he'd said his name was Jim Smith, but she called him Mr. Smith—gave Bunny a peanut butter and honey sandwich from his backpack. Trish had turned down beef jerky, which was the only other thing he had. Then they'd doubled back along the trail, since Mr. Smith said it would be fastest to take it back to the one that led to their campsite. He assured Trish he'd spent a lot of time out there and knew the trails really well. That made one of them, anyway. She was relieved to turn navigation over to him.

The going was slow, because Bunny was wiped out and the trail was steep. The little girl refused to let Mr. Smith give her a piggyback ride, too. Trish had tried to carry her for a while, but they'd finally had to stop so she could rest. Bunny had fallen asleep sitting straight up on the ground, head bobbing on her chest.

"Let's give her ten minutes," Mr. Smith said.

"But mine and Bunny's parents will be worried about us."

Mr. Smith nodded. It was funny, but when she wasn't looking at him, she couldn't remember anything about his face. It was ordinary, with dark brown eyes like saddle leather. "I'll bet. But ten minutes won't make much difference. It's still faster than you would have gotten back without me."

"That's true."

"How long have you been gone?"

"Two hours? Or maybe longer, I guess."

"How did you get separated from your family?"

"We were going fishing and gold panning on Trout Creek. But Bunny threw a fit, so they made me take her back to camp by myself.

Then I missed the trail. I thought I could get to the river and find my way from there, but that was harder than I expected it would be."

He pulled at his chin. It was smooth. No whiskers. "Trout Creek, huh? Pretty. Did you see anyone else on it?"

"No. But I didn't get very far. I didn't see animals either. Our group scares everything off."

"That's a good thing in grizzly country."

"Yeah. I was a little wigged out when I was alone with Bunny."

"So, you're with a big group?"

"Really big. My grandparents. My aunt and uncle. My seven cousins. My parents. And my brother Perry and me."

"Wow. That's a lot of people."

She nodded. "I'm going to be in so much trouble. We were supposed to canoe down the river to a new campsite this afternoon. I'm ruining things for everybody. And they came all the way from Texas for this."

"They'll be so glad to see you, they won't even care."

She sighed. "I'm trying to convince my parents to let me get a car. They're probably going to tell me no, since I can't find my way around by myself."

He laughed. "Everybody gets lost sometimes. And the woods are a lot harder to navigate than roads."

"I hope so. Do you have kids?"

"Me? No."

"Well, I'll bet you'd be a cool dad."

"Maybe someday."

Bunny stretched and started to wake up. When she opened her eyes, they landed on Mr. Smith first. She started to cry. "I want my mommy."

Trish held out her arms. "Let's go see your mommy, Bunny. Right now."

Bunny launched herself into Trish's chest. "Really?"

"Really." Trish stood up and put Bunny on her own feet.

"My feet hurt."

"Mine, too. Can you go a little further, though?"

Bunny nodded, her face solemn.

"Follow me, girls." Mr. Smith set off down the trail in front of them.

Trish gave Bunny a gentle push to send her after him. His blue jeans had dirt and twigs on his bottom from sitting on the ground. He walked slowly so Bunny could keep up, his big work boots thudding on the path.

Trish brought up the rear. Earlier, she and Bunny had sang songs. But that didn't feel right in front of Mr. Smith. They hiked in silence.

After about five minutes, Mr. Smith said, "Wait here for a second."

"What is it?"

"I thought I heard something." He walked ahead.

Nervous butterflies took flight in Trish's tummy, dipping and swirling. What could he be checking on? She didn't want to be alone in the forest with Bunny again. She hoped he didn't walk so far that he was out of sight. Right now, she could still see his red shirt through the trees.

Then he was heading back to them, smiling. "I guess I was hearing things. Good news, though, I think we're at the place where your family camped last night."

"Really?" Trish couldn't help herself. She ran ahead into the clearing. It looked familiar—a fire ring and flattened grass inside a semi-circle of trees with a view of mountains from the open side—but there were no tents, no sleeping bags, no backpacks, and no people. She turned back toward Mr. Smith, her cheeks aching from the effort of holding back tears.

He'd followed her. "The bad news is they're not here." He didn't sound like it was bad news to him though. But why should it be? They weren't his family.

Trish turned in a slow circle. "Are you sure we're in the right place?"

"Doesn't it look familiar to you?"

"Yes, but . . . I just . . . I . . ."

He pointed at the ground. "See here, the holes from the tent stakes? And the fresh ash in the fire ring?"

"Yeah. But maybe it's someone else's camp."

He shrugged. "Maybe. Except not many people camp back here, and this is where you said it would be."

Bunny put her hand in Trish's. "Where's my mommy?"

"I don't know sweetie. We'll find her."

Bunny released a wail that pierced Trish's heart. "I want my mommy. I want her right now!"

Trish would never have said it out loud, but inside her head, the words were strong and clear. *I want my mommy right now, too.*

CHAPTER TWENTY-SEVEN: DISAGREE

Patrick

Patrick watched as the youngest of their group wandered off the trail, kicked a rock, and held up the line behind him, again. "Come on Bert. You need to hike a little faster."

There were a lot of rocks to kick. They covered the steep trail. Small, loose rocks. They made the footing precarious, and the traction terrible. More than once, one of the kids had gone down. There had been tears. He'd have some patching up of hands and knees to do later.

Bert's voice was wheedling. "I can't, Uncle Patrick."

"You can do it. I know you can."

"My legs hurt."

"So, don't think about your legs. Think about something else. Something you like. What's your favorite sport?"

"Soccer."

Soccer was starting to catch on in Texas. It was nowhere near as popular as football or baseball, but there were kids' leagues in all the bigger cities now. "Playing it or watching it?"

"Both."

"Are you on a team?"

"We're called the Dynamos, and I play forward." Bert grew more and more excited as he talked about the game.

Patrick kept the conversation going and encouraged the other kids to join in. It was the best thing he could think of to keep their minds off what they were going through. Not just the steepness and altitude, but the punishing sun. The tree cover was only intermittent, and he was starting to notice pink noses and necks along with sweaty armpits and foreheads. He knew he was pushing the group to hike faster than the youngest kids were comfortable with, but what choice did he have? Between Perry's condition, the encounter with the prospectors, and the uncertainty about Trish and Bunny—and his dad—they had to hurry.

For the millionth time, he considered taking Perry and pushing ahead of the rest of the group. If he did that, though, they'd have to take one of the canoes. There wouldn't be enough space left in the others for the rest of the family. He could solve that by bringing Brian along. It wouldn't resolve the bigger issue, though. And that was that he could not and would not split this group up any further, and he could not and would not leave them out here. Maybe he hadn't been able to prevent the catastrophes that had happened so far. He couldn't have foreseen Perry's accident. And he never would have guessed Trish would get lost. Or that Pete would run into gold-greedy murderers. But he still felt responsible. Guilty. Like a failure. Like a man who had a lot to make up for.

He sensed a shift in the mood of the other adults toward him in the last half hour, too. Portaging was hard work, and it was giving everyone too much time to think. He suspected what they were thinking was that this was all his fault. That it wouldn't have happened if he hadn't taken them on this trip on the Tukudika River and then camping along Trout Creek. Susanne had rebuffed his hug. Vera was shooting him dirty looks. Pete wasn't speaking to him. Even his mother had been avoiding him.

It was my job to keep them out of harm's way in the first place. It's my job to protect them now. Putting everything on Pete's shoulders wouldn't be fair. Worse, it would mean their fate would be outside of Patrick's control. He wasn't going to leave anything else up to chance.

The conversation between the kids continued without him, and he became aware of another one going on at the same time, at the front of the line, between Pete and Booger. He strained to hear them, eager to learn more about this guide who had magically appeared in their lives. He hoped it was providence and not more bad luck that had brought them together. They were due to catch a break.

Booger said, "Vera told me you had a scare this morning, Pete."

Pete's answer wasn't immediate. "Um, yeah. Perry was injured, but you already know that. It's why we're, like, in a hurry to get to Jackson, to get him treated at the hospital. Patrick is a doctor, but he can't fix a head injury out here, you know."

"A doctor, huh? I'm hanging out with rich folks."

Patrick ground his teeth. He hated the perception that all doctors were rich. He did well as a family practice physician in a small town, but rich? That was the stuff of big city surgeons whose parents had paid their way through medical school, not small-town doctors who'd footed their own bills. His salary was in line with the principal at the high school, and no one was calling principals rich.

"He's the successful one in our family. I'm the starving musician."

"Your job sounds more interesting in my book."

"I think so."

"But when I asked you about your scare this morning, I wasn't talking about the boy's injury."

"Well, also, our daughter and my niece are lost. My dad went back to find them. So, yeah, a few scares."

Vera piped in. "I told Booger what happened to you, Pete. When you ran for help for Perry."

Patrick stiffened. With everything happening so fast, there hadn't been a chance to talk to Vera, Susanne, and the kids about keeping that incident to themselves. He was highly uncomfortable sharing it with strangers in the wilderness. It was a story for law enforcement, when they were safely back in civilization.

Pete cleared his throat. "That was nothing, honey."

"But you said—"

Patrick raised his voice. "Booger, how much further do we have to go? Didn't you say a mile or two? We should be about halfway, right?" Today he was the master of the conversational redirect.

The silence from Booger was deafening.

But then Pete jumped in. "A little downhill would be a relief about now. Are we almost to the highest point?" Happily, the group had just entered another thick stand of trees. Shade. Protection. Cooler temps.

Patrick relaxed a little. Pete was in sync with him, at least. *Good.*

Because he was certain he'd just hurt Vera's feelings, which would make Susanne even less happy with him.

Finally, Booger answered. "If you look there to your left, through the trees, you can see out over the river. Perfect spot for a break. I need to make a pit stop." He set his canoe beside the narrow trail, then turned to face them. "Listen, folks. I don't know why you don't want to talk about what Vera told me."

Susanne interrupted him. "We have our children here, Booger. I'd ask you to please think about what you're about to say next."

Patrick put down his canoe and moved to help Susanne, Brian, and Vera with theirs. Vera shot him the reproachful look he'd anticipated. He'd apologize to her later. Right now, he felt a fierce pride burning inside him for his wife. She might be unhappy with him, but she was backing him and Pete up. When the canoe was on the ground, he put his arm around her. Again, she didn't hug him back. Her rejection made his gut ache.

Booger raised both his hands. "I gotcha. I gotcha. Back in a few." He disappeared into the forest.

Lana led the kids to the overlook. "Stay back from the edge, everyone."

Patrick heard ooos and ahhs. It must be beautiful. He wanted to go take a look himself.

"There's a herd of bighorn sheep!" Perry shouted, and then flinched, like the loud noise in his brain had hurt. He pointed along the cliff, a little uphill from where the kids were gathered.

Patrick's eyes followed his son's finger. A ram was facing them. His chest grew tight. Three ewes and several kids sprinted across the trail and disappeared up into the rocks on the other side. The ram snorted and pawed the ground. Then he whirled and followed his herd in agile bounds and a clattering of hooves.

"Bighorn goats." Brian laughed.

Patrick didn't care. He was mesmerized and searched for them long after they were gone.

Pete put a hand on his arm. Vera was standing with her husband, her expression sullen. "A word? Just the four of us?"

Patrick nodded.

Pete motioned toward the overlook. The four of them walked halfway to where Lana was entertaining the kids. Patrick still couldn't see the water from where they stood, though.

Pete leaned in, his voice a whisper that made the others lean toward him, too. "I think we should downplay what happened to me, until we get to town."

Patrick nodded. "I agree."

Vera looked on the verge of tears. "No one told me it was some big secret."

Pete kissed her forehead. "We didn't. My bad."

"I'm sorry for cutting you off back there," Patrick added.

She looked back and forth between the brothers. "Fine. I get it. I won't talk about it anymore."

Patrick nodded. "Thank you. We need a united front. Things could get even worse if we don't work together."

Susanne hugged her arms around her middle. "We weren't working together when you sent Trish and Bunny back to camp alone."

Patrick cringed. *Who is she talking to?* He glanced at the others. But she was looking at him. Her words were like a branding iron to his chest. He didn't blame her, though. He *shouldn't* have let Trish walk Bunny back to camp. He should have made them stay with the group. Then they wouldn't have gotten lost. And Patrick shouldn't have walked off alone when he was upset. *He* should have stayed with the group. Then he could have told Perry to get off the rocks, before he fell. Then Pete wouldn't have run into the prospectors.

Vera snapped at Susanne. "Are you blaming me? I'm not the one who got lost."

Susanne reacted like she'd been physically struck. "I wasn't blaming you."

"It sure sounded like it."

"She was blaming me." Patrick put a hand on Vera's shoulder. "I was responsible. I thought Trish could handle it, and I feel terrible about it. More than you'll ever know. But Dad is going to find them."

Vera stared into his eyes, like she was looking for a sign that he blamed her, too.

He kept his mouth shut, even though he wanted to add *And if you'd been concerned enough about Bunny that you thought she should go back to camp, you should have taken her there yourself.* But what good would it have done if she had? She might have gotten just as lost as Trish. But he didn't mention that. While he was at it, he could have mentioned that he wished she and Pete had kept an eye on Perry for just five minutes so that he wouldn't have gotten hurt, especially after everything he and his family were doing to help them with their kids. But he didn't say that either.

Finally, she shrugged. Patrick dropped his hand, and Vera moved closer to Pete.

Pete sighed. "We just need to get out of here. All of us. We can count on Dad."

Patrick couldn't help noticing his brother let him take the blame for Trish and Bunny. *Great. Susanne blames me. Vera is mad at Susanne. And Pete won't even take my side.*

From right behind them, Booger said, "I feel better. Ready to hit the trail, folks?"

The man hadn't made a sound. Patrick whirled, trying to read Booger's face to see how much of their conversation he'd overheard. But Booger's expression was neutral.

Maybe he didn't hear any of it. A man can be hopeful, anyway.

"You heard him," Patrick called out. "Everybody back on the trail. If we hurry, maybe we can make it back to Jackson by tonight."

CHAPTER TWENTY-EIGHT: CRUSH

Trish

Trish felt like she was about to crumple with the weight of her disappointment. She looked around the campsite, or the empty clearing where the campsite had been, anyway. Their families hadn't waited on them. She didn't understand it. She'd never even considered the possibility that her parents would leave her and Bunny lost out in the wilderness. *Why?* But then she realized the more important question was *where,* as in *where would her parents go and where are they now?* It wasn't like they were going to pack up and go home without her. Without Bunny. That was too ridiculous to even think. They probably were trying to figure out where Trish was. Where she'd go. Where they could go that would make it easiest for her to find them.

"They'll be at the river." Trish nodded. *Yes.* Hearing the words come from her lips, she was even more sure. "They'll be waiting for us by our canoes."

Mr. Smith touched the ash in the fire ring. "Unless they forgot you."

His words were like a face slap. She backed up a step, pulling Bunny with her by the hand. "They wouldn't forget us."

Bunny looked up at her. "Did my mommy and daddy forget me?"

Trish threw some heat into her words. "No, Bunny. They did not. They wouldn't ever. They couldn't."

Mr. Smith shook his head. "Sorry. I didn't mean *forgot you*. More like *lost track of you*. You said yourself it's a big group."

Trish pulled Bunny closer and hugged the girl's shoulder against her leg. "They wouldn't lose track of us."

He stood and held up both of his hands. "Okay, okay. I know a shortcut to the river. How about I get you there before they take off without you."

A loud squawking noise startled Trish. It sounded like it came from Mr. Smith. He slapped a hand at his chest.

"What's that?" she asked.

"I had something stuck in my throat. I'll be right back."

His chest squawked again. Either he was choking to death or lying, and he didn't look like he was choking. As Trish watched him trot off into the trees, it seemed to her that he unbuttoned his shirt, then pulled something out. *What in the world?* She thought about the squawk. *A bird?* Maybe he had a pet bird in an inside pocket that he was embarrassed to tell them about. It wasn't a very manly thing to do. It also wasn't very likely. She narrowed her eyes at him. At first, she'd been thankful for his help. But she wasn't feeling that way anymore. She didn't like how he'd talked about her family. Something about him felt . . . off. Of course, he was a man alone in the wilderness. Most people didn't wander around out here by themselves if they were completely normal. They were the outcasts. The misfits. Sometimes, criminals. Kids at her school told stories about hermits who lived alone up in the mountains. There was a man who'd moved into a cabin in the Bighorns after his wife and children died when he'd wrecked their car. People said he would sneak up on hikers, scream at them, and chase them away. Mr. Smith didn't seem that bad, but he was acting weird, and now he had something in his shirt that was making funny noises.

What else could make that noise, if it wasn't his throat or a bird? She wanted to find out, but she couldn't leave Bunny to follow him, and taking her would make it impossible to sneak up on him, since Bunny was prone to blurting out whatever crossed her mind, whenever it did.

Trish strained to see if she could hear the squawking thing again. Instead of squawks, she heard Mr. Smith's voice.

"Ran across two girls who were on Trout Creek earlier with a big group. He might have been with them. Their campsite is empty. I still have the girls with me. What should I do with 'em, Les?"

Chills ran up Trish's arms. *Someone else is out there.* Then she heard the squawk again.

A new voice spoke. A man. But Trish found it really hard to understand what he was saying. "Bring . . . here . . . bargaining chip . . ."

Mr. Smith said, "You've got him?"

"Soon."

"10-4. Over and out."

". . . out."

And then Trish understood. Radios. Walkie talkies. Like the CBs Papa Fred—her other grandfather—used. Similar, at least. There was no other man *here*, but there was another man out there *somewhere*. Her breath caught in her throat, and for a moment she couldn't breathe. Mr. Smith wasn't trying to help them. He was trying to find someone, and he planned on using Bunny and her as bait.

"Just a minute longer, girls. I have to go take care of some personal business in the woods."

This is our chance.

Trish leaned over and took Bunny's face in both her hands. In her softest whisper, she said, "Mr. Smith is a bad man. We have to be very quiet and run to the river. Can you run with me, without making a sound, Buns? Like hide and go seek, but for real."

Bunny nodded, her mouth hanging open.

"Good girl."

Trish scooped up Bunny's hand and gave it a tug. The two of them took off as fast as Bunny's legs could carry them down the narrow trail back toward the Tukudika.

CHAPTER TWENTY-NINE: OPPOSE

North of the Tukudika River, Bridger-Teton National
Forest, Wyoming
Friday, June 24, 1977, 3:30 p.m.

Susanne

Stomping down the trail under the unwieldy canoe, Susanne
fumed. Her anger increased in pace with her fear. Feelings about
Patrick that she hadn't even known she'd been suppressing were
starting to erupt. It wasn't that she'd opposed this trip. She'd thought it
sounded like a great idea, at first. Taking his parents fishing in the
Bighorns had turned into a fishing trip on the western side of the state
when Pete and Vera had signed on and asked to visit Yellowstone. *Okay.*
That was still fine by her. Things had started to get iffy when Patrick
had decided it needed to be a multi-day camping, canoeing, fishing, and
gold panning adventure in the Gros Ventre Wilderness. Yet, she'd
supported it and thought it was feasible.

What she had opposed—and still did—was Patrick's *rigidity*. When
his brother and Vera had shown up with the kids, Patrick had been obsti-
nate about sticking to his plan, even though it wasn't appropriate for
young children. When they'd reached the Yellowjacket guard station,
he'd been determined to take the group far upriver for a wilder experi-

ence, instead of just letting the kids eat and fish and play and relax. Be kids. When he'd led a group up Trout Creek, he'd sent Trish to bring Bunny back to camp alone, instead of just slowing down and matching the activity to *all* of the family members. When he'd known the inherent dangers of the area, yet he'd failed to supervise Perry. While the results weren't directly his fault—Trish and Bunny lost, Perry hurt, and Pete attacked—he could have prevented them at any juncture if he'd been flexible.

Which begged the question of whether she could have prevented them if she'd spoken up. If she'd told Patrick *no*. The thought of sharing the blame made her even madder at him, and herself.

She shifted the canoe, pinching the skin on her palm. The pinch ripped it open. Not a mortal wound, but painful, and, to her current way of thinking, also something Patrick could have prevented.

Ahead of her, Brian tripped. He lost his grip on the canoe as he fell to his knees. The increase in the weight made her lurch forward, off balance. Vera stumbled, the canoe wobbled sideways, and it was all Susanne could do to hold the back end aloft. The canoe rammed a tree, sending a thundery rumble through its interior and her head. She planted her feet wide and held on tight.

"You all right, honey?" Vera tried to turn back to look at Brian, but the canoe didn't bend. It threw Susanne a step to the right, but she fought it back under control. Again.

Brian climbed to his feet, rubbing his hands on the thighs of his jeans. "Yeah. My hands sting, though." The trail was gravelly where he fell.

"Uncle Patrick can fix you up later." Susanne's words sounded like they were trapped in a box with her. They sort of were, bouncing around inside the body of the canoe.

"It's not that bad." Brian got back into position.

The three of them walked the canoe the last ten yards to catch up with Booger and Pete at the base of the descent, a few yards from the banks of the Tukudika. Susanne gazed out from under the canoe. The water surged by like a slate green sheet. Yellow, purple, and white flowers in a patchwork quilt alongside it. Birds swooped to its surface to fish and drink. Forested hills backed the river, each promontory rising higher than the next in stair step to a snow-topped peak.

It didn't seem like anything could be wrong and stressful in a place as beautiful as this one. As a young girl, she had daydreamed from sweltering, humid College Station, Texas about visiting the mountains pictured in her geography textbook. She never had, not until Patrick had interviewed for the job in Buffalo. In her dreams, the mountains had been peaceful, like heaven. A mosquito buzzed her face. She let go of the canoe with one hand to slap it. It stuck to her palm. The bug made a star-shaped splat the size of a smashed pea. Certainly, there had been no flying, biting insects in her dream version. And definitely there had been no crazy prospectors chasing her family down a river.

Dreams can be misleading. Appearances can be deceiving.

Patrick walked up beside them and put his canoe down. Without a word, he took their canoe and set it on the ground for them. Susanne shook her hands to get the blood flowing, then she sucked on the rip in her palm and wiped the other on her shirt.

Booger was staring upriver. He turned to them, scratching his neck. "We've run out of time to do the next leg before sundown. We'll need to overnight here."

"What? No." Patrick frowned at the sun-lit sky, then at the river. "There's plenty of daylight left. We have to keep going."

"I hear ya, but, with all due respect, I'm guiding you because of my knowledge of the river."

Susanne almost corrected him. *You're guiding us because you needed a ride and Vera can barely paddle a canoe.*

Patrick set his feet apart, crossed his arms over his chest, and glowered at the man. "We didn't delegate decisions for our group to a man we met in the wilderness less than two hours ago."

Booger started pacing. "We've got two more sets of rapids, the second of which is followed up by a waterfall. That's a lot of hiking and portaging. Your group could use some food and rest, since there's no way to make it tonight anyway. And you'll want to get your camp set up before the storm blows in."

"What storm? I don't see any clouds."

Booger waved a hand in the air. "I feel it."

Susanne looked at her son. He hadn't been vomiting in the last hour, but he was still pale and a little hollow-eyed. Not as energetic as normal. She hated to admit it, but she agreed with Booger about stopping. They needed to rest, eat, and set up camp, and soon.

"Patrick? Can we talk?" she said.

Her husband stalked over to her. Everything about his posture screamed agitation. His high shoulders, furrowed brow, clenched fists, and rapidly moving lips. She tried to relax herself, knowing that the clash of their moods would only lead to an impasse. She forced herself to focus on the man, not the situation. Even though she was frustrated with him, he was a good person. He was still her Patrick. Handsome, hard-working, brave, and smart. With his cornflower blue eyes. His light brown hair, albeit thinner every year. His slim, muscular physique. Some of the stress inside her eased. *God, help me handle this well.*

Patrick nodded at her to speak.

She put her head next to his, conscious of the eyes of the group upon them, especially Booger's, although he was feigning nonchalance. "Everyone making it to Jackson safely is the goal."

He cut her off. "That and making it there as fast as we can."

Some of her good intention slipped. "As I was saying, it won't do any good to hurry if we only end up delayed as much or more because we get ourselves in trouble."

"We won't."

"We haven't done a very good job of that so far. And the weather. That's a problem."

His eyebrows soared. "There's not a cloud in the sky."

But Susanne felt the change in the air, too. Electricity, even though it was still hot as blazes. She'd started having headaches a few months ago. Migraines. Patrick had insisted she be checked out in Denver by a neurologist. Her appointment was next month. But she'd begun to notice a correlation between her head issues and changes in pressure before storms. Like right now. It wasn't something she could prove. She just knew it was real. The expression on Patrick's face was intractable, so she decided against trying to convince him about her newfound psychic ability to read the weather.

Instead, she crossed her arms. "I really want to overnight. To give Joe a chance to catch up to us with Trish and Bunny."

"And I want to press on. For Perry's sake. And so the lunatic fringe doesn't ambush us in our camp."

Her irritation was rising. It came out in her voice and word choice. "How has pressing on worked for you so far?"

"Have you forgotten that these people tied up Pete and were going to kill him? That they killed one of their own partners?"

"Of course not."

"So what was that supposed to mean then?"

She bit down on the inside of her lip. She could enumerate all the times the group had followed his agenda to their detriment on this trip. That would end in an argument, though, and fighting in front of the family would make things worse for everyone. But when they got home, she and Patrick were going to have a *serious* talk about the pressure he put on everyone, and about him dismissing her ideas.

"Never mind." Her voice was clipped.

They stared at each other for a few seconds, then he turned to the group. "Time to get moving while there's still plenty of daylight."

CHAPTER THIRTY: FLIGHT

Trish

Trish couldn't tell the pounding of blood in her ears from the pounding of her feet against the trail. She thought she and Bunny had a pretty good head start on Mr. Smith, but it was hard to know for sure. She wasn't about to look back. A few times, Bunny tripped over rocks and Trish had to pull her up and along by her hand to keep her from falling, but, for the most part, the girl ran like someone twice her age. Trish felt a strange sense of pride in her cousin. She also felt terrified. Mr. Smith wasn't a good man, and Trish had trusted him. Well, at least he had gotten them back to the campsite, so they were no longer lost. But she was responsible for keeping Bunny safe. She had to get them away from him, to the canoes and their family.

She whispered. "Good job, Bunny. Run. Run. You can do this."

Ahead of them, she saw magpies alight from trees, cawing their protest at a disturbance. A pinecone fell from a tree and hit her on the shoulder, startling her. For a moment, she thought Mr. Smith had thrown something at her. Then she almost laughed. A squirrel, she realized, remembering how the little animals knocked pinecones from trees then scampered to the forest floor to eat the nuts from them.

She prayed silently in rhythm with her feet. *Please God, help us find our parents. I'm sorry for getting mad at my mom and dad and for the times I haven't been nice to Perry. And help me keep me and Bunny safe from Mr. Smith. Amen.* She had promised God she'd be nicer and go to church last time he'd helped her out of a jam, and she'd backslid a lot since then. She amended her prayer. *I'll do better. I promise I will.*

The trail in front of her twisted and turned and seemed to go on forever. Panic crept over her, and her breaths became pants. If Mr. Smith was coming after them, he had to be gaining on them. Had she gotten on the wrong trail again? Surely, they'd gone far enough to reach the river by now? She was giddy with relief when she recognized Teddy Bear Rock. Not far to go now. Not far at all. If she could keep Bunny running, they were going to make it. In fact, they were close enough to call for help now.

"Dad," she screamed. "Dad, help! There's a man. A man chasing Bunny and me. Somebody, help us!"

The silence of the forest mocked her. No answer. Not from God. Not from her dad or anyone else.

Suddenly, a heavy weight crashed into her back, flattening her against the forest floor. *Grizzly.* Her chin connected with something hard, and her teeth bit through her bottom lip. Pain shot flashing lights in front of her eyes, like the Fourth of July fireworks at the Johnson County fairgrounds. She tried to cry out, but the ground had knocked the air from her lungs. Her mouth filled with dirt. She bit down. It felt gritty. Muddy. Gagging and spitting, she lifted her head and saw blood dripping to the ground. The mud. The mud was dirt and *blood.* She groaned. What was she supposed to do if she was attacked by a grizzly? Play dead? What would happen to Bunny if she did? But what would happen to them both if she didn't?

She tried to curl in a ball, but the weight lifted, and she became aware of the sound of someone sobbing. Something grabbed her shirt by the back of her neck, choking her as she was jerked to her feet. She tried to fight back, flailing her hands and feet, looking for something to connect with. Her feet found the ground, her arms, only air. Then she was upright. *Not a grizzly.* She glanced up long enough to see her attacker. *Mr. Smith.* She clawed at the neck of her shirt, loosening it, then touched her mouth. Her fingers came away slick. She gasped for breath, then leaned over on her knees, watching drops of blood plop to the forest floor.

"Don't do that again, Trish. I don't want to have to hurt you," Mr. Smith said. "I'm bigger and faster and stronger than you. And I have a gun." He held a handgun in her line of vision, then worked the action.

At the sound, a muffled whimper escaped her before she could hold it in. If it was possible to be more terrified than she already was, that was the moment. Her dad had taught her to shoot. Taught her all about guns. Mr. Smith had just chambered a round. His gun had a live bullet in it, and with one pull of the trigger, he could end her life. Or Bunny's.

Bunny. The sobbing had intensified. Her eyes followed the sound to her cousin. She tried to smile at her, even though she imagined it wasn't a pretty sight. Bunny was curled in a ball on her side, but her eyes were glued on Trish.

"We're going to be all right, Buns." Trish flashed the little girl a thumbs up.

Something in the trees behind Bunny caught Trish's attention. Movement. A shape and color that didn't belong in the forest. She squinted. If only she hadn't bitten her lip so hard. Her vision was still kind of messed up. But squinting helped, and the image came into focus. What she saw filled her heart with hope again, although she did her best not to let it show on her face. Not with Mr. Smith watching her.

It was Grandpa Joe, hiding behind a bush, a finger to his lips. He held his other hand up, his forefinger and thumb making the "okay" circle.

Trish knew then that God had answered her prayer. She and Bunny just had to hang on a little longer.

CHAPTER THIRTY-ONE: REPULSE

Perry

Perry's dad had just announced they were leaving, but Perry didn't care whether they stayed the night where they were or continued down the river. He didn't care about anything. He was *so* tired that he was having trouble understanding what was happening anyway. He'd thrown up everything in his stomach, but he was still dizzy, and his headache wouldn't go away. Stay, go—it didn't matter. Wherever he was, he'd still feel awful. He sat down on a rock and stared through the group into the rocks, at nothing. But he didn't see *nothing*. A figure took shape. His headache must be making him see things, because he could have sworn it was an Indian. Perry tilted his head. *What?* The man didn't have on a shirt, just some funny buckskin pants with a flap across his personal parts. No headdress, but he wore some feathers in his long black hair and had red paint under his eyes. When he caught Perry's eye, he pointed at Booger and shook his head. Perry rubbed his eyes then squeezed them shut. *I'm not crazy. It's just my headache.* He turned back toward his family.

His Uncle Pete looked at Aunt Vera. She shrugged.

He said to Booger, "You heard the man. We're moving out."

Booger shook his head and pulled out a handgun, pulling back the slide as he did. Confusion swept over Perry. *A gun? Where did that come from?* "I don't think so."

Perry's dad didn't hesitate. Faster than Perry's eyes could follow, his dad leapt on top of Booger from the side, knocking him to the ground. Booger's weight landed on his gun hand. He wasn't a small guy. It was a lot of weight. The gun went flying. Perry watched the gun tumble through the air and cartwheel across the ground. He winced, waiting for it to fire on impact, but it didn't. He shifted his attention back to the fight. His dad was on top of Booger, and Booger was struggling. His dad lifted his arm high over his head. Perry saw his dad's .357 Magnum in it. His dad cracked it down on Booger's head. Booger quit fighting.

"Oh, my God," Aunt Vera said.

Perry's mom had her hand to her chest. "I never trusted him."

"Somebody help me. I need rope to tie him up," Perry's dad shouted.

Perry forgot all about the Indian, seeing things, his head, and how he felt. He ran to the stack of backpacks the grown-ups had dropped by the canoes, Brian right behind him. A coiled rope was attached to each pack. Perry brought one to his dad. Uncle Pete had joined his dad, putting a knee between Booger's shoulder blades in case he woke up and tried to get away. His dad cut the rope in half. He fastened Booger's hands behind his back with one length of the rope, moving so fast he looked like a calf roper tying a pigging string around a calf's hooves. The only thing he didn't do was throw his hands in the air when he was finished. Instead, he moved on to Booger's feet, making quick work of securing them as well.

"I'd feel a lot better if he wasn't breathing." Uncle Pete stood, brushing dirt off the knees of his pants.

Perry's dad put his gun back in the holster and limped over to Booger's. "I'm not a murderer." He'd moved so fast when Booger pulled the gun that Perry had forgotten his dad's ankle was even hurt.

"It would have been self-defense."

His dad ejected the bullet from the chamber, added it back to the magazine, then put the cartridge back in and handed the gun to Uncle Pete.

Uncle Pete stared at it like it was a rattler about to strike. "What do I do with it?"

"Defend yourself."

Uncle Pete took it and, after a few awkward attempts, managed to stick it in his waistband.

"Now what?" Perry's mom said.

His dad said, "Pete, check his ID, if he has any."

Perry watched his Uncle Pete search the man's pockets. He pulled out a fancy Indian knife, fishing line, and chewing tobacco, but no wallet. Uncle Pete patted Booger's shirt pocket and frowned. His hands probed something that looked rectangular under his shirt. Rectangular, with a long pointy thing sticking out of one end. "I found something."

Perry's dad knelt beside his brother. When he felt the object, he ripped open Booger's shirt.

Underneath it, Perry saw a walkie talkie. Perry thought of the CBs in *Smokey and the Bandit*. His other grandfather, Papa Fred, had explained CBs and other radios to him last winter, since Papa Fred was into them, big time. Police band radios worked over longer distances. CBs a little less. Walkie talkies, only a few miles. Mountains could shorten their range. But Booger having a walkie talkie still meant he could talk to people miles away from where they were right now.

Hadn't he said he was alone out here, though?

Uncle Pete grabbed it, turning the dial on and cranking the volume. The walkie talkie squelched. He pressed and released the mic button. "I'm going to give them a piece of my mind.

Perry's dad snatched it away from him. "Don't. Booger proves there's more of them than we thought, and they're not rational. They're coordinated and in communication with each other. They probably know exactly where we are, and my guess is Booger had us staying the night here so they could catch up with us. If they know we're on to them, they'll speed up their plan. At least now we can monitor them."

Uncle Pete threw his hands in the air. "There goes Patrick being right again. Always putting himself in charge."

Perry's dad dropped the radio down his shirt. "Someone has to lead. And think."

Uncle Pete snorted. "And that someone is always you."

His dad's voice grew hard. "Unless you have someone else you'd like to nominate for the job? But make it quick, Pete, because people are after us, and we have to get going."

Uncle Pete shook his head, his face disgusted. "No, Patrick. Just tell us how high to jump."

Perry's dad ground his teeth. His lips were moving as he walked to a canoe and started carrying it to the river. Uncle Pete did the same with the second canoe.

Brian whispered in Perry's ear. "I've never seen Pete mad like that. I wish they wouldn't fight. What do you think? Should we keep going?"

The fighting had made Perry's headache worse. He wanted things to be peaceful, and he wanted to go to sleep. That was all. "I think we should listen to my dad."

Uncle Pete and his dad came back for the other two canoes.

"Load up," his dad called over his shoulder. "And don't forget any of our stuff."

Perry grabbed a backpack, life jacket, and paddle. He wondered if he should tell someone about the Indian, but decided not to. They were already treating him like an invalid. Admitting he was seeing things wouldn't help that situation.

He cast one last glance at Booger. The man was still out cold. "Are we just leaving him here?"

No one answered him. He hustled behind his mother to the river.

CHAPTER THIRTY-TWO: ALLY

The Tukudika River, Bridger-Teton National Forest, Wyoming
Friday, June 24, 1977, 4:00 p.m.

Patrick

The group loaded up without a peep, not even from the kids. Patrick stood in ankle deep water beside his canoe. The cold was the only painkiller he had, and it helped. So did the break from being the bad guy to everyone. The incident with Booger had sobered them all up. Taken the heat off him.

Booger. He felt sick with self-disgust. He should have seen through the man from the beginning. He'd put his family at risk, again, by inviting an enemy into their midst. Yes, he'd felt like he had to, because Pete and Vera had asked for Booger to join them. Still, Patrick accepted the responsibility for going along with them. He should have trusted his instincts and stood his ground.

He looked up the river, re-living his wife, brother, and sister-in-law turning on him on the trail, then his argument with his brother at the river. He'd known they were upset with him, but they hadn't made him feel any worse than he already did. Then and now, he couldn't let anyone guilt him out of doing what he believed—what he knew—was best for the group. Their lives were at stake. He'd put them in this situation. He was the one who would have to get them out of it.

Just as he was about to vault into his seat, an image took shape on the water. Then two images. Canoes gliding toward them. *The prospectors.* And they hadn't even pushed off yet.

"Pete, canoes." He pointed, his voice tight. "They ran the rapids and caught up with us."

His brother turned his head to face the flow of water. "I see them."

Patrick raised his voice. "Run for cover. Everyone. Behind the rocks."

Susanne leapt out of the canoe. Patrick watched in horror as Booger's walkie talkie fell out of the side pocket of her backpack. It landed on a rock then fell into the river. Completely submerged. *Can't anything go right?* Susanne didn't seem to notice. Patrick's eyes met Pete's. His brother shook his head. Patrick had to shake it off. *Easy come, easy go.* At least the knife Patrick had found on Booger was safely zipped inside. He suspected it was a genuine Sheep Eater artifact. Stone, bifacial, and beveled. A thing of beauty.

For a split second, his mind filled with a vision. He wasn't an Anglo doctor from Texas transplanted into Buffalo, Wyoming. He was a Tukudika man, toughened by a life at altitude and savvy to the ways of the wilderness. At lower elevations, Tukudika were often considered medicine men, which he felt a sense of kinship to as a doctor himself. Had they faced enemies by water? He knew from his reading that they preferred retreating to higher ground where they had the tactical advantage over combat—like the bighorn sheep the Flints had seen earlier had done. Both were capable of fighting. The Tukudika with bow and arrow, the sheep with their massive horns. Neither sought it out.

Like him. Like now.

"Come on. Faster," he urged his family.

Twelve bodies splashed through the water. Bert and Barry both fell and ended up dragged out of the river by Pete. No one spoke as they ran, other than Vera, calling to Danny and Stan to hurry when they started to fall behind the group. When everyone was hidden behind rocks, Patrick and Pete walked back to the bank. They huddled behind a cluster of trees.

"You know how to use that gun?" Patrick said to his brother.

Pete retrieved it from his waistband and stared at it. "I haven't handled a gun since we were kids. And then it was, like, a pellet rifle."

Patrick worked the action. "This is a 9mm. Pulling the slide back puts the first bullet in the chamber. So, you've got a live round in there now." He flicked the safety off. "This is the safety." He flicked it back on again. "Now it's on. Turn it off when you're ready to fire. The rest of the bullets will load automatically."

"How many do I have?"

Patrick said, "At least eight. I'm not familiar with this gun. Make them count. Wait until your target is ten feet away or less. Aim for the thickest part of the body. It's hardest to miss the torso."

Pete nodded. He took the gun back from Patrick and turned the safety off and on, then he pointed the business end downward. "I'm sorry. For what I said a minute ago."

Patrick swallowed a sudden lump in his throat. "It's nothing. I'm the one who's sorry. For everything."

They stood together, watching the canoes approach. A solo paddler piloted one. There were two people in the other. All of them looked male. As they drew closer, Patrick thought the soloist seemed older and smaller than the men in the second canoe. Then the older one shouted out and waved at them in a friendly way.

"Do we know them?" Pete asked. His shoulders were hunched from his tense, two-handed grip on the gun.

Patrick studied the men. "Is that the father and his sons from Trout Creek? What were their names—the Hilliards?"

Pete cocked his head. "I think it might be."

"They don't look anything like the prospectors." Patrick lowered his revolver. Faces came into focus. A John Deere ball cap. A couple of cowboy hats. Fishing vests. "Yeah, I think it's them." He waved back at the men.

Pete's hands were shaking as he put the pistol back in his waistband.

Mr. Hilliard held his paddle in the water and his canoe pivoted toward shore. "Hello, there. How'd you fare on Trout Creek?"

"Not so well. It's a long story. How about you guys?" Patrick grabbed the nose of the boat and pulled it in to shore.

Pete did the same for the second canoe.

"We'll be fat as a black bear after berry season on the trout we caught."

"We?" The older of the two boys adjusted his John Deere ball cap over dark curls. "I think that was mostly 'me.'"

Hilliard laughed. He and the boys were all brown-skinned, brown-eyed, and short—probably not much taller than Susanne. While they didn't look alike, all three had angular cheek bones. The two boys were muscled up so much that Patrick guessed they were gymnasts. Or wrestlers, more likely, since they'd said they lived in Wyoming. Their dad had a slim build.

Hilliard said, "I deserve partial credit since I taught him everything he knows. Where's the rest of your tribe?"

Pete gestured to their hiding place.

Patrick adjusted his hold on the canoe, which was struggling to break free of his grip in the current. It was putting a lot of pressure on his ankle, but the cold water was numbing, so he didn't care. "Perry, the Hilliards are here. Bring everyone out."

Perry and Brian walked over, waving, and the rest of the family followed. Mr. Hilliard and his sons exchanged confused glances. Patrick supposed it did seem odd. He wrestled with telling them everything, but he didn't want to bog everyone down. He'd roll it out as needed. Then he thought about Booger, bound on the bank. There was no time for all the explaining it would take if the Hilliards saw or heard him. He wished he'd gagged the man.

After greetings and introductions, Mr. Hilliard zeroed in on Perry. "Good grief, young man. Is that blood on your shirt?"

"Hi, Mr. Hilliard. Yes, sir, it is."

Patrick said, "That's part of our long story. We're in a bit of a predicament, actually. We're short one paddler for a canoe, since Perry fell and hit his head earlier at the waterfall on Trout Creek. He has a concussion."

"Sorry about your injury, Perry. That waterfall is pretty slippery."

The younger boy—with the same dark hair as his brother, but a cowboy hat on— pointed at a scar on his cheek. Patrick hadn't noticed it before. "I got this there a few years ago. Falling on a rock."

"Ouch." Patrick went on with the story. "We're trying to hurry down to Jackson. I'd like him to get checked out at the hospital there. But my sister-in-law Vera is worried about handling the canoe in the white water."

Hilliard tipped his fishing hat at Vera. "Nice to see you again, ma'am. Well, if you'd like, my crack fisherman Buzz here could paddle for you. He's a student at the University of Wyoming, and he's not bad if you like Cowboys who are really Indians.

"What does that mean?" Annie said.

"My family is from these mountains. We're Shoshone. My wife and I are first generation off the Wind River Reservation. I'm a geologist out of Laramie."

"Oh. Then you eat sheep," Bert said.

Hilliard laughed. "My ancestors did."

"The Toocoodoocoo." Barry looked very mature as he mispronounced the word.

"Someone knows their history." Hilliard nodded. "Buzz is a Tukudika Cowboy now, since that's his school mascot."

"Is that weird?" Perry asked.

"It's cool," Buzz said.

Hilliard looked at his son. Clearly from the expression on his face, he was proud of the boy. "Anyway, we could travel together. Even share our fish dinner with you tonight."

Patrick shook his head. "We couldn't ask that of you."

"You're not asking. I'm offering."

"Well, then." Patrick looked at Pete, Vera, and then Susanne, a question in his eyes. They all nodded. "We accept. Thank you."

Hilliard grinned. "With your four and our two canoes, we'll be a regular flotilla."

Vera put a hand over her breastbone. "Thank you so much, Mr. Hilliard. And Buzz."

"Son," Hilliard said, motioning him to get out, but the boy had beaten him to it and was already wading over to the Flints.

"Already on it, Dad," Buzz said.

The younger boy laughed. "Now I don't have to listen to you screaming like a baby on the whitewater."

Buzz made a rude gesture behind his back at his brother. "Shut up, Cliff."

"Dad, did you see what he just did?" Cliff said. His eyes danced.

"No reason to sit around jawing, then. Gotta get my boy down to the hospital." Patrick smiled, but he was eying the river. It was still clear of the prospectors, but for how much longer? They needed to get gone. "We appreciate your help, Buzz."

"No problem, sir."

"How far are we going, Flint?" Hilliard asked.

"Let's regroup after we see how we do on this next set of rapids."

"Good enough."

Everyone got back in their respective canoes and pushed off into the middle of the river. When they were underway, Patrick let out a heavy sigh. Every minute counted, and they'd lost half an hour between the altercation with Booger and connecting with the Hilliards. Not that the Hilliards were a negative. Quite the opposite. Buzz was saving the day by paddling Vera's canoe. Suddenly, Patrick realized that the canoes he'd seen upriver near the guard station might not have been the prospectors. They could have been the Hilliards. Or even someone else altogether.

No matter who it had been, where were the prospectors now? Booger had been in contact via radio with someone. They could be preparing to ambush the Flints at any minute. He should tell Hilliard all of it and tell him soon. But right now, he couldn't afford to let anything else slow them down.

"All right. Let's pick up the pace, everyone." Patrick dug his paddle in and pulled, sending the canoe surging forward. After a few power strokes to gather speed, he settled into a steady, river-gobbling cadence.

They needed to put the greatest possible distance between them and where they'd left Booger on the bank, pronto.

CHAPTER THIRTY-THREE: YIELD

East of Trout Creek, Bridger-Teton National Forest,
Wyoming
Friday, June 24, 1977, 5:00 p.m.

Trish

Trish alternated between carrying Bunny on her front—the little girl's head on her shoulder, arms around her neck, and legs around her middle—and on her back. Either way, she was getting heavy. It had been a long hike from where they'd seen Grandpa Joe to wherever Mr. Smith was taking them. Trish kept looking behind her the whole way, trying to catch another glimpse of her grandfather. Had he really been there? The further she went without seeing him, the more she worried that she'd imagined him. Plain old wishful thinking? Although, if she could have wished for anyone, it would have been her dad.

"Where are we going?" Bunny whispered.

Trish wished she knew.

Mr. Smith turned around, walking backwards. She tried to make him trip with the power of her mind. It didn't work. "My camp."

Trish kept her eyes averted from his. "Okay."

He started hiking forward again.

Great. His camp. In the wilderness. With no one around to help us except for Grandpa Joe, if he was really there and is still following us.

Bunny put her lips to Trish's ear. "Are you scared?"

Trish was petrified about what would happen when they got to the camp, but she didn't want Bunny to know it. "It's going to be okay, Buns."

Trish's dad had always coached her to fight back. To not let herself be taken somewhere remote. "Whatever a bad guy is going to do to you somewhere else is always worse than what he is going to do to you right here. So fight, fight, fight," he'd say. When she'd been kidnapped by Kemecke and his gang, they'd blindfolded and bound her. Even gagged her for a while. That had been worse than this. She couldn't fight back against them at all. Here, at least she could see where she was going.

But her dad hadn't counted on Bunny. If Trish ran for it, Bunny wouldn't be able to keep up. She'd already proven that—no matter how well the little girl had done, she'd slowed Trish down. Trish doubted Mr. Smith would have caught her before the river, if she hadn't had to slow down for Bunny.

And if Trish fought Mr. Smith and lost, she'd strand Bunny alone with him.

Trish couldn't let that happen. She'd just have to bide her time. She'd trust that she really had seen Grandpa Joe, and that he would think of something to get them free of Mr. Smith.

Then she had a horrible thought. What if they reached the camp and found more men? Then Grandpa Joe would be outnumbered. He was just one old man. Not young and tough like her dad.

The frantic spinning wheel of her thoughts was exhausting her brain. She had to make it stop. She'd never been more tired in her life, mentally or physically. *How many miles back and forth have I walked today?* She'd thought she was in good shape, from basketball and running for cross country. But nothing had prepared her for this.

Mr. Smith was standing on the bank of a creek. Not big like the river. Smaller, like Trout Creek. It might even *be* Trout Creek, although she'd gotten pretty turned around with all the twists and turns and ups and downs on the trails. Had it only been that morning that she was on the creek with the whole family? It seemed like a lifetime ago. She stopped. She was closer to him than she wanted to be. He tugged on the sleeve of her shirt. Trish clasped Bunny tighter to her chest and jerked her sleeve from his hand.

He made a funny noise in his throat, like he was laughing at her. "We cross the creek here."

Trish eyed the boulder-strewn water in front of them. It looked pretty deep in a few places, and the water was flowing fast. "How?"

"See the line of rocks to your left? You can step from rock to rock like a bridge."

What about Bunny? The little girl rubbed her eyes against Trish's shoulder. Bunny couldn't make the crossing on her own. Trish would have to carry her. She remembered gymnastics lessons a few years before. The balance beam. Trish had been the worst one in the class, falling off every few steps. If she fell off here, she and Bunny were going in. They might land in one of the deep parts. They'd be stuck wearing their cold, wet clothes. Could Bunny even swim? And what if they fell on the rocks and one of them broke an arm or a leg?

Mr. Smith reached for Bunny. "I'll take the kid."

"No." Trish drew in a deep breath and clutched her cousin to her chest. "I've got her."

Trish tried to remember the suggestions her gymnastics coach had given her about balance. *Thighs together.* She squeezed them tight. *Arms narrow.* She tucked her elbows in under Bunny. *Imagine myself being pressed in by the walls of a tunnel.* It wasn't a pleasant thought, but she fixed it in her mind. *And eyes ahead, on something that isn't moving.* She locked hers onto the trunk of a big pine tree on the other side of the creek. She could "dismount" when she reached it, then and only then.

"Bunny?" she shook her cousin.

"Hmm?" Bunny didn't lift her head.

"I'm going to carry you across a bridge, and you need to be really still so we don't fall in the creek. It's very cold. Okay?"

"Okay." The girl's voice was a whimper.

"Promise?"

"I promise."

Trish hoped she meant it. With one last breath, Trish stepped carefully onto the first rock, checking to be sure it was steady before she put all of her weight on it. It stayed in place. No problem. *Phew.* Once her weight was centered on it, she lifted her other foot off the bank and moved it to the next rock, repeating the process of ensuring stability before trusting it with her body weight. That rock went well, too. She took another step, then another, until she was out over the stream. The sound of water rushing beneath her made her dizzy. Her eyes flitted down to the creek, and her whole body wobbled, shifting the rock. *Keep your eyes up.* She fixed them on the tree trunk and breathed, waiting for her equilibrium to return. She became aware of butterflies dancing above the stream. Of brilliant bluebirds hopping from limb to limb on the pine. Of swarms of insects so tiny they were almost invisible.

She took three more steps. Mid-creek. *Good.* As she pushed off to take another step, the rock under her back foot tilted. She lurched forward. Bunny screamed and scrambled upwards in her arms like a baby monkey, pulling Trish further forward. They were going to fall. She had no choices left, except to move her feet under her body as fast as she could, before she went down. Without checking her footing, she half-ran, half-fell the rest of the way across the rocks, landing on her knees on the other side of the creek, where Bunny fell on her tush.

"Ouch," Bunny said.

A stone dug into Trish's knee. Ouch was right, but she didn't care. She'd made it across without falling in or getting Bunny hurt. She stood and flexed her knee. It would probably bruise, but she'd be fine.

"Are you all right?" She reached down and pulled Bunny to her own two feet.

"Yeah." She giggled. "You dropped me on my bottom."

"I did. I'm sorry."

"That's okay."

Mr. Smith hopped off the last rock, landing beside them. "You should have let me carry her."

Trish ignored him.

He pointed into the woods. "It's not far now."

Trish followed the direction of his finger. All she saw was tree trunks, bushy plants, and giant boulders on the forest floor. "There's no trail."

"Look closer. See the tent?"

At first, she didn't. But as her eyes adjusted to the lines of the forest, they finally picked out a shape and angle that didn't belong. Triangles and rectangles forming the body of a tent.

She crouched. "On my back this time, Buns."

"I wanna walk."

Hallelujah. Trish offered her hand instead. Bunny took it, and the two of them walked together, winding between trees, climbing over semi-flat rocks, and walking around taller ones. When they reached the campsite, Trish's stomach tightened. It wasn't one tent. It was three of them. A gang of men was a very bad thing. In her experience, whatever the worst of them wanted was what the others did. She looked around wildly, trying to get a fix on where they were.

Behind her, Mr. Smith's walkie talkie squawked.

He said, "We made it back to camp."

A man answered, but it was hard to understand him because of all the static. ". . . out of range . . wait for us . . . back . . . hours."

"10-4. Over and out."

"-ver . . . out."

Did that mean the other men weren't here but were coming back soon? If so, that was good news. It would give Grandpa Joe time. It gave Trish time. She would come up with a plan. She couldn't rely on anyone but herself, even if she hoped Grandpa Joe would show up. But first, she needed to find a weapon. She started a visual search, trying to make it look like she was just casually surveying her surroundings. A few feet from camp, she saw what appeared to be the mouth of a cave with a pile of dirt and rocks beside it. *Bears like caves.* But that was in winter, wasn't it? Still, something about the cave made her feel anxious.

Mr. Smith was shaking his head. He put the radio back in his shirt, but he kept muttering. "Bad luck. Bad luck ever since Les took the bighorn bow from the cave."

What did that mean?

Mr. Smith interrupted her thoughts. "I'll bring food. You'll make us some dinner."

Cooking meant forks and knives. *Weapons.* Trish nodded. "Okay."

He pointed at Bunny. "You. Make yourself comfortable, because this is where you'll be spending the night."

Trish gritted her teeth. Not if she had anything to say about it.

CHAPTER THIRTY-FOUR: DEFY

The Tukudika River, Bridger-Teton National Forest,
Wyoming
Friday, June 24, 1977, 5:00 p.m.

Susanne

Susanne's second whitewater experience wasn't as frightening as the first, but it was still a rush. Adrenaline-fueled excitement and even joy competed with underlying frustration, anger, and fear she was feeling toward Patrick and about their predicament. For the moment, the excitement was winning.

When she had almost brought her canoe all the way through the rapids, she hit a rough patch. The tip of the canoe plunged into the water, sending icy spray up and over Brian and Annie, and all the way back to her. Annie squealed. Brian bellowed with excitement. Susanne held her paddle at the ready, in case she needed to give their boat direction. But the nose burst up and brought the rest of the canoe along with it. For a moment, the back of the canoe dipped, and they seemed to be stuck, like they had fallen in a hole. Annie turned frightened eyes on Susanne. Before she had time to panic, though, the canoe broke loose.

And then the water calmed, as if by magic. Within seconds, they were floating, albeit at a good clip, on a flat surface. Susanne paddled on her left toward the riverbank. She beached her canoe next to Pete's in a line of four. Patrick floated up just to her left.

"Everybody good?" he asked.

Obviously, Susanne thought, as affirmative replies bounced back to Patrick from everyone else. Her eyes sought out her son. He was the one she was worried about. He seemed the same to her. *Not worse is good, right?*

Patrick's voice was no-nonsense. "We need to keep going, then."

Lana met Susanne's eyes. She cut them down and away so fast, Susanne wasn't sure it had happened at first, but then she realized that her mother-in-law had looked . . . *what?* . . . disappointed in Susanne? Like Susanne needed to do something. Assert herself. Heat rose from Susanne's neck to her face. Maybe it was easier for Lana to imagine Susanne standing up to her son than it was for Lana to stand up to her grumpy husband. A stab of pain behind her eye made Susanne wince. She knew she wasn't being fair. It was possible Lana *did* assert herself with Joe, outside the eyes and ears of her family. Maybe she had a far greater positive influence on him than the rest of them would ever know, although it was horrifying to think Joe could act any worse.

Then again, maybe all Lana was trying to convey was that she was counting on Susanne to temper Patrick because Susanne was the group's only hope. It wasn't like he would listen to anyone else.

Either way, Lana's point was well-taken. And it was Lana's husband and granddaughters somewhere out there, separated from the group. Susanne drew in a deep breath. Lana was right. Susanne did need to speak her mind. She was done deferring to Patrick. He wasn't always right. He was smart, he was strong, he was well-intentioned, but that didn't make him infallible.

So, Susanne bristled up. Lowering her voice, she turned away from the group and leaned toward him. "Absolutely not. We need to feed these kids."

Patrick moved his canoe closer. His expression was tight and grim, but he also kept his voice down so they could talk somewhat privately. "Perry needs treatment. And we need to stay ahead of . . . you know."

No one had told the Hilliards about their pursuers yet. There just hadn't been time. Susanne felt a little guilty about it, but not enough to stop this conversation and remedy it. She had to make Patrick see reason.

She lowered her voice. "Your mother and Perry are tired. If you're determined to make us try to go further tonight, they need rest and food first."

"The only way we have a chance to make it tonight is to keep going now. Otherwise, we'll have to wait for morning."

"Fine. Then there *is* no chance, Patrick."

He mumbled and rubbed his forehead. After a few seconds of communing with himself, he sighed. "We have to at least do something to hide. To protect ourselves."

"I don't disagree. I'm scared of Booger's friends, too. Can't we hide from them, though?"

He pondered in silence for long seconds. She waited, glancing at the rest of the group. Pete and Mr. Hilliard were in a spirited conversation, but everyone, those two included, were sneaking looks at her and Patrick.

Finally, he said, "How about we go to the point just before the next set of rapids. That shouldn't be more than a half hour or so. Then we hike off the river and set up camp there."

Susanne gripped the paddle until her knuckles were white. He was pushing her. But meeting him partway meant her family could rest and eat. And it gave Joe a chance to catch up to them, *with* Bunny and Trish, because she had to believe he had the girls by now. And if Patrick's plan kept them safe from the prospectors, then she could be flexible, too.

"All right."

He nodded. Turning back to the group, Patrick cleared his throat and raised his voice. "Change of plans. We'll camp tonight before the next set of rapids and push off at dawn tomorrow. This group could use some rest and food."

Susanne raised her eyebrows at the last part. Well, maybe she *had* converted his way of thinking.

Mr. Hilliard raised a paddle. "The fishing here is great. Why don't we catch up with you guys in the morning? We could get down to where you're going to camp by an hour after sunrise? You don't need Buzz for this stretch, anyway. All Vera has to do is float down river."

"Sounds good. But there's something we need to tell you before we take off." Patrick rubbed his forehead again. *He's going to have a divot in it if he keeps that up.* "We had, um, a pretty serious altercation with a couple of gold prospectors on Trout Creek. They might be following us. They're not nice guys. If you run into them, you don't want to mess with them."

The brother in the cowboy hat—Cliff?—said, "Whoa. Sounds like *Deliverance*."

Susanne had heard about the disturbing movie where four friends were ambushed on a river by men who did unspeakable things to them. She and Patrick didn't go to many movies, and that one hadn't appealed to her. And she didn't want to think about their situation being anything like that.

Mr. Hilliard looked back and forth between his muscular sons. "They probably don't want to mess with us. My boys are plenty tough. If we see them, we'll be smart. And we'll tell them we saw a group matching your description going over the next set of rapids."

Patrick smiled. "That would be great."

Susanne looked upriver, searching for canoes, hoping to see Joe and the girls, and not a deranged group of gold prospectors. All she saw was a bull moose standing hock deep with its head in the water. She felt a renewed sense of determination. She'd pushed back on Patrick and made him see sense.

Now, she just had to hope she'd done the right thing.

CHAPTER THIRTY-FIVE: CLOTHESLINE

The Tukudika River, Bridger-Teton National Forest, Wyoming
Friday, June 24, 1977, 5:15 p.m.

Patrick

Half an hour of canoeing later, the current was gathering force, and Patrick knew it was time to get off the river or they'd be swept into the next stretch of rapids. This time he was paddling in the lead position, so he signaled to the group behind him to move to the riverbank on their left.

BOOM. The air around him vibrated. *Gunfire?*

"Down! Everyone down!" he shouted.

Bert and Barry hit the floor of the canoe. Patrick leaned low, but he kept his eyes above the edge of canoe as he followed the sound, looking for its source.

BOOM. BOOM. BOOM.

Definitely gun shots. But there were no watercraft or people in sight. No sign he could see that the shots had been fired in their direction. No birds alighting, squirrels complaining, splashes in the water, or telltale whisps of smoke from gunpowder. That didn't mean the Flints hadn't been fired on, though, only that he hadn't seen where the bullets came from or where they ended up. The sounds had come from upriver. But from how far away? Distance was hard to figure with the competing noise of the water and the way sound carried out here.

Could it have come from where the Hilliards were fishing and camping out? Just about everybody from Wyoming carried a firearm, and an even higher percentage of them carried one in the wilderness. Maybe they were chasing off a bear or a mama moose. For that matter, it could be a poacher shooting at game.

But it could be someone shooting at a human. That was the possibility that troubled him most. What if Joe and the girls had made it downriver—could they be the targets? *Please, God, no.*

In his gut, he knew it wasn't a poacher. And he highly doubted the Hillards would be fazed by a moose or bear. The most likely scenario, then, was the one he feared—that the prospectors weren't far behind the Flints. That his family was the target.

He had to do something.

"Susanne!" he shouted. Hers was always the first name on his lips.

"I heard them!" Susanne shouted back. Her voice was steadier than he would have expected. *That's my girl.*

Pete called out, "What do you think, Patrick? Keep going or hide?"

He'd promised Susanne the group could rest and eat. But he couldn't let his word be the deciding factor now. He had to make the right decision for the circumstances. Patrick glanced downriver at the white water, then at the bank where they'd planned to stop. He had to make a choice fast or the river would make it for them. They'd be sucked into the rapids. Once that happened, they wouldn't be able to get to shore until they were through them. And if they didn't make a dash for the shore quickly, they wouldn't have time to find a good place hide.

He looked up at the sky, and what he saw made the decision easy. Black clouds were barreling down on them from the north. As if to emphasize the point, an explosive gust of wind rocked his canoe to the side. Thunder boomed. Lightning streaked across the horizon.

"Get to shore." Patrick dug his paddle into the water. He pulled with all his strength on the right side, aiming for a pebbly stretch of beach. He grunted, then stroked again and again. "Unload as quickly as you can. We've got to get everything and everyone off the water and out of sight."

"The current," Vera shouted. "It's got my canoe."

Patrick turned to look at her. She was still in the middle of the river and had only managed to turn the bow toward the shore. The canoe was now riding the current at a slant.

"Paddle harder, honey!" Pete yelled. "I'm coming for you."

In Vera's canoe, Perry grabbed the spare paddle from the floor. He might be hurting, but he still had more fight and try in him than most men ever had. Perry started paddling, his body in a crouch with his behind hovering over the seat. Patrick was just close enough to see his son's face turn red with strain. Slowly, the canoe started breaking to the left. Perry was doing it. He was breaking the current's grip on the canoe. Patrick's heart swelled with pride. Then he realized he'd lost traction in his own canoe against the current. He hadn't quit paddling, but his cadence and pull had tapered off as he'd watched Perry.

He redoubled his paddling efforts. "Susanne?" He swiveled his head around, looking for her, but he didn't stop paddling at one hundred percent.

He found her, already at the shore. He couldn't keep from smiling. She didn't have an abundance of upper body strength, but, like Perry, she had heart. His canoe broke free. Without the pull of the current, he was able to get to the bank easily. He paddled up beside Susanne. Without need for a word, they worked as a team, disembarking, donning backpacks, handing paddles to kids, and pulling their canoes further ashore.

Pete escorted Vera's canoe in. The two of them started doing the same things as Patrick and Susanne.

"Brian and Perry, you're going to need to help your moms carry the canoes. Can you handle it?" Patrick said.

"No problem." Brian made a muscle. "I did practically all the work for Mom and Aunt Susanne earlier."

Susanne rolled her eyes, but she grinned and buckled the waistband of her backpack. Then she made eye contact with Patrick. He read the fear in them. She was doing a good job of hiding it from the kids, but he could see it.

"Everyone, drag the canoes into the trees as far as you can."

"Kids, help. Everybody grab and pull," Pete added.

It was a good thing the kids pitched in, because Susanne and Vera struggled under the combo of heavy canoes and packs. With all of the canoes and family members well inside the trees, Patrick moved back to where he could see upriver. His heart nearly arrested. Two canoes came into view around a bend, just visible in the distance, up a long, straight stretch of river, maybe a half mile or more away. Could the people in the canoes see them on the shore?

The Hilliards or the prospectors? Joe and the girls? Or someone else? There was no way to know. He would hope for the best, but he had to assume the worst. A calmness came over him, and the beginnings of a plan took shape in his mind.

"Wait here for a minute, everyone." He pulled his brother aside, under cover of the trees. "Two canoes. Heading for us."

Pete's face was stoic. "Not good. Can you tell who it is?"

"Too far away. I've been thinking about how to thin out their numbers. The prospectors, I mean. To improve our odds, in case we do end up having to . . . face them."

"What are you thinking?"

"That you and I take our canoes down the rapids, then run a rope line across the river."

Pete nodded, his lips pursed. "We clothesline 'em."

"Yes. If I were them and hit a line, I'd assume we'd put it up to slow them down. To keep them from catching up with us. I wouldn't think about doubling back, which is what we are going to do, of course."

"And it will just be dusky enough that they won't see it until it's too late." Pete gestured toward the darkening sky, visible in patches above the trees. "Those storm clouds will help, too."

"I think we should hike downriver a bit ourselves before we put in, so the canoes upriver don't see us. There was a nice bend coming up. But we've got to get going immediately."

Pete looked at Brian, who was listening like he'd been invited to the conversation and was going to be asked to offer his opinion. "Get us some rope, Brian?"

"How much?"

"All of it," Patrick said.

Brian untied a coil of light gauge rope from the pack on his mother's back. Patrick and Pete set their own packs on the ground and did the same.

"Patrick, what's going on?" Susanne asked.

Wasting no extra words or time, he explained the plan to her.

She shook her head and hugged herself, rubbing her hands on her upper arms. "Don't leave us."

"I'm not leaving you. We're thinning out their numbers."

"Bad things happen when you split the group up."

He kissed her forehead. She stood still for it, but she leaned away ever so slightly. "I'm sorry we're in this situation. I promise, we'll be back in an hour."

Brian ran his ropes back to Pete. "Here you go."

"Thanks, bud." Pete clapped Brian on the back.

The brothers tied the ropes together, then added the rope from Pete's and Patrick's packs. Pete coiled the now-lengthened stretch of rope. The two men walked to the canoes. They flipped Vera's and Susanne's canoes.

Patrick held Susanne's up. Pete did the same for Vera.

Susanne stared at Patrick, her eyes sending him a message. If he'd thought his wife was unhappy with him before, she was twice that now.

He stepped closer to her. "Take it. Please. We've got to hurry."

"I don't like this, Patrick Flint," Susanne said. Her voice was taut and thin. But she stepped under the canoe, where Brian joined her.

"We'll be fine. I promise."

She turned away from him. She and Brian started walking their canoe into the forest. Patrick's chest ached, but he went to Bert and took back a paddle, then wrestled his canoe over his head.

Susanne was just visible in the twilight, looking back at him. Patrick waved at her. She waved back, and he took a mental snapshot. Red bandana holding back long brown braids. Frayed blue jeans and a long-sleeved t-shirt. Hiking boots. A canoe over her head, her nephew beside her. God, he loved her. He counted on her. He needed her. His eye burned. Had he gotten something in it? He wiped underneath with his thumb and was surprised when it came away wet.

Then he turned away. He was vaguely aware of Pete and Vera making their goodbyes. Were they doing the right thing? He thought about the natural inhabitants of the area, like the Tukudika Indians. Like the bighorn sheep. They both chose to move to higher ground when threatened, where they had the strategic advantage.

Higher ground. Not just *off* the river, but to *higher ground.* That's what his family needed to do. Hike upward, across the road that ran along the river, and into the forest on the other side. It would be harder for the prospectors to find them there. Maybe they'd even pass a vehicle driving into the wilderness and could flag it down for help.

He shouted, "Susanne."

She looked back at him.

"Don't stop until you cross the road. Camp on the other side. No fires. We'll find you. Have one of the kids make piles of rocks to show us the way."

"Okay," she called back.

Annie raised her hand. "I'll make the rock piles."

Patrick borrowed her nickname from Pete. "Thanks, Annie Oakley. Just find a big rock, and put a medium one on it, and a little one on top. Do it every few minutes. Okay?"

She smiled at him. "Okay, Dr. Uncle Patrick." She'd borrowed Danny's nickname for him.

Susanne said, "Come on, everyone."

Two four-legged canoes, one grandmother, and five lifejacket- and paddle-bearing kids disappeared from sight into the woods, like they'd never been there at all.

Patrick felt hollowed out as soon as he lost sight of his wife and son. But he shook it off and ran his canoe downriver. Pete's footsteps were close behind him. The terrain was boggy and choked with willows. It made a hard right, and he followed its curve. When he calculated they'd gone far enough to enter the water without being spotted from the other side of the bend, he cut over to the water and launched his canoe.

He levered himself up and onto the seat and wedged the coil of line between his feet. "Come on, Pete!"

"Right beside you, brother."

They eased into the fast-moving, choppy current, side-by-side. Patrick fought to hold his canoe back so he could talk to his brother.

"When we get past the rapids, pull close and I'll toss you the other end of the line. Then you go left and I'll go right. Once we're on shore, let's walk back up to the white water and tie off on either side there, then run up the river, but out of sight in the woods. When I get back here, I'll cross and join you, and we'll go find the family."

"Sounds good. Except for the part where we run upriver carrying canoes."

Patrick laughed. He wasn't sure how something could be funny at a moment like this, but the laughter helped.

"Maybe I should leave mine hidden?"

"I'd hate to be short one if we needed it. And if the prospectors found it, they'd know we hadn't gone further downriver."

"True. I'll suffer through it."

"See you in a few, my brother."

"See you in a few."

Patrick paddled like a mad man. The sun was sinking behind the Tetons, which made the surface of the river dark—a navy that was almost black. With the clouds moving in from the north and the shadow from the west, it was eerie, and Patrick had to shake off a feeling of doom. But then the rapids snatched his canoe and propelled it down-river at a dizzying pace. The canoe dipped and rocked. It scraped and jarred. It hit a boulder so hard he was sure it would crack down the center and break open like a watermelon. But it kept going, and so did he, paddling to match the river's pace, and asking it for more.

A fallen tree—its crown submerged and its trunk slanting up to where it was snapped in two and still rooted into the bank—stretched over and into the river. Branches protruded outward like spears aimed straight at his head and torso. He was on a trajectory that would take him past it without a problem, though, and didn't worry until the current started sucking him toward the tree. He frowned, fighting against it, but the pull was incredible. With all his strength and speed, he fought to paddle away from it.

The water's strength was greater than his own. It was too much.

"Argh!" Pete yelled.

Patrick couldn't spare a glance to see why his brother was yelling. All his attention and all his fight were focused on the tree and the weird gravitational pull it was exerting. Around him, the water looked like soup through a blender. He was down to fractions of a second before he was impaled on a tree limb. *Should I ditch?* If he did, the current could suck him under and surely drown him. *Should I lay down in the belly of the canoe?* It might be his best bet, but it was no guarantee. A branch could still skewer him through the side of the canoe, or the tree could sweep the canoe over and dump him in. *Strainer*, he thought, remembering the name of this type of obstacle, right when it didn't matter.

No. He would ride it out and try to stay as much in control as he could, until the last second. He strained against the water, biting down on his lower lip and tasting blood. The tree reached out for him with long, lethal fingers.

Then the back end of the canoe sunk, and the front wandered to the right, bringing him broadside to the tree. *Great. Now the tree can poke it all full of holes. Me, too.* He was paddling across the current now, but without making any progress, and he had the uneasy feeling the backend of his canoe was sinking lower than the front. The sharp tip of a branch was inches away from his temple. At water level, two boulders were breaking the surface a foot in front of him, just out of his reach. If he could get to them, he could stick his paddle in and use it as a lever, to shove his canoe away and hopefully out of the tree's grip.

He sprint-paddled on his downriver side, ignoring the fatigue burning through his shoulders. He was maintaining his distance from the branches, and his canoe was inching forward, toward the rocks. Closer. Closer. Almost close enough. He didn't dare stop paddling until he was certain he was in position. Closer. Closer.

Now.

With a lightning quick move, he jammed his paddle into the slot between the boulders. The wood chattered between the rocks with the energy of the powerful current. But it gave him the control he was hoping for. Now he was able to hold his canoe off the tree with much less effort. But what he really wanted to do was to propel himself back into the center of the stream. He held himself there for a moment while he caught his breath. Pete shouted something to him as he passed by.

"I'm okay," Patrick yelled back.

He had no idea if his brother understood him, but it didn't matter anyway. Pete was already downstream and there was no turning back for him. Patrick was on his own.

When he was breathing more normally, he knew it was time. He positioned both hands low on the handle of the paddle and pulled. It was harder to lever the canoe than he'd expected. Sweat beaded on his forehead even as the river doused him with a continuous mist and an occasional splash of the bone-chilling water. Muscles already pushed to their limit protested, but Patrick believed in the superior strength of his brain. *Mind over matter.* He willed his arms to do his bidding. *PULL,* he shouted to them. *PULL.*

When the canoe broke free of the sink hole, it shot forward almost like a slingshot. The paddle wasn't quite as lucky.

SNAP.

The wood cracked in two, right at the base of the handle. *Fine.* Patrick hit his knees in the floor. *I'll use the spare.* But even as he searched, he knew it was futile. He'd only taken one paddle from Bert before he left. He was, quite literally, up a river without a paddle. There was nothing in the floorboard to use as a rudder, only the coil of rope for their mission. And what had looked like the end of the rapids felt a lot longer now that he was at the mercy of the water.

And then, suddenly and magically, the water calmed. Where there had been a raging beast, there was now a languorous kitten. Patrick floated up to his brother's canoe. He was shaking all over, but he was alive. Pete caught the side of Patrick's canoe and held it beside his as they continued drifting downriver. A few sprinkles of raindrops fell on his head and arms. Patrick looked up. The sky was dark and angry. A gust of wind whipped the surface of the water and chilled Patrick's wet body. Their canoes sped up.

"What happened to you back there?" Pete asked.

Patrick grinned. "Got stuck in a hole, and nearly impaled in a strainer."

Pete shook his head. "Whatever that means. Where's your paddle?"

"In two pieces back there. It's all right, though." Patrick tossed the coil of rope, letting out a little line. It landed in Pete's canoe, and his brother scrambled forward and picked it up. He saluted Patrick.

Patrick said, "I think we'd better hike around those rapids with the group in the morning. They're too much."

Pete laughed. "For sure."

He gave Patrick's canoe a push toward the riverbank. Then he paddled toward the opposite shore as the coil unwound itself and followed him from the floor of Patrick's canoe.

Patrick tied the other end of the rope around his torso. He stuck his right arm in the water and splayed out his fingers. As a crude rudder, it was better than nothing. His canoe veered toward the bank. He ended up further downriver than Pete, but not by too much. When he was fully beached, he dragged the canoe out of the water, emptied it, and stashed it in the bushes. Then he ran back up the riverbank, keeping pace with Pete on the opposite bank and taking care not to catch the rope on any rocks. He stopped when they'd reached the faster section of water. There, Patrick looked across the river. Pete was tying his end of the rope to a tree. He finished and gave Patrick a thumbs up. Patrick pulled the line tight, eying its height above the water. He selected a stout aspen almost on the bank and tied the rope low on its trunk, compensating for a slight rise in elevation from the river. The rope sagged in the middle, which he hoped would make it the right height to snare their targets. In the twilight, it was practically invisible. But was it invisible enough? Was it low enough? Would it even work?

It would. It had to. But he wasn't going to be sticking around to confirm it.

He waved at Pete, who waved in return. He pointed east up the river. Pete nodded. Then Patrick went back for his canoe, hoisted it over his head, and began to run. The ankle wasn't feeling any better, and he knew he was limping even though he fought against it. The weight of the canoe and its length sent it knocking into tree branches every few steps, which put a lot of torque on it, too. He had no choice. And it wasn't like he had a bone sticking out of it. *Just a sprain.*

He hadn't gone fifteen yards when he had a soul-crushing thought. What if the clothesline caught the Hilliards and not the prospectors? For a moment, his steps faltered. But the Hilliards had said they'd meet the Flints upriver from the rapids an hour after dawn. Not below the rapids at dusk.

He had to trust them at their word.

Still, he prayed as he sped back up. *Please God. Don't let our rope hurt an innocent person.*

After nearly ten minutes, he was even with the strainer tree that had nearly done him in. *Not this time,* he thought. *Not this time.* He gave its trunk a kick as he passed by. While he was slowed down, he saw two canoes, one coming down the river right after the other, barreling through the roughest stretch of water. His heart leapt when he recognized the men in the canoes. Les and Winthropp were in the first one, with Les in front. Diego was in the front of the second, and Booger was in the back. *Booger.* They'd found him. Patrick wasn't a murderer, he was a healer. But he couldn't help wishing he'd done more permanent damage to the man when he had the chance.

He set his canoe down and ducked behind a rock to hide and watch.

The first canoe was bearing down on the rope. Patrick couldn't help it. He stood up from his hiding place, holding his breath as he watched the action.

The rope caught Les and swept him backwards. The canoe jerked sideways. Les went over the side. The line hit Winthropp next. He followed Les into the water a second later. Their canoe continued down the river without them. Diego and Booger were so close behind them that they didn't have time to react. The rope hit both of them. One of the men shouted before they both disappeared into the white water. Two heads popped out of the water. Canoe number two careened downstream with no one to paddle it.

Patrick wanted to whoop, but he didn't dare.

His elated feeling was quickly replaced by unease. He ignored the powerful urge he felt to go to their aid. The Hippocratic Oath required that physicians do no harm. He'd gone beyond doing *no* harm and caused quite a bit of it. The men might have broken their necks. They might be paralyzed, or unconscious and drowning at that moment. The physician side of him felt like he should attempt a rescue. The husband and father side of him disagreed violently with the physician. *Besides,* he told the physician side, *there are plenty of other people who need my help.* The Hilliards, possibly. His son. His father, daughter, and niece. The rest of his family.

So why was he still frozen in place, staring at the water, waiting for the rest of the prospectors to surface?

A sense of calm stole over him. What would the Tukudika have done? This land was theirs, after all. And he knew the answer from all that he had read about them, as well as in his heart, where he felt a kinship to them and their land.

They would have retreated. Lived to fight another day. Protected themselves and their families. But, they respected life and weren't known as blood thirsty. So, first, they would have gone back to cut the line so no one else could get hurt.

So that is what he would do. He started running downriver, and he didn't stop until he'd slashed the rope. As soon as he'd done it, an immense weight lifted from him. He put his knife back in his pocket and set off, back to his canoe and his family.

CHAPTER THIRTY-SIX: ENDURE

South of the Tukudika River, Bridger-Teton National
Forest, Wyoming
Friday, June 24, 1977, 7:00 p.m.

Perry

Perry tried to have a good attitude about most things. But as he trudged up the steep incline from the Tukudika, the road was still nowhere in sight, even though it felt like they'd been hiking forever. His socks had soaked up water like sponges, and now his wet boots were too tight. The blood had run out of his arms, and it felt like they were being stabbed with a billion needles. The sky had turned dark. Dark like the time there'd been a tornado near his house back in Texas. Raindrops were starting to fall on the canoe. Not many, but enough to drive him crazy. And everything hurt his head. The canoe, every sound, every movement, even breathing. His own breathing, his mother's, everyone's he could hear. And the kids just could not be quiet. They'd probably get murdered because anyone who wanted to find a group this noisy wouldn't have a lick of trouble.

Yeah, he decided, it was okay to have a bad attitude this once. Even a really bad one. Because this trip was getting worse by the second.

His dad was back in front, where he always liked to be. Dad and

Uncle Pete had caught up with the group about an hour into the hike. Annie had left the rock piles so they could find their way, and they'd slobbered all over her. So much praise for that simple little thing. Meanwhile, even though he felt like dog poop, Perry was carrying one end of a heavy canoe.

Not fair. Not fair at all.

His dad and Uncle Pete were pretty cagey about how their clothesline plan had worked, other than to say it went as good as they could have hoped. So even though everyone was relieved they were back, they were also on edge. They'd been hoping for a home run. That his dad and Uncle Pete would come back and say everything would be okay now. Bad guys weren't after them anymore.

They didn't.

Perry's breaths were coming in short pants. He readjusted his hands on the sides of the canoe and his arms quivered. His Aunt Vera was balancing the front of the canoe on her head, but it had hurt so bad when he tried that he was having to hold it in the air. His arms were quivering from tiredness, and that stabbing feeling that he'd decided was more jellyfish stings than needles.

A jolt jarred his arms. Aunt Vera lost her grip with one hand and the canoe crashed onto his head.

"Ow." His vision tunneled and bile rose in his throat. It wasn't the first time Aunt Vera had bumped into a tree. There was nothing he could do to help her navigate, since all he could see was the back of her head and the ground in front of his feet. It was like someone was squeezing his head over and over with a giant pair of pliers, and that every step he took was the pound of a mallet to the back of his skull. He couldn't get away from the pain. It was as if his head was immobilized in a vise. He owed an apology to every block of wood he'd ever worked on in his dad's tool shed.

"I can't hold on," he said.

"No!" Aunt Vera said. "Don't drop it. If you need a rest, we should get Pete to take it from us and set it down."

I need a rest. But Perry didn't say it. Not with his dad listening. He'd rather eat a handful of live grasshoppers than admit weakness in front of his dad. *Mind over matter,* he thought. Then, out of nowhere, a picture flashed in his mind of his fist punching his dad's mouth. Right in the kisser, as his dad would say. Perry was horrified. His dad was his hero. Why would he want to punch his dad? He banished the image. *Mind over matter,* he told himself again. Then it started to rain. Not just little sprinkles every now and then like it had been doing. Bigger ones, falling faster and faster and faster, the sound of every drop hitting the hull of his canoe a new knife in his skull. It didn't help that the group was carrying the canoes through the forest where there was no trail. The perfect combination of dust and rain made the pinecones slippery, and the rocks were even more slick because of moss and lichen.

He just kept moving forward, dizzy, hurting, and nauseated.

"Stop it!" Stan hollered.

Perry heard the sound of flesh on flesh.

"He hit me!" Danny yelled.

His cousin's voice hurt Perry's ears like someone had stuck a hot branding iron in them.

Aunt Vera said, "Annie, I'm carrying a canoe. Make them stop."

"Why do you always make me do everything?" Annie was walking right beside Perry, and he saw her roll her eyes. She was starting to sound like Trish.

"Annie Oakley, no backtalk. Help Vera." Uncle Pete sounded stern.

"Gotta love stepdaughters," Vera muttered.

Perry's dad paused to eye the line of hikers. They all kept going, filing past him. Perry's mom and Brian were right in front of him and Aunt Vera. His mom stopped, so everyone behind her stopped, too.

Perry's dad said, "Susanne, you're holding everyone else up. What's the problem?" He sounded irritated.

She looked mad enough to spit. Perry had never actually *seen* her spit when she was mad, but she'd been saying it since he was little, so he knew what it looked like. "Can't we leave the canoes here and pick them up in the morning?"

His dad waved his hand around. "Where? There are no trees."

It was true. The trees had disappeared, and Perry wasn't even sure when it had happened. Now there were none to be seen anywhere near them. Just sagebrush, rocks, and mud. The thought of sagebrush brought rattlesnakes to his mind. His dad said they liked to hide under it. Were there any up here in the mountains? He would have to watch where he put his feet, just in case.

"Well, my foot is killing me," his mom snapped. "I think I have a blister."

"I'll take care of it when we make camp." Perry's dad inserted himself into the hiking lineup in front of Perry and Aunt Vera.

"When will that be?" Gramma Lana had stopped beside Perry. He thought she was probably the prettiest grandmother in the world. She hardly even looked like a grandmother, usually. More like a model. But not now. Now, she looked older and more tired.

His mom and Brian started forward again, and the rest of them followed. Perry's dad twisted his ankle on a rock, and he started limping worse.

"We haven't even crossed the road, and I want to get on the other side before we camp."

Bert collapsed on a rock and started crying. "I'm tired."

Barry plopped down beside him. "I'm hungry. Can we have something to eat?"

"Hold up," Uncle Pete said. He was behind Perry. "Maybe we can leave the canoes and come back for them later after we find a spot. That way we can help everyone get to camp where they can rest."

"And eat," Barry reminded him.

"And eat."

"And I have to go to the bathroom," Danny said.

Perry's dad set his canoe down. "Good idea, Pete."

At least his dad and Uncle Pete weren't mad at each other anymore. It seemed like everybody else was, though. Not like fist-fight-mad. Just a little bit irritated. On edge. The two men lined up their canoes, then helped with the others while Gramma Lana took Danny into the forest, which she called "the men's room."

Perry sat down. He was so sleepy. Maybe he could just close his eyes for a second. He must have fallen asleep, because when he opened them, Danny and his grandmother were back, and his dad was ordering everyone into a line. Perry stood, trying to shake off his fog. For a minute, he had trouble remembering what they were doing and where they were. Then it came back to him. Hiking to camp on the other side of the road. Because they were canoeing back to town. To get Perry to the doctor. *Yeah, that's it.* At first, he'd thought his dad was being overly protective when he'd insisted on getting Perry back to Jackson to be checked out. But now he was beginning to think his dad was right. Perry didn't feel so hot. The sooner he got there, the better.

"We're going to be using the buddy system," Uncle Pete announced. "Bert, you're with me, Barry, you're with Uncle Patrick. Danny, with your mom. Stan, with Aunt Susanne. Brian and Annie, with your grandmother."

Perry almost raised his hand to ask if they'd forgotten him. He decided he was happier on his own, though. He waited for everyone else to walk ahead, then fell in line at the end. Since they'd have to come back for the canoes later, he made rock piles to mark their path, like Annie had earlier.

"There's the road," his dad called out from the front of the line.

Everyone came to a dead stop.

"Great. Can we camp here?" his mom said.

"Let's move past it. I want to be close enough that we can hear a vehicle if it goes by, but out of sight."

"I'd like to be close enough that we can flag one down."

"That, too. Just give me fifteen more yards once we cross the road."

Perry's mom sighed. It was the sigh he heard whenever she'd had it with his dad. She always said that his dad didn't know when to say when. When they went hiking, he always wanted to go further than anyone else. When they were driving, he always wanted them to wait "one more town" for a bathroom break. Now it was just "fifteen more yards." His mom was pretty smart.

"Joe will never find us," his mom muttered to his dad. Her voice was so low that Perry barely heard her.

Perry thought about the rock piles. They were good markers, if you knew to be looking for them. Grandpa Joe didn't. Perry hadn't thought much about Trish and Bunny. With his head hurting and how bad he felt, it was all he could do just to keep going. But now he imagined them spending the night out in the forest alone, without a tent. He would be really scared if he were them. He hoped Grandpa Joe had found them, and that they'd catch up with the group tomorrow.

Lana walked Brian and Annie over to Perry's mom and Stan. "Come here, everyone. I have something I need to say."

Perry couldn't remember ever hearing Gramma Lana give an order, but it was clear that this time, she had.

Everyone did as they'd been told.

When her family was clustered around her, Gramma Lana took Brian's and Annie's hands and held them up. "Everyone join hands." There was some jostling and sniping amongst the younger kids as everyone grabbed the hand of the person next to them. Then Gramma Lana bowed her head. "You know I love each and every one of you, but I don't like how you all are treating each other in this family right now."

Perry squirmed. He hoped she was talking to everyone else. He thought he'd been pretty nice. It was a major accomplishment since he felt bad, too.

"You think this is tough? Imagine Grandpa Joe, Bunny, and Trish out there. Or Perry, who feels so rotten he keeps throwing up. Now, all of you, stop complaining, and help your parents get us to camp where we can rest and eat, and be quiet, so no one finds us. But most of all, be nice. Can you do that?"

"Yes, ma'am."

"So let's pray about it." There were a few groans. "None of that. I'll make it fast." She cleared her throat. "Dear God, we can't do this without you. We need your help. We're asking for your help. Amen."

Perry's eyes tickled and burned, but he held back the tears. It was bad enough being hurt and having everyone running down the river to get him to Jackson like some wimp. He was a teenager now, nearly a man, and he wanted his family to see how grown-up he'd become. Normally, he didn't put much stake in praying either. It was just something his mom made his dad do before they could eat. But something about Gramma Lana's soft words got through to his heart. They did need help. They needed it bad. He knew that from the tension between the grown-ups and the look in his dad's eyes. Gramma Lana's prayer made Perry believe it was possible God would help them. He felt . . . better.

Maybe there was more to this praying thing than he thought.

"Amen." Perry's dad kissed her forehead. "Thanks, Mom."

The others took turns pressing their lips to her cheek.

Perry went last, and after he kissed her, he was caught up in an impulse. He threw his arms around her. "I love you, Gramma Lana."

"I love you, too, Perry-winkle."

Perry-winkle. He had never really liked the nickname, but it was all right from her.

"Back in line, everyone," Perry's dad said. "Last leg before we make camp."

There were groans, moans, and mutterings, but the family complied and lined up with their buddies.

"Why did the chicken cross the road?" Uncle Pete shouted.

"To get to the campsite on the other side," Brian shouted back.

Stan slapped Brian a high five. Then the group started forward again.

Within five minutes, Perry's dad had selected a campsite, and the dads had gone back for the first two canoes. Unfortunately, no vehicles had driven by when they crossed the road. Worse, the rain had gotten heavier. It was officially pouring. Water ran down Perry's head and face, in his eyes. Lana and Vera sheltered under a large pine tree and made sandwiches—no fire, per Perry's dad, so the bad guys wouldn't see it and find them—and Brian was helping Susanne and him erect tents. Just being at rest made Perry feel a little less bad. Or maybe his concussion was getting better. He sure hoped so.

By the time all the canoes were stowed near the camp and everyone had been fed, the rain was bombarding them. Water rushed in streams around Perry's feet. Full dark had set in. He could barely keep his eyes open. Had he ever been this tired in his life? He crawled inside their tent, unrolled his sleeping bag, and snuggled down into it, sighing.

His dad sat down beside him. "Not so fast, son."

"Huh?"

"I've got to keep you awake tonight."

"Why?"

"Because of your concussion."

Perry groaned. "Please, Dad. I'm so tired."

His dad sat down beside him and drew him into a hug. "I'll be with you every minute, buddy. Somebody has to keep lookout and be ready in case there's a problem, anyway. I guess that's us."

At that point, Perry would have willingly given himself over to the prospectors, if it just meant he could close his eyes.

CHAPTER THIRTY-SEVEN: AMAZE

Trish

Trish slid the spatula under a pancake in the cast iron skillet that Mr. Smith had set on a wire rack over the fire. The pancake stuck, and she pried it loose, then flipped it over. The odor of burnt food wasn't as nice as the campfire. She flipped the other two in the pan quickly so they wouldn't burn, too. Cooking had turned out to be a bust as far as finding a weapon was concerned. No forks. No knives. Not even a can of food. Just a spatula, which wasn't much of a weapon. She guessed she could slap him with it, if it came down to it. Or hit him with the skillet, as soon as the handle was cool enough that she could pick it up. She transferred the pancakes to a plate and finished making the rest of them from the batter.

When she had exhausted the batter, she turned to Mr. Smith. "The pancakes are ready."

"Eat up." Mr. Smith grabbed the top four pancakes.

Trish hesitated. "Don't we get plates?"

"Nope. Just use your hands."

Bunny gasped. "My mommy doesn't let me eat pancakes with my hands."

"Your mommy isn't here, and what she doesn't know won't hurt her. Or you."

Bunny's mouth fell open. "That's not nice."

"Don't eat them if you don't want to. I don't care."

A raindrop pinged Trish on the nose. She picked up a pancake and ripped a bite off with her teeth. It tasted chalky. She gagged a little in her throat. Syrup might have made them taste better, but they were so bad, that, if she wasn't hungrier than she'd ever been in her life, she would have given hers to the birds and chipmunks. "You should eat, Bunny. Aunt Vera won't be mad at you."

"Promise?"

"I'll tell her you had to do it."

The little girl nodded, but she still looked doubtful. She stuffed a pancake in her mouth. Her face crumpled. Trish nodded at her. Bunny chewed with tears in her eyes. Trish sat and patted her lap. Bunny brought her half-eaten pancake and took the seat offered. The two of them managed to finish off a pancake each in silence. Before Trish could decide whether to choke down another, the skies opened up and rain began pelting them. Bunny squealed. It was surprisingly cold, and they were drenched in seconds. Bunny's teeth started chattering. Trish wrapped her arms around her. Suddenly, she wanted to lie down on the wet forest floor and not get up. She felt utterly defeated. They were in a pickle, and she had completely failed to keep her cousin safe.

The rain started to hurt. It was so hard. Trish wanted to cry. Because it was hailing now, too.

"Get in the tent now, before you get so wet that you spoil the inside." Mr. Smith's voice was snappish.

He walked under a tarp stretched between two trees, where he dug in an oil skin bag. He came out with a rain jacket, which he put on, without offering anything to Trish or Bunny.

Trish would have rather spent the night out in the cold rain than go in a tent with Mr. Smith. So far, he hadn't tried to hurt either of them. But that didn't mean she trusted him in close quarters. She didn't move.

"I'm c-cold," Bunny said. "The rain hurts."

The fire was dwindling in the rain and hail. It wasn't warm enough anymore to ward off the bone deep cold, Trish knew. Not for long, anyway, even with their body heat. Indecision wracked her. Which was worse—freezing Bunny to death, or taking her into the tent where bad things might happen to her? Or to both of them?

Mr. Smith stared at them across the fire. "Why are you just sitting there? I said for you to get in the tent."

Trish stared at him.

Mr. Smith shook his head. "I'm not going to follow you in there, if that's what you're worried about. I'm not like that. Just get in there, be quiet, and go to sleep. We'll be waking up early tomorrow."

"Where will you sleep?"

"Out here under the tarp, where I can make sure the two of you don't run off."

Trish wanted to believe him. She needed to believe him, so she could stomach going inside with Bunny. "Come on, Buns."

She set her cousin on her feet then stood and led her by the hand into the tent, careful not to bump the sides. She'd learned the hard way that water would soak right through if that happened. The small space was darker even than outside, and the patter of the rain and thunk of the hail on the tent gave her the sensation it was shrinking around them. It smelled like wet, dirty socks.

"Shoes off," Trish said.

There were two sleeping bags on the floor and nothing else. Bunny sat down on one of them and stuck a foot out. Trish untied one tennis shoe, then the other. Sitting beside Bunny, she removed her own shoes. She tucked all four of them to the side of the door of the tent. On all the camping trips in her life so far, it had always been one of her parents telling her to take her shoes off, helping her, and setting them by the door. Now it was her turn. She was only sixteen. Not old enough to be responsible for a five-year-old little girl. But she had no choice. And that meant she needed to make good decisions about everything, not just do them automatically.

She didn't have much she could do to protect them from Mr. Smith, but she could set a trap of sorts. She scooted her hiking boots and Bunny's tennis shoes directly in front of the tent door. It wasn't much, but if Mr. Smith came into their tent, maybe he'd trip, and Trish would hear him in time to fight.

"Which sleeping bag am I in?" Bunny yawned.

Trish imagined men sleeping in these bags the night before. Dirty, smelly men. Bad men. Possibly men with bed bugs, ticks, or fleas. She wanted to say, "Neither." That wasn't realistic, though. She wanted

Bunny to have the best one, but to Trish they looked identical in the dark.

"You pick."

Bunny twisted her lips, considering, then crawled to the other sleeping bag from the one she was sitting one. "This one is farther from the door."

Trish thought they were equally close to the door, but she didn't say it. "Then it's all yours."

Bunny slid in, yawning. "Can you tell me a story?"

"I don't have a book."

"You can make one up."

Trish didn't feel very creative at that moment. Her dad had always sung to her and Perry at bedtime. Not her mom, who claimed she couldn't carry a tune. Her mom was always doing laundry or packing lunch bags for the next day. Tucking in was her dad's job when he wasn't at the hospital. Her mom would stop in their rooms and kiss them goodnight after he'd turned out their lights. It was all Trish could do not to sob at the thought. She would have really liked her dad's songs and her mom's goodnight kiss about then.

"How about I sing to you instead?"

Bunny nodded. "Like my daddy does. My mommy reads the books. He sings."

Like my parents, Trish realized. She'd never really thought before about the similarities in her life to those of her cousins. Their dads had grown up best friends, sharing the same bedroom, one year apart in school. They seemed so different in some ways. But her dad had a great voice, and so did Uncle Pete. Her mom was always telling her dad he should go to church so he could be in the choir. When he said no, his excuse was that he felt closer to God in the wilderness than he did in a building, and he knew God would forgive him for sleeping in and working around the house one of the few times he wasn't at the hospital or on call.

Trish smiled. "I won't be as good as your daddy, I'm afraid."

"That's okay."

She cleared her throat, trying to remember the lullabies her dad used to sing to her. The opening words of one came back to her. She lay down beside Bunny and began to sing. "Go to sleep little baby, go to sleep little baby. For when you wake, you'll find a cake and two pretty little ponies."

Bunny smiled and her eyelids fluttered.

Trish sang the words again and again. She was pretty sure Bunny was asleep after a few times through it, but she kept going for herself. It was calming, and she needed some calm. Finally, she started feeling sleepy herself. The words were coming out slower and slower. But then, outside, she heard the sound of footsteps.

"Hey," Mr. Smith said. His voice sounded surprised.

She stopped singing and sat up, bumping her head on the ceiling of the tent. Drops of water plopped on her face and the sleeping bags. There were more sounds outside. Scuffling. Breathing.

THUD.

OOMPH.

Her heart started thumping hard inside her chest, the sound in her ears like a basketball in an empty gymnasium, picking up speed like a fast dribble. *A bear?* She was more afraid of Mr. Smith than any bear, even a grizzly. Bears were just bears. They were either hungry, or they weren't. They either had cubs to protect, or they didn't. Mr. Smith wasn't as straightforward. He was unpredictable. He did things that weren't right and didn't make sense.

She held her breath, listening to what was happening outside through the pounding in her ears. A snuffle, a grunt, a growl? The sound of ripping, like a bear would make if it were tearing into a backpack or tent, looking for food?

But she didn't hear anything that sounded like a bear. There wasn't a sound from Mr. Smith either. Or at least she didn't think there was.

She needed to know what they were up against. Bunny looked like she was sound asleep. Moving quietly past the girl, Trish eased the zipper up on the tent—wincing at the zzzzzz sound it made—and leaned low to peer out. If there *was* a grizzly out there, she didn't want to offer herself up as its next meal. *Is it wrong to pray a bear got Mr. Smith?*

Her eyes were already adjusted to the darkness, and she swept them around the camp. She saw movement. Instinctively, she withdrew further into the tent. But an after image of what she'd seen was imprinted on her brain.

It wasn't a grizzly. It was two men, dragging Mr. Smith by his heels over to the fire. One was a stranger. A weird stranger without a shirt on. Light colored pants that looked funny in the seat. He had black hair down to his shoulders with something hanging from it in the back. She couldn't see his face. But she knew the other man. It was her grandfather.

"Grandpa Joe!" she whispered.

He looked up at her and nodded. "Come help me tie him up."

She wondered why he didn't just get the other guy to help him, but that was okay. Her heart pounded with a new kind of excitement now. Grandpa Joe had come for her and Bunny. It was going to be all right. They were going to be reunited with her family. Luckily, she and Bunny had stayed completely dressed because of Mr. Smith. She crammed her feet into her hiking boots. When she had them tied, she lifted the zipper too fast. It got stuck and she had to do it over. *Measure twice, cut once,* her mom would have said. That or *haste makes waste.* Maybe her mom was right. Sometimes.

By the time Trish made it out of the tent, her grandfather was tying Mr. Smith's arms behind him around the tree closest to the fire. The other man was gone.

He finished and stood. "Got it done without you."

"Where did your friend go?"

He tilted his head and scowled. "What friend?"

She hesitated. Had she been seeing double in the light of the fire? "Never mind." She threw her arms around him. "I'm so glad you're here. Where's my dad?"

He hugged her back, pulling her into his chest with both arms. Trish couldn't remember him ever hugging her like that. "Perry got hurt real bad. Your dad's canoeing him down to town. I came to find you." He released her.

Trish was shocked. But mostly because Perry was hurt bad enough to end the trip. He did get hurt fairly regularly. Trish never did. Her mom said it was because he was a boy. "Is he going to be okay?"

"I expect he will. You'll hear all about it later."

"Okay." Her grandfather wasn't much of a talker.

"This man that had you is camping with a group. We need to get out of here before anyone else shows up."

Trish hugged her elbows. "They have walkie talkies. They took us to use as bait, Grandpa Joe. I don't know what's going on for sure, but it sounds like they're upset with someone, and they think we were with him. Do you think it's my dad?"

Grandpa Joe grunted. "No way to know." He went back to Mr. Smith and rummaged under his raincoat. He backed away and held up the walkie talkie.

"I told you," Trish said.

He stuffed the radio into his waistband. "Where's Bunny?"

"In the tent. Are we leaving now?"

"Yes."

Grandpa Joe always sounded mad, but her dad had told her that he just didn't have much to say. Her grandfather's curt ways had never bothered her. He did seem shorter than usual, though, except for the long hug.

"I'll get her shoes on and bring her out." Trish crawled back into the tent with renewed energy. She wanted to get out of this creepy campsite and away from Mr. Smith as fast as she could.

Bunny was sleeping peacefully. Trish paused, thinking. In her experience, Bunny was easiest to deal with when she was asleep. Maybe she could get her out of the tent without waking her. She pulled her from the sleeping bag and put her shoes on. Bunny didn't stir`````````. Then Trish carried her out to their grandfather. She was still asleep. He held out his arms, and Trish transferred the limp girl to him.

He shifted Bunny's cheek onto his shoulder and placed a hand over the back of her head. "Keep up."

He speed walked ahead of her into the wet night. Trish scrambled after him. Moving quickly through the mountains in the dark reminded her of the night a year before when she'd ridden, blindfolded, behind Ben on her horse Goldie, up the mountain, not sure whether Kemecke would kill her when they reached his camp.

Ben.

She missed him. She'd grown to count on their unlikely friendship. When she got back from the trip, she wanted to see him. Maybe . . . maybe . . . she wasn't sure . . . but she might want him to be her boyfriend. But she was sure that she wished she had Goldie with her for this midnight hike. She was completely out of breath and stumbling all over the place.

After they'd crossed the creek, Grandpa Joe slowed down, but it was still faster than Trish had ever hiked before. It was spooky on the trail in the dark. She imagined Mr. Smith's friends around every bend, mountain lions crouched behind every boulder. But the hike was uneventful. In less than half an hour, they'd made it to the river. By then the rain had stopped, but it was still pitch dark from the clouds. They couldn't even see the moon, which had been big and bright the night before.

Grandpa Joe handed Bunny back to Trish, then pulled a canoe out of a hiding place and dragged it down to the water. The rest of the canoes were gone.

"Get in," he told her.

"We're going to canoe down the river in the dark?" she asked. It seemed dangerous. What if they hit rapids or a waterfall? There was no way Grandpa Joe would see them coming. She could barely see her own fingers.

"No better time not to be seen."

"Where are we going?"

"The cars. The guard station."

Bunny's eyes popped open. "Where are we?"

Trish shifted her to her hip. "Grandpa Joe is taking us to your mommy."

Bunny smiled and put her head back on Trish's chest.

Trish waded to the canoe, carrying Bunny. She set the girl in the middle seat, then followed, careful with her footing. "Where are the life jackets?"

Bunny said, "I'm sleepy."

"Don't have any." Grandpa Joe pushed the canoe off the bank. It rose in the water, and Trish felt a weightless sensation when it started to float.

There was the sound like knocking on the canoe, then Grandpa Joe flopped in.

He grunted. "Good. A paddle."

He lifted it out of the bottom of the canoe and navigated down the far side of the river. He paddled fast, without pausing between strokes. To Trish, it felt like they were flying down the river. Something dark loomed overhead and she realized it was the footbridge. They passed under it. Then Grandpa Joe cut left. The canoe scraped over rocks, and they came to a stop.

"We're already to where we parked the cars?" Trish was disoriented.

Only an hour before, she and Bunny had been Mr. Smith's captives, hidden away in a tent in his campsite. And now they were free, across the river, and all the way down to their vehicles. She had felt isolated and like they were a million miles away from the world when Mr. Smith had them. But they weren't really far away at all.

Grandpa Joe got out and reached back in for Bunny. Trish held the girl's waist as Bunny stood and let her grandfather lift her from the canoe.

"Huh," he said.

"What?" Trish replied.

"No canoes."

"Should there be some?"

"Dunno. Follow me."

She moved to the front of the canoe and got out without tumping it or falling, which she considered a pretty major accomplishment in the dark. By the time she was on dry land, Grandpa Joe was nearly out of sight. No way was she getting left alone out there. Even though it had gotten brighter. She looked up. The clouds had parted. The moon shone through like a spotlight.

Trish sprinted to catch up with her grandfather. She'd only thought they were going fast before. Her grandfather's long legs ate up the ground, and she jogged to keep up.

Within a few minutes, they were at the vehicles.

Grandpa Joe cocked his head, then walked around the station wagon, with Trish on his heels. "Son of a . . ."

"What is it?"

He didn't answer. He repeated the head cocking as he paced the perimeter of the Suburban. He turned, hands on hips. "Cabin. Now."

"What's wrong with the cars?"

"Flat tires." He spun on his heel and jogged toward the cabin. Or where she thought the cabin should be. It was too dark to tell.

She jogged after him. The ground was wet and mushy. Water splashed from puddles onto her ankles, but it didn't matter. Her jeans and boots were already sopping wet, like the rest of her. She figured that if someone rung her out, it would be enough water to fill a bathtub.

Grandpa Joe rapped his knuckles on the cabin door. Even his knocking was clipped and a little bit grumpy. "Hello? Anyone home? I've got a little girl out here." *And me*, Trish thought. "We need shelter."

There was no answer.

The clouds pulled together again, leaving only a sliver of moon. It spilled meager illumination on the little log cabin. Grandpa Joe handed Bunny back to Trish and motioned them to the side of the door. Trish moved a few steps away. He opened the door and peeked in. After a moment, he walked through it. The sky lightened again. Now Trish could see the Suburban across the clearing. She could even see the trees on the riverbank. She stood without moving a muscle, waiting for

Grandpa Joe to signal her in, but, when he hadn't after a few seconds, she joined him anyway.

When she saw the inside of the cabin, her mouth fell open. Even in the low light, she could see the place was trashed. The bedding was on the floor along with curtains, metal dishes and utensils, and what looked like an emptied bag of flour. If she hadn't been holding Bunny, Trish would have gasped. Cars with flat tires? The cabin tossed? Something had happened here. Something scary.

She scanned the room for a second, looking for whoever had done these things and ready to hightail it out of there with Bunny. To where, she didn't know. A hiding place. Maybe the back of the Suburban. Then her eyes lit on her grandfather. He was standing at a table with some kind of electronic gadget on it. *A radio*, she decided.

He picked up the mic, then muttered something under his breath that was probably curse words. Grandpa Joe had a potty mouth. Dad said he got it honestly in the Navy. "Broken."

"The radio?"

"Yes."

Trish bit her lip to keep from crying. "Where do you think our family is, Grandpa Joe?"

"Dunno. But one thing's for sure."

"What's that?"

"We aren't going to find them standing around here. We'll leave at daylight."

CHAPTER THIRTY-EIGHT: GORGE

South of the Tukudika River, Bridger-Teton National
Forest, Wyoming
Saturday, June 25, 1977, 1:00 a.m.

Susanne

Susanne's eyes flew open. She'd heard something. Or sensed something. Of course, there were lots of sounds she wasn't used to, it being the wilderness at night. She'd been able to sleep through most of them. Not this one, though. She lifted her head and moved her hair aside so she could hear better.

CLANK.

There it was again. Outside the tent. Metallic. Loud.

"Patrick." She pushed on his shoulder.

He snored in response.

She raised her voice to a shouted whisper. "Patrick. Wake up."

"Huh?" He sat, bumping his head into her chin. "Ow."

She forgot about the strange noise. His skull didn't feel great on her chin. She was already irritated at him. He wasn't making it any better.

"I thought you were staying awake to keep Perry up and listen for trouble?"

"Perry. Yes. Sorry. I must have dozed off."

"Must have." Not that she'd stayed awake herself, but Patrick had promised her he wasn't going to fall asleep. She had counted on him, and now trouble was in their campsite. She was sure of it.

Patrick jostled his son. "Wake up, Perry."

Perry moaned and rolled over.

"Shh." Susanne's voice was tight. "There's something outside the tent."

Patrick went on immediate high alert. She could feel intensity radiating from him. He grabbed her arm and leaned closer. "What did you hear?"

THUMP.

"That. And a CLANK a second ago. Something is out there. Or someone."

Patrick inhaled sharply. "Did anything sound human?"

"I don't know. I can't tell."

Patrick's holster was lying at the head of their double sleeping bag. He freed his revolver, then held it awkwardly as he crawled on his knees and one hand to the tent zipper and eased it up.

"What are you doing?" Her words were sharp. She couldn't help it. She might not be happy with him, but she didn't want him to leave.

"Gotta see what's out there."

Now it was Susanne's turn for a quick breath. "You're not leaving?"

"No, just looking."

"Be careful." Her eyes had adjusted to the darkness, and she could see Patrick leaning over and peering out the small opening he'd made.

CRASH.

GRUNT.

"Well, that's not good." Patrick crawled back to her.

"What is it?"

"Bear."

"Black bear?"

"No. Grizzly."

Susanne clutched his arm. She'd never been so close to a grizzly, with only a thin layer of fabric between it and herself, her husband, and her sleeping child. "Will it attack?"

"No. We just need to stay quiet and be still."

"Are you sure?"

"Pretty sure, since it's found our food backpack. I expect by now it's eating everything we have left." He shook his head. Her eyes had adjusted to the dark, and she could see his face crumpled in confusion. "I thought I'd double checked it was hung from a tree. Maybe I didn't. Or maybe someone had one last snack before bed." He muttered for a few seconds, chastising himself for the backpack getting left outside in grizzly country on his watch.

No food for the kids in the morning. She wondered who had left it out there, but there was no time for the blame game.

SNORT.

No food wasn't as bad as a bear attack, so she prayed that Patrick was right and held on tightly to his arm.

RIP.

"What was that?" She knew her voice was starting to edge toward panicky. Could the animal sense her fear? Would it be attracted to her weakness? She needed to dial it back.

"Something tearing. Only the backpack, I hope."

Pete's voice sounded like a bellow in the quiet of the night. "Patrick, is that you out there?"

Patrick's voice was a loud whisper. "No. We've got a visitor."

ROAR.

The hair on Susanne's arms stood on end. The unearthly sound seemed to go on forever. She forgot about being mad at her husband and buried her face in his shoulder. She could imagine the grizzly's long, sharp teeth, his lips pulled back, his eyes beady and enraged. A gust of wind rattled the tent, and to her, it seemed like it was the breath of the bear as he exhaled with all of his might.

"Patrick," she whispered.

From the other two tents, she heard whimpers, then someone started to cry.

"Is your mother alone in her tent?"

"No. Brian's with her. But everyone needs to be quiet." Patrick's whisper sounded terse.

Susanne didn't like this. Not at all.

ROAR.

A scream pierced the night. Perry didn't stir. For a moment, Susanne worried. How could that not have woken him? Then she was relieved. He didn't have to go through the terror that would probably take a decade off her life.

She stayed huddled against her husband. Her voice was shaking. "Could it have gotten one of the kids?"

"No. I still hear it out by the backpack. But they've got to be quiet. The way to avoid a grizzly attack is to play dead, not squeal like a wounded prey animal."

"Does Pete know that?"

"I hope so."

Susanne's breaths were coming in pants. It was hard to be sure, but it sounded like the crying had stopped. The whimpering faded away. The grunting and snorting and roaring had stopped, too. Slowly, Patrick began to rock her side to side. Small, gentle rocks. His hand stroked the back of her head. Her breathing returned to something closer to normal.

She swallowed. "I don't hear anything."

"Me either."

"Is it still out there?"

"Only one way to find out."

"No."

He squeezed her. "I'm not leaving. Just peeking out. I'll be right here. And I have my gun."

"Okay."

As Patrick crawled to the tent door, Perry woke. "Mom? Dad?"

"Shh, son. We need to be very quiet." Susanne scooted toward him and put her hand on his shoulder.

"Are the prospectors here?" His voice sounded woozy.

"All clear. I think." Patrick sat beside her. "You okay, Perry?"

"What's the matter, Dad? Who's here?"

"Was here. A grizzly. It seems like he's gone now."

"A grizzly. Right outside our tent?"

"Yes. And he got the last of our food." Patrick raised his voice. "The bear's gone, but everyone needs to stay in the tents and keep quiet. Roger that?"

"10-4," Pete said.

"Um, okay." It was Brian, and his voice was vibrato with tremors.

Susanne felt sorry for the kid. Alone with his grandmother with a grizzly in camp. "Are you sure it's gone?"

Patrick shook his head. "The only thing I'm sure about is that I won't have any more trouble staying awake tonight."

CHAPTER THIRTY-NINE: SHOULDER

South of the Tukudika River, Bridger-Teton National
Forest, Wyoming
Saturday, June 25, 1977, 5:00 a.m.

Patrick

As Patrick disassembled and packed up their tent, he kept an eye on his son. They were running late. The sun had risen half an hour before. It would take them at least an hour to get down to the river. He hated the thought of the Hilliards having to wait on them.

Perry was stumbling around the campsite, stuffing things into the remaining backpacks. Shredded paper, crumpled aluminum foil, a flattened, bear-shaped plastic bottle that formerly held honey, an empty peanut butter jar with teeth marks in it, and ripped pieces of the canvas from what used to be the backpack. All of it still soggy from the rain the night before. The bear hadn't left a scrap of food. Luckily, no one had snuck any food into the tents.

Patrick still couldn't believe the food had been left out. *My fault.* His entire family had been a hair's breadth away from a bear mauling and today they would have no food until Jackson, and it was his fault. It didn't matter whether someone else had left the backpack out. Either he hadn't impressed strongly enough upon them how dangerous it was to leave out food, or he'd failed to ensure it was put away. His trip. His watch. His fault.

It made him feel incapable. Unmanly. How long would he have lasted in these mountains back when the Tukudika had lived here? They'd co-existed with the grizzlies and other predators successfully for centuries, without permanent structures and thick walls. By using their brains, they'd kept their families safe. Patrick didn't feel worthy to roam the same mountains.

He yawned, which also made him frustrated. The catnap he'd accidentally taken didn't make up for the rest of his sleepless night. Sleep deprivation didn't improve the mind's function, that was for sure, and he needed every brain cell he had left for their journey today. After the bear had disappeared, he'd listened for it the rest of the night. He hoped it was the only one in the area, since Trish was out there somewhere, without even tents. He hated the thought of the grizzly between him and his daughter. He hated even more that she'd been gone for nearly twenty-four hours. *Come on, Dad. Bring Bunny and Trish back safe.*

Perry had stopped and was standing slumped. The backpack he'd been carrying was resting on the ground, dangling from his limp hand.

"You okay, son?" Patrick zipped the tent into a backpack.

"Tired." Perry stared at the ground, unmoving. His voice was the slurred mumble of a drunk. "You made me stay up all night."

"Part of it. You slept half."

"Doesn't feel like it."

"You're just lucky I fell asleep so you could, too."

"If the grizzly hadn't come, I could have slept more." Perry turned to face him. His dark-circled eyes looked past his father. "Since I didn't die in my sleep, does that mean I'm okay?"

It was hard to tell how much of Perry's symptoms were due to lack of sleep and how much to his condition. The bottom line was that Patrick had no idea, which scared him, so he avoided answering the question.

"How do you feel?"

"Awful. And my head hurts."

"I'm sorry, son. I know. I'm proud of you. You're a tough kid."

Many people with head injuries like Perry's were fine up until the moment they weren't, and, by then, it was often too late. Patrick wasn't going to tell him that, though. And he was absolutely taking him to the hospital as fast as they could get down the river.

"Young man."

"What?"

"I'm a teenager now, and that makes me a young man."

Patrick smiled. "Young man. Of course."

Around the clearing where they'd camped, the rest of the group was finishing getting dressed and packing up.

Patrick clapped his hands softly. "Look alive. We're leaving in five minutes, everyone."

Danny let out a war whoop and chased Stan through the clearing.

"Shh. Sound carries out here," Patrick reminded them. "We're trying not to attract grizzlies or bad guys."

Danny whooped again. Patrick decided to change the boy's seven dwarves name to Unruly.

Pete snagged Danny by the arm. The boy jerked to a stop. "Did you hear your Uncle Patrick? Be quiet. You can do it. Just one more day."

Danny jerked his arm away. "This is no fun."

"Tell me about it." Pete sighed. He turned to Patrick. "My clan is ready."

"Me, too," Lana said.

She had wrapped Danny in a bear hug to stop his shenanigans. He giggled and struggled against her half-heartedly, shaking her hairdo. Patrick wasn't sure how she'd managed it, but she'd caught her blonde hair in an orange and brown scarf. Not a wisp was showing, except for her bangs under the jaunty knot she'd tied in the scarf at the crown of her head.

Patrick shouldered his backpack. It was heavier and bulkier than it had been the day before. "Everyone ready for their canoes?"

He was met with dead silence, but Perry and Vera shuffled over to theirs. Vera's eyes were red, like she'd cried herself to sleep. Patrick lifted the canoe for them. Pete did the same for Brian and Susanne's canoe. Susanne avoided eye contact with Patrick. The thaw the previous night when he'd held her and comforted her during the grizzly's visit to their camp had been replaced by an even thicker layer of ice that morning. She hadn't said a word to him. Susanne was usually his biggest supporter. He drew strength from her confidence in him. More than he'd realized. He tried not to let it deflate him.

Pete said, "New buddy assignments today. Keeping it fresh, guys. Bert, you're with Gramma Lana. Barry with Annie, Danny with Stan."

Bert did a victory dance, then he ran to his grandmother.

"We don't have to hold hands, do we?" Stan said.

Pete made a serious expression that didn't hide his laughing eyes. "The whole way."

Both boys groaned, but they linked hands. Immediately, Danny tugged on Stan and then tickled him. Stan wrestled away from his brother and nearly went down. He yelled in protest.

"Boys," Pete said.

They straightened up and pretended to hold hands, without actually touching. Pete ignored them.

Patrick led the way down the trail. Water was rolling onto his fingers down the sides of the canoe. Instead of the canoes drying, water dripping from tree branches was continually recoating them with water. The footing was terrible. Wet, muddy, and slippery, where it wasn't wet, rocky, and slippery. Little mushrooms had sprung up overnight.

Patrick had wrapped his ankle as tightly as he could in a wool sock. It wasn't a perfect bandaging job, but the extra support helped some. He scrambled onto the roadbed and scanned it in both directions. Based on the lack of tire tracks, not a single vehicle had driven by the whole night. He slid down the other side of the road embankment.

Behind him, he heard Vera say, "Are you okay, Perry?"

"I'm all right," Perry replied.

"What's the matter?" Patrick turned to them, holding up the line.

Perry didn't answer.

"He tripped," Vera said. "He nearly dropped the canoe on me."

Patrick got too close and his canoe bumped into and rattled theirs. "Sorry. Son, will you tell me if you're getting worse?"

"Dad, I already did tell you. I'm *tired*."

Patrick knew that's what Perry had said. To be honest, though, he wasn't sure what he'd do if Perry did tell him he was getting worse. It's not like he could drain fluid from inside his skull to reduce the swelling. Not out here.

He walked faster.

But Perry wasn't the only one he was worried about. He couldn't forget the gunshots they'd heard the night before. It would be a load off his mind when they met up with the Hilliards, everyone safe and sound, and got on the river. He felt responsible for the well-being of the three men, too, since he'd roped them into helping the Flints. Patrick slipped on a mossy rock, tweaking his ankle again. Complaining was out of the question, but he wished he could curse like his father. It suddenly seemed like it would make his ankle more bearable.

He quickened his pace. Time passed in a blur as his brain tried to work out solutions to every problem they were facing. He didn't get anywhere on them, but he covered a lot of ground on the trail. He became aware of a rushing sound growing louder with every step. Then, through the thinning trees, he saw water. The river was in sight. Not close, but in sight.

He walked faster still.

"We're having trouble keeping up, Patrick." Susanne's voice sounded far away.

THUD.

"Ouch," his mom said.

"Hold up," he replied. As treacherous as the wet ground was, Patrick didn't want to cause a pile-up. He turned back to the group. Behind Vera and Perry, his mother was crumpled on the ground, a bird-like mound of safari-tan fabric. "Mom, are you okay?"

She sat up, cradling her left arm. "I fell. I'll be fine."

"Are you sure?"

"Of course." She waved him off with the other hand but grimaced. *Pain.* "Stop fussing."

"I think I should look at it."

"It's not bleeding, Patrick. Bert, be a good boy, and help me up, okay?"

Patrick frowned. "If you're sure. It could be broken."

"I'm sure. It's already feeling better."

"Just a hundred yards to the river. Maybe less."

Vera's eyebrows lifted. She looked refreshed just hearing the river was close. He sensed the rest of the group perking up, too. Even Perry nodded, like their proximity met with his approval.

He smiled encouragingly at the group. "We've got to be quiet, and we have to be observant. Let me know if you see or hear anything." He signaled to move forward with two fingers.

Patrick led on, more careful than ever. His group was physically, mentally, and emotionally spent, which made them more prone to accidents—like his mother. The ground was rockier this close to the river. Big, buried rocks half-covered with pine needles, mud, and lichen. A fall could result in an injury like Perry's. They were banged-up enough as it was, and he couldn't afford to put anyone else on the injured reserve list.

His stomach rumbled. And they were hungry. When they made it to Jackson, they'd have to find hotel rooms. Everyone needed rest and good, hot food.

As the cover of the trees broke at the riverbank, he held up a hand. He scanned the river and its banks, looking for signs of the Hilliards. They didn't know exactly where the Flints would be, just that it would be on the south side of the river, before the rapids. He also kept an eye out for the prospectors.

But he saw nothing, other than a vixen fox, her red coat lustrous, dashing into the forest across the river with her three bushy pups. No canoes, no gear, no people. *That's strange. We're late, but they wouldn't have left us.* They knew the Flints couldn't shoot the rapids without their help. In his mind, he heard the gunshots again from the night before, and his throat felt tight. *They just overslept. Everything's okay.* Still, there was no reason for him to stand here waiting for them. He decided he would meet them partway, or, failing that, walk until he found their camp, to make sure they were all right.

His wife arrived at the bank. He set his canoe down and reached for hers. She let him take it without a word. *Icy.* He didn't push her.

When the canoe was on the ground, he went to his mother. "Can I see that arm of yours?"

She was holding the weight of her elbow with her opposite hand. "I feel so foolish."

He straightened it as gently as he could, but he saw the discomfort that clouded her watery blue eyes. "Don't be silly. I was the klutz who twisted an ankle yesterday." He ran his hands down her arm, from above the elbow to her palm. "Where does it hurt?"

"Up close to my elbow."

He focused his attention there. "I don't feel a break. But I can't be sure without an x-ray." He peeled off his flannel shirt and the t-shirt underneath. He put the flannel back on, then fashioned a rudimentary sling out of the t-shirt. "I'm sorry. That will have to do for now."

"It's perfect." She beamed at him. "I can't believe how lucky I am to have a doctor as a son. Thank you, Patrick."

He didn't feel like he deserved her praise. Certainly not on this trip. But he dipped his head. "You're welcome, Mom."

He walked to his wife and stood close to her. Perry was sitting with his back against a tree about five yards away. The other kids were on the ground, so close that they looked like a litter of kittens curling up for a nap in the sun. Pete and Vera had put their canoes beside his and Susanne's and were standing with her.

He pitched his voice so that the kids couldn't hear him. "The Hilliards should have been here already."

Susanne scowled. *Why is she even more beautiful when she's upset with me?* "What if they left us?"

"They wouldn't have. They're not that kind of people."

"You barely know them."

Her tone raised Vera's eyebrows.

Patrick might not have known them long, but he'd gotten a sense of them, and he felt sure he was correct. "I need to check on them to be sure."

"Wait. What about getting Perry to the hospital?" Susanne's face was stormier than the rain clouds from the day before.

Pete put his hand on Vera's arm, and the two of them seemed to move away even though they didn't go anywhere.

"We need help getting down river."

"Which we'll have, if they show up. And we won't if they don't."

"Standing here waiting on them for hours doesn't get Perry to the hospital any faster. If I get there and they're gone, then we know to push on without them."

"On the rapids?"

The river had come close to eating his lunch the evening before. Vera and Susanne couldn't paddle that stretch of the river. He barely could. He wasn't even sure if he'd make it through them a second time. "On foot."

"The group isn't up for another hike carrying canoes."

"I know." He kept his voice neutral. Her feelings were valid. He just knew she might not have a choice.

She put her hands on her hips. It emphasized her tiny waist, and he could see her chewing the inside of her cheek. It was a gesture he was familiar with, and he braced himself.

"I don't want you leaving us," she said.

He put the last of his cards on the table, wanting to persuade her to see things as he did. "Susanne, I feel like they were in harm's way because of us. Those gunshots last night. I'm worried about them. If something's happened, I need to try to help them."

Susanne's eyes drilled into his. "I don't agree. If you get stuck there, your son is stuck, too. Here. Not getting medical care."

Anger flickered inside him, then faded. Why should he expect Susanne to agree without reservation? Besides, she wasn't incorrect. He just knew deep in his gut what the right thing to do was. And sometimes the right thing to do felt all kinds of wrong.

He drew in a deep breath, held it for a moment, then released it. "I hear you. I'll hurry back."

"Patrick Flint . . ." she sputtered to a stop. Then she huffed. "Be careful."

"I will." He started to kiss her cheek, but she pulled away. It was like a knife between his ribs. He cleared his throat. He turned to his brother, who he knew had been listening, Vera by his side. "Pete, you've still got the gun?"

Pete patted his back with one hand. "Yep. Don't worry. We'll stay back from the river and out of sight. You can count on me."

His words made Patrick's throat close. He tucked his own gun in the waistband at the small of Susanne's back, then he cleared his throat. "You know how to use this if you have to."

She started to protest, but he held up a hand, giving her a look that told her not to waste her breath. She nodded instead.

"Somebody hand me a paddle and a life jacket?" he said to the kids.

Stan handed him a life jacket. He put it on, then took the paddle Danny brought to him.

"Thanks, guys. I'll meet you all in an hour or less."

He took off up the river, jogging briskly, with a limp.

CHAPTER FORTY: RISK

Yellowjacket Guard Station, Bridger-Teton National
Forest, Wyoming
Saturday, June 25, 1977, 5:00 a.m.

Trish

Trish woke to see Grandpa Joe rifling through the ancient wooden cupboard in the cabin. Sunlight was flooding through the windows. The radio was making static noises, but no voices were coming out of it. Bunny was standing behind Grandpa Joe, eating something out of her hand.

Trish sat up and stretched. She let out a big yawn. "Hi, Grandpa. Good morning, Buns."

He held up a Tupperware bowl, its lid in his other hand. "I found dry granola. Breakfast."

Trish nodded. She was starving. She reached for it, but he put the lid on the container.

"We eat on the way. Let's go."

Trish hadn't even had time to wipe the sleep out of her eyes. "Can I go to the bathroom first?"

"Hurry."

"Bunny, do you need to go, too?"

Bunny nodded and wiped her hand on her leg. Granola rained onto the wooden floor. Grandpa Joe didn't seem to notice. *That will make the forest mice happy.*

Holding hands, the girls went outside and walked into the trees. It was shady and almost cold without the sun. When they finished and came back, Grandpa Joe was standing outside. The door to the cabin was closed. He handed Trish the granola. In one smooth motion, he lifted Bunny to his hip and whirled toward the river. Across the clearing, a couple of cow elk were grazing with calves by their sides. The long-legged animals spooked and disappeared into the forest like vapor as soon as the Flints headed toward them. Trish's mouth fell open. Had they been there when she and Bunny went into the woods? Elk were shy, and beautiful. Grandpa Joe and Bunny hadn't seemed to notice them at all.

Grandpa Joe began marching toward the river, his pace brisk, as usual. Trish looked at the grass. There were standing puddles from the storm the night before—a real downer. She was sick to death of wet shoes and clothes. Stalling, she ripped the lid off the Tupperware, stuffed a handful of granola in her mouth, then put the lid back on. She splashed after her grandfather, crunching, chewing, and trying not to choke on the dry cereal. When she'd swallowed it all, she made a face. No more for her.

She caught up with Grandpa Joe at the water's edge where he'd set Bunny down. He went back into the trees and came out with the canoe.

"I'm thirsty," Bunny said.

Grandpa Joe pointed at the river.

Bunny giggled. "Like a dog?"

Trish remembered how sick her dad had gotten the year before from drinking unsterilized stream water in the mountains. She also recalled that it was because she hadn't boiled it when he asked her to. Not her finest moment. She couldn't let that happen to her cousin.

"Let's wait, Buns. It can make you sick. We'll get a drink when we catch up with your mommy and daddy."

Bunny frowned but she nodded.

Trish asked her grandfather, "Are we going through the rapids?"

He nodded.

"Without life jackets?"

He pulled off his belt. "Put Bunny in the middle seat."

Trish did as she was told. Her back and arms ached from carrying her cousin the day before. She could barely lift her high enough to put her in the boat. As it was, Bunny landed halfway on the side. She kicked her legs up and over.

"Good job, Buns."

She rewarded Trish with a grin.

In the meantime, Grandpa Joe had fastened the belt around Bunny's seat. He buckled it and pulled against it. He grunted.

"Hold this strap, Bunny." His face was stern. "Really tight and don't let go."

Bunny's eyes were big brown buttons. "Yes, Grandpa Joe."

"Promise me."

"I promise." She smiled at him like a little angel.

Trish wrestled down a lump in her throat and climbed into the front seat.

Her grandfather drilled his eyes into Trish's. "And you. Don't you fall out, no matter what. You hear me?"

"Yes, sir." How could she really promise that, though? She practiced holding on to the seat and bracing her feet against the inside of the bow. It didn't feel right, and she moved her hands and feet around until she found a more secure position.

Grandpa Joe nodded. "Good. I may need your help. Got no idea what's ahead of us." He pointed at the floorboard. Trish turned and saw an extra paddle behind her. "Be ready to use it." She scooted it within reach.

The canoe rocked violently as Grandpa Joe climbed into it. "We're off then."

Trish wished she could just *hike* out and meet the rest of the family when they got back to town. She clung to her seat and clenched her jaw. Well, it didn't look like she had a choice. It was the river. Or nothing.

Right now, she would have gladly picked nothing.

CHAPTER FORTY-ONE: SICKEN

Patrick

As he trotted up the river, Patrick kept an eye out for people he didn't want to encounter. Animals, too. Wherever the grizzly went the night before was a place he didn't want to be. He glanced over his shoulder every few yards. His skin prickled like eyes were watching him. He'd stowed the canoe a quarter mile back. It had slowed him down too much. He could pick it up on the way downriver with the Hilliards.

Running uphill at this altitude, his breathing was loud and heavy. He wouldn't be able to hear anything coming up behind him. But turning his head was risky, too. The footing was challenging, even though it was a relatively obstacle-free section of the river. It alternated between stretches of small rocks to grassy, almost boggy patches still seasonally wet, to rough boulder-strewn areas he skirted around. His ankle was unstable and it hurt like the dickens. But, still, he marveled at the beauty around him. Across the river, the entire face of one peak had been reduced to a scree-and-boulder slide. Movement in the rock caught his eye. He stopped dead in his tracks. A bighorn ram was watching him. Patrick willed time to stand still, so that he could marvel at the majestic animal. He felt the pressure of its passing and the urgency of their situation, though, so he nodded to the animal and ran on, holding a picture of it in his mind.

He wished the circumstances were different so he could have slowed down to enjoy the animal and his surroundings. Maybe his family would want to come back someday. Unlikely, he knew, after how this trip had gone. He'd probably missed his one good shot to enjoy the area. The thought made him a little melancholy, but he knew it was small potatoes compared to everything else he had to worry about.

After about five more minutes of painful running, he stopped, winded, to catch his breath. He evaluated the shore and river further up from him. It looked familiar. He was pretty sure that they had split up from the Hilliards near here. Anytime now, he should find their canoes. And then a camp with three men—sheepish about sleeping late—throwing coffee grounds in the ash from the fire, loading up their canoes, and ready to strike out with him to meet up with the rest of the Flints.

Rounding a bend in the river, he spied the canoes on the bank and sped up. His heart rate, already high from exertion, accelerated to a scary pace. He wanted to call out to the Hilliards, but he didn't dare. Hector hadn't been with the prospectors he and Pete had clotheslined on the river the night before. For that matter, even those guys could have hiked up the river during the night. He was making too much noise running pell-mell through rustling bushes, loose rocks, and wet, splashy areas. He slowed to a cautious walk and raised his alert from high to critical.

He scanned the area for movement, colors, and shapes that didn't belong. Something out of place beyond a stand of trees caught his attention. A red glint in the sunlight. Definitely not a red native to the forest. He fox-walked silently toward it, taking extra care with his footing.

CAW. CAW. CAW.

A flock of crows—he couldn't call them a murder, never had been able to use the term—startled and winged away. Their presence was unnerving. If the Hilliards had been there, the crows probably wouldn't have.

Fishing, he decided. They'd decided to get in one last hour of fishing before they canoed the last stretch of river back to civilization. It was their vacation. They'd want to make the most of it.

The thought *sounded* good, but it didn't relieve his anxiety.

He slowed down even further as he reached the stand of trees. Using both hands, he pushed aside branches and made his way through.

GRUNT.

He froze. The noise didn't sound human. It sounded like it came from an animal, and a big one. He separated two branches and peered through.

What he expected to see in the clearing was a tent. A fire ring. Gear bags. Fishing poles and tackle boxes.

What he hoped to see was a father and sons bonding over their annual wilderness adventure. Maybe one of them would be laughing and making the weird noises he'd just heard.

What he actually saw was the stuff of nightmares. Three bodies in unnatural positions on the ground, completely still.

And one grizzly bear, feeding on them.

CHAPTER FORTY-TWO: STICK

The Tukudika River, Bridger-Teton National Forest, Wyoming
Saturday, June 25, 1977, 6:00 a.m.

Trish

Trish braced herself as they approached another set of rapids. Her arms and legs were shaking. The first stretch of white-water hadn't been that bad. Bunny had squealed the whole way, happy squeals. Trish thought it was kind of exciting, actually, but she was tired from holding herself wedged in the bucking canoe. She would have rather been with her dad, but she felt okay with Grandpa Joe. He was good at the whole canoeing thing, especially for an old man.

The river narrowed, and the canoe picked up speed. Tall, gray rock walls rose on either side of them. All of a sudden, the boulders in the water were bigger. And then . . . the riverbed just fell away. From her position at the bow, she had the first glimpse of what was in front of them, and below them. It wasn't exactly a waterfall. More like a night-mare version of the Log Ride at Six Flags over Texas. She'd never liked that ride, either.

Trish gulped, then screamed.

"Hold on, Bunny." Grandpa Joe's voice sounded funny.

Bunny didn't squeal this time. She let out a blood-curdling wail.

Down, down, down the canoe went. Trish gripped the seat and braced her feet in the V of the canoe's nose. And none too soon. As the canoe plunged, her bottom separated from the seat. Icy water rushed over her, drenching her entire body. She screamed again from the shock of it, but she held on as the bow landed in flatter water, dipped, then rose. Her tush slammed back into the seat.

She was still in the canoe.

SMASH.

The canoe careened off a boulder beside her.

Bunny's wails escalated like a siren. There was nothing Trish could do for her. She couldn't even turn to see if she was all right.

"Don't let go, Buns!" Trish shouted. She got a mouthful of water for her efforts.

The canoe crashed into something below the waterline. The impact jarred Trish so hard that her front teeth snapped shut, and she was afraid she'd broken them. The canoe strained forward over the obstacle. The scraping noise was terrible, like a shriek. *Is the bottom of the canoe ripped out?*

WHAM.

The canoe broke free only to slam into another boulder, this one on its opposite side. All around Trish, the water boiled, pummeling and drenching her relentlessly. She could barely get air without choking, and she couldn't see in front of her to time her breaths with what was coming next. Her hands ached from the cold, and it was getting harder to hold on to the seat. The noise of the water shooting through the canyon drowned out Bunny's wails now.

Without warning, the canoe dropped, and with it, Trish's stomach. Her bottom floated off the seat. It felt like the time she'd been bucked off her first pony, a bad-tempered, furry little beast who bit and kicked. And those were his good qualities. Not like Goldie, her beautiful, perfect girl, her current horse, the one of her dreams. The pony's name had been Cotton. Something had spooked him—something was always spooking him—and he'd ducked his head and kicked his back legs up and out. She hadn't been ready for it. The next thing she knew, she had the sensation of air between her and the saddle. Of her thighs losing their grip and her knees and feet coming up, limp and loose like the limbs of a rag doll.

WHAM.

Of her hands on the reins and the saddle horn her only tether to the crazed animal.

WHAM.

Of the pull on her fingers as they slowly lost their grip.

WHAM.

And then the feeling of . . . flying . . . time slowing . . . wondering if it would hurt when she landed . . . would she be on her back? Her head? Her butt? Her stomach?

That was how she felt now, too, as she was catapulted up and out of the canoe.

She was pretty sure she landed hands and face first in the river, but it hurt everywhere. Everywhere. She'd only thought the water was cold before. When she went under it, she felt like she'd been electrocuted. The current didn't give her any time to get her bearings either. She hurtled down the river, unsure which way was up. Unable to see anything. *Air. I need air.* She scrambled and flailed her arms. They found nothing to grab onto. Her lungs were burning. She couldn't keep her mouth closed much longer. Her legs smashed into a rock. The pain was intense, but she managed to kick off from it. When she did, her face broke the surface of the water. Her eyes and mouth flew open at the same time. The breath she drew in was wonderful for a fraction of a second, until water poured in after it. She gagged. But as she gagged, she kicked her legs in front of her, threw her arms out to the side, and tilted her head up. Her dad had told her what to do. She wasn't going to drown out here. She was only sixteen. She had friends. Her best friend Marcy. Goldie. Her silly dog Ferdie. Her family. And she had her—her Ben. *How odd that I think of him now when I'm about to die.* She wanted to see Ben. Her parents wouldn't like it. But she wanted him to be her boyfriend.

She gasped for another breath.

She wanted a driver's license. She wanted to be on the cross-country team. She wanted to buy a car. She wanted to go to her senior prom. To the University of Wyoming. Become a wildlife biologist. Get married. Have kids. Again, Ben's face flashed in her mind.

Another breath, less water this time.

Was it her imagination, or was the river slowing down? Her eyes were on the blue, blue sky, so she couldn't judge distance. But in her peripheral vision, she thought the rock walls had disappeared. That trees had replaced them. *Yes.* Trees, and they were growing further apart. In the water, there were less obstacles. Just a few rocks she hit with her feet.

Another breath, no water.

"Grandpa Joe!" she screamed, then coughed and gagged again when she slurped in more water. She choked it back out. "Help! Help me!"

"I'm coming." It was her grandfather's voice.

She heard the fast, rhythmic splash of his paddle. Her teeth were chattering. Her right calf was cramping with a Charley horse. "Hurry. P-p-p-please."

Then the nose of the canoe passed her, and there was Bunny, crying. Something hard hit Trish's hand. The paddle. She tried to grab it, but her fingers wouldn't bend. She shouted. "Argh!" She tried again, and this time she got hold of it. She rolled over and hugged it to her.

Grandpa Joe pulled her toward the canoe. "I'm going to lever you up, and you're going to have to climb in."

"I'm c-c-c-cold."

His voice was hard. "I don't care, Trish. You need to get in this canoe, without flipping us, on your first try, or we'll all go in. I can't help you and Bunny at the same time. Do you understand?"

Grandpa Joe was right. He didn't make her feel good, but he was right. She loved Bunny. She'd worked really hard to keep her safe. She couldn't be the reason Bunny drowned with no life jacket. *No life jacket.* She'd just survived getting dumped in freezing whitewater with no life jacket. She nearly laughed aloud.

Of course I can do this. This was nothing compared to what she'd already done.

She kept her eyes on Grandpa Joe as he muscled her upwards by the other end of the paddle. His teeth were gritted and the veins in his neck bulged. His shoulders were shaking. But she rose a few inches out of the river. She hadn't realized how strong he was. She'd always thought of him as old and weak, but he wasn't. He was as strong as her dad. She wished she could make this easier for him, but all she could do was hold still.

When he had her high enough, he braced the paddle on the far side of the canoe. "Now. Climb in now."

Trish reached her arms across the canoe, between Grandpa Joe and Bunny. She let her weight flop onto the canoe's edge.

"Lean, Bunny. And scoot to the edge of your seat, away from Trish," Grandpa Joe ordered.

The little girl whimpered, but Trish heard a rustling sound as she did what she was told.

Trish's legs felt like they were anchored to the bottom of the river. She had to get them out of the water. There were no good handholds. She wriggled and scrambled to get her hips over the side, dragging her legs after her. *So heavy.* Finally, her upper body was far enough in that it tipped the scales. She flopped onto the bottom of the canoe and rolled into an inch of standing water. She stared upward, blinded by the sun, and panted. Air, with no water. It felt wonderful.

"Good job." Grandpa Joe patted her shoulder.

His hand was warm. So was his voice.

She tried to smile.

"Trish!" Bunny cried.

"I'm okay, Buns."

"Back in your seat, Trish. Now." Grandpa Joe's voice was hard again.

"Okay." The canoe rocked as Trish slithered over the middle seat, pausing to kiss Bunny's warm hair. Then she was on her knees and crawling on to the bow seat. She adjusted herself in the seat to take full advantage of the sun's warmth. She closed her eyes. Time slipped away from her. She wasn't sleeping. Not really. Just recovering.

Grandpa Joe's voice jolted her to alertness. "Time to hold on again, girls."

Trish wasn't ready for more rapids. She looked ahead of them. "No," she whispered.

She braced and gripped. She had to stay in the canoe this time. She thought about climbing back on Cotton after he'd bucked her off. She'd landed on her butt on the ground. It had hurt, but her dad hadn't let her quit.

"Trish, that pony needs to know you'll always get back on. Otherwise, he'll buck any time he wants to be done for the day, from here on out. Is that what you want?"

Tears had been streaming down her face. She'd shaken her head. Her dad had tossed her into the saddle. Cotton had started to get shifty immediately.

"He's going to buck, Daddy."

"What will you do this time?"

"I don't know."

"You're going to put weight in your feet like you're standing on them. Then you're going to make your bottom the heaviest part of your body. You're going to glue it to that saddle. Show me."

"What do you mean?"

"Show me what it looks like. Use your imagination, then do it."

Trish had pushed down in her stirrups, thought about it, then slumped down a little in the saddle. It *did* make her bottom feel heavier. She imagined it glued to the leather.

"Good." Her dad had let go of Cotton's bridle.

Trish had walked the pony away, and, sure enough, he'd bucked. But this time was different. She was ready, and she'd stayed glued to the saddle.

"Did you see me, Daddy?" she'd crowed.

Suddenly, she wasn't a little girl on a white pony anymore. She was a shivering young woman in a canoe hurtling toward whitewater on the Tukudika River. The nose of the canoe fell and along with it her stomach. *Here we go again. Feet like you're standing. Glue your bottom to the seat.*

With all the strength in her mind and body, Trish willed herself to stay molded to the canoe seat. Water cascaded over her. She spluttered, but she stayed put. The canoe bucked. It rocked, and it shuddered, but she stayed put. It careened off boulders, jolted against others, and slammed into more. But Trish stayed glued to her seat.

And, then, as quickly as they had started, the rapids ended. Trish wiped water from her face and tried to slow her breathing. Was it really over?

"Nice of you not to go swimming that time," Grandpa Joe called out to her.

Trish threw her head back. She laughed and laughed and laughed, until Bunny and Grandpa Joe were laughing along with her.

"Hello! Over here! Hello!" a man shouted.

Trish looked to the left, toward the riverbank. A man was walking and waving. "Is that Dad?" She squinted. "Dad!" She started waving back so hard it rocked the canoe, although nothing like the rapids had.

"Where's my daddy?" Bunny said. "And my mommy?"

"I don't know, Buns. We'll ask Uncle Patrick, okay?"

Bunny didn't answer.

Grandpa Joe turned the canoe and it shot toward her dad. In mere seconds, he was pulling the nose of their canoe onto the shore. Two other canoes were stashed side by side a few feet further into the trees.

Trish stood. The canoe lurched, but she didn't care. Her dad threw his arms around her. It was the best hug of her life.

"I'm so glad to see you, Trish. You have no idea how worried we've been." Was his voice quivering?

She wiped her face on his shirt. The flannel was soft and smelled like him. "Oh, Daddy. Grandpa Joe saved us."

She felt her dad's hand lift off her back and shake something. She looked over her shoulder and saw her dad's and Grandpa Joe's hands were clasped. Grandpa Joe had Bunny on his other hip.

Her dad released her. "Dad, what happened to your face?"

Trish looked at Grandpa Joe. Blood had dried on his forehead.

"He hit himself in the face with the damn paddle," Bunny said.

There was a moment of silence, then a laugh exploded from Patrick, so Trish joined in. Bunny looked confused. Grandpa Joe's expression never changed.

"Well, thank God you guys are okay, except for that, um, paddle." Her dad took Bunny from Grandpa Joe and hugged her, too, then handed her back. "I hate to do this, but I have to get us out of here." He nodded back over his shoulder. "There's, um, there's a grizzly over there with, um, fresh kill. I'll take one of those canoes and you guys can follow me to catch up with the others. But whatever we do, we have to do it very, very quietly." He looked away from the river, frowning. "Then we have to get to town fast."

"A grizzly?" Trish whispered.

"Do you have any life jackets?" Grandpa Joe said, keeping his voice low. "I'd like to get some on Bunny and Trish."

Trish would love that, too. "I went swimming, Dad. In the rapids."

"You're kidding me? You went in?" Her dad's throat moved like he'd swallowed a frog.

Grandpa Joe put his hand on Trish's shoulder. "She scared us good, but she did what she was told, and lived to tell about it."

Her dad hugged her again "You'll have to tell me all about it when we get to safety. I'm just so glad you're all right." When he released her, he walked to the other canoes. He brought back three life jackets. "These will be kind of big for you girls, but there are three here you can use."

"Don't those people need them?" Trish said.

A funny look crossed his face. "No. They'll . . . understand."

"Okay." Trish took the life jacket he handed her and slipped into it.

"Grandpa Joe said Perry has to go to the hospital." She tightened the straps as far as she could. It was still a little big.

Her dad gave one to Grandpa Joe, then crouched to adjust a third one on Bunny. It swallowed her. "Yes."

"Is he okay?"

"He hit his head. But I think he'll be fine."

Grandpa Joe pushed the canoe back onto the water. Her dad put Bunny on the middle seat. Grandpa Joe motioned for Trish to get in.

"Can I ride with you, Dad?" she said.

"Sure." He walked quietly over to the canoes.

Trish went with him. "Are there bad guys chasing you, too?"

Her dad cocked his head at her as he pulled on the canoe. "How did you guys know that?"

Trish went to the other side of it to help him push.

"One of them got us." Bunny's high-pitched voice sounded wise beyond its years.

Trish's dad shook his head. "Yeah. We've got them on our tail, too. Dad, we need to talk about—"

She heard a now-familiar squawk. For a moment, she worried the grizzly would hear it, too, and come after them. She shoved harder on the canoe.

A man's voice said, "Hector, do you read me? Hector, come in." The radio. It was muffled, but Trish could understand every word.

"What was that?" her dad said. He stopped pushing the canoe, and his face was scary.

She said, "Grandpa Joe took the man's radio. That's one of the men he was talking to. I recognize his voice."

Grandpa Joe fished the radio out of the backpack.

The voice grew much louder. Grandpa Joe dialed back the volume, watching the trees like dad had been doing. Grizzlies tended to make people nervous like that.

"Hector, if you can hear us, we found 'em. I thought I saw one of 'em running up the river after they attacked us, and I was right. Booger's unconscious. Diego is dead. Me and Winthropp are gonna make 'em pay for what they did to us. I don't think they've seen us, so we're going after them on foot. Meet us near the last stretch of whitewater before the falls. South side of the river."

Trish frowned and started looking all around them, even across the river. "Found them? Does he mean us?"

Her dad shoved their canoe the rest of the way into the water. It began to float. "Not us. The family. All the kids. Your moms. I've got to warn them. Help them. Trish, ride with Grandpa Joe. Dad, you find a place to hide the girls. Keep them safe. You can't stay here with this bear."

Trish's mouth went dry. *Her family. All of them.*

Grandpa Joe frowned. "Be careful."

"I will." Her dad leapt in the canoe. He started paddling so hard that it shot away from them down the river, disappearing around a bend. He was gone so fast, Trish was dazed.

She turned to her grandfather. "We have to do something, too."

Grandpa Joe grunted. "We're staying out of your dad's way. Now, get in the canoe before that grizzly finds you."

Staying out of the way wasn't enough. She lowered her face in her hands and started to cry.

CHAPTER FORTY-THREE: LEAP

Susanne

"Patrick should be here by now." Susanne paced back and forth near the rest of the family. Her mother would have told her she was wearing a hole in the ground, she'd made so many loops of the small clearing in the trees. Her chest hurt like she was having a heart attack and she was short of breath. The thought of sitting made it worse.

Everyone else was sitting down, backs against rocks, backpacks, and trees. They'd left the canoes close to the river but moved further into the woods. The youngest of the kids had fallen asleep with their heads in adult laps. Lana was stroking Bert's hair with her uninjured hand. Danny and his big sister were whispering about something and looking mischievous.

Susanne's eyes lit on her son. Perry didn't look good at all. His face was so pale and his eyes so dark that he was a miniature of Lurch from *The Addams Family*. Worse than that, he seemed uncoordinated and confused. He'd been lethargic and was having trouble staying awake. She was worried about him. She was worried about Patrick, about Trish,

Bunny, and Joe, too. For that matter, she was worried about everything and everyone related to this trip.

She decided to expand her pacing a little further. Walking was the only thing she could think of to release some of her killer anxiety. "I'll be back in a second."

Vera nodded. Pete saluted. Perry didn't look up.

"Want me to go with you, Aunt Susanne?" Brian stood.

He was such a great kid. "No, I'm good. I'm, uh, just making a trip to the ladies' room. Thanks, though."

She took off down river at a loose walk that was almost a trot. *Slow down. Toe first. Weight on the back foot. Ease yourself forward. Repeat, slowly.* She stopped and closed her eyes. She was silent fox-walking. Taking instructions from Patrick, even when he wasn't here. Didn't it just figure? She was so frustrated about the situation he'd put them in. And yet his was the voice she heard in her head, all the time. *All the dang time.* Right now, even though she was mad at him, she needed him more than ever. She hated that the group was separated. Hated being apart from him. Even at the worst of times, he was her one and only. Her partner. Her love. Her anchor. And without even meaning to, she'd been avoiding twigs, pebbles, and other noisemakers, because he was with her. A sad smile moved across her lips, and she started walking again.

A male voice carried through the woods to her.

Her smile drooped. She didn't see anyone, but that didn't mean the man wasn't close. She moved behind a stand of trees and froze, listening.

"Me and Winthropp are gonna make 'em pay for what they did to us. I don't think they've seen us, so we're going after them on foot. Meet us near the last stretch of whitewater before the falls. South side of the river."

She heard the electronic squawk of a radio. *Or a walkie talkie.* It was the men after Pete. The ones that had sent Booger. It had to be. She closed her eyes and tried to breathe without making a sound.

"Whatta we do now, boss?" It was a second male voice.

The first man answered him. "We need to go stash our canoes in the woods first. Then gather up our stuff. Follow me and be real quiet. They'll never know we're coming."

All the blood rushed from Susanne's face. No time. They had no time. She opened her eyes and nearly screamed. A hand clapped over her mouth. She started to struggle before she could see who had her. An arm pinned hers to her sides. She relaxed. *Live to fight another day. Pick your battles.* Again, it was Patrick's voice in her head. She looked down at the arm encircling her. It was olive-skinned and bare. Further down she saw feet in tall moccasins, almost moccasin-boots. *What the heck?* Above the moccasins was a pair of buckskin pants. Light in color, scratched, worn, and soiled. *Who has me?*

The arm released her, and she turned and scuttled back so fast that she fell on her bottom. That was okay. She was so shocked, she couldn't have stayed on her feet if she'd tried.

A man was staring at her. Slim, toned, shirtless, and terrifying. His hair was black and straight. It touched his shoulders. Two eagle feathers hung from a piece of leather that was braided into it. Stripes of red paint on his cheeks emphasized his sharp features.

An Indian. Here. Now. She didn't understand. Couldn't understand.

"Who are you?" she whispered.

He motioned for her to follow him.

She stood, ready to run in the opposite direction. But if she did, she'd run into the prospectors. *Fine.* She'd run back to her family on the path she'd taken to get here instead. But which way was that? She looked around and recognized nothing. A cry died in her throat. The man motioned for her again.

He held out his hand, then touched it to his chest. In a deep voice, he said something in a language she'd never heard. Then he reached his hand toward her again, palm up, fingers outstretched.

Behind her, she heard the voices of the prospectors as they walked back to their canoes.

No choice. She took the man's hand.

Without another sound, he took off, guiding her through the woods. Susanne scrambled to keep up with him, to keep her feet under her. She was running. Running like the wind, pulled along by the man's strong hand. Away from the prospectors. But even though they were running, they were silent. She slipped, she tripped, she stumbled, but he didn't let her fall. Her terror ebbed. She felt something stronger than fear. Faith. She had faith that this man didn't mean her any harm. That he wanted to help.

For long, heart-pounding minutes, they ran. Then the woods around her started to look familiar. As quickly as he'd taken her hand, he released it and pointed. She caught sight of her family through the woods.

She nodded. This wasn't a game or a drill. They'd been discovered. She had to tell them. She had to get them moving.

In quick, silent strides, she burst into their midst.

Pete jumped to his feet, his expression alarmed. "What is it?"

She held a finger to her lips. Whispering, she said, "Don't be scared of him. He's helping me."

"Who?"

She turned around. The man had disappeared. She hadn't even had time to thank him. *No time for that.* "The prospectors found us. They're coming. They're on foot. We've got to get on the water. Now."

"But Patrick—"

"We can't wait for him. They said they're going to make us pay. Come on." She ran toward the canoes, then turned back. "Everyone grab a kid and *move it.*"

Finally, her hushed voice and words broke through to them. The group mobilized, running for the river. When they reached the spot where they'd left the canoes, though, they were gone.

"Did the prospectors beat us here?" Pete said. "Where are they?"

Susanne looked out to the river. Four canoes were lined up half-in, half-out of the water. "There." She pointed.

"What the heck?" he breathed.

No time. "Come *on.*"

She sprinted to a canoe, and the others followed.

"The backpacks," Vera said as she climbed in the rear of a canoe.

Perry loaded himself in front. Pete lifted Bert and Barry in and sat them together on the middle seat. He gave Vera's canoe a push, and it sailed out toward the middle of the river, where it was widest.

Susanne looked downriver before getting in the rear of her own canoe. A hundred yards ahead, the water narrowed as it approached the rapids.

"No time to go back," she shouted to Vera. "They have guns. Get to the other side."

Vera started paddling. With all the weight in it, the canoe rode low in the water. "It's too heavy."

"You can do it, Vera," Pete said. He turned his attention to the rest of the family. "Mom, you and Annie will be with me. Brian, Danny and Stan, you go with Aunt Susanne."

"Yes, sir," Brian said.

Pete helped the three kids in, then shoved Susanne's canoe into the current. "Put your life jackets on."

Brian shot him a thumb's up.

From the trees, Susanne heard one of the men's voices from earlier. "They're getting away, Winthropp. Stop them."

"Pete, they're here. Hurry," Susanne shouted. She paddled hard, harder than she thought she could, and pulled near Vera. "Vera, faster."

Tears stained Vera's cheeks. "Pete."

"He's coming. You can do it, Vera."

Vera snuck a glance behind her, eyes wide. Then she wiped her face, nodded, and set her mouth in a grim line. She picked up her cadence.

Susanne felt something warm and soft mushroom inside her as she watched her sister-in-law. The woman seemed to mature and harden before her eyes. Vera would be okay. "Looking good," Susanne said.

CRACK. CRACK.

"They're shooting at us," Brian screamed.

Susanne's heart started beating like it was going to explode out of her chest. "Kids, get down."

Danny, Stan, and Brian scrambled to the floor of the canoe.

CRACK. CRACK.

"That was me," Pete called out. "They're retreating."

Susanne had forgotten about Booger's gun. *Gun.* She had one in her own waistband and hadn't even remembered it.

"Susanne." It didn't sound like Pete.

She couldn't slow down, but she allowed herself a quick glance. The face she saw on the man paddling the canoe toward her was a Flint's, but it was her Flint. Patrick was alongside her in a few strokes.

Susanne held back tears. "You made it. Thank God."

"I hurried as fast as I could."

"The prospectors found us. They're shooting at us.

Pete pulled up on the other side of Patrick. "Were. They headed back into the woods. Is everybody okay?"

Slowly, children's heads rose in all the canoes. Voices started shouting out reports. The consensus was that they were all fine, if a little scared.

"Uncle Patrick," Brian sat up from the belly of Susanne's canoe. "You made it."

"I did." Patrick stuck his paddle in the water, slowing his canoe down to keep pace with Susanne. "And I have good news. Dad found the girls."

"Are they okay?" This time Susanne let her tears fall.

"They are. And they have one of the prospectors' radios. We heard them transmit about finding you guys and coming after you. Dad is hanging back to keep the girls safe."

"Thank the Lord," Susanne said. It was the first good news in what felt like forever, even though it had been less than twenty-four hours since everything went haywire.

"That's *great* news," Pete echoed. "Vera will be so relieved."

Patrick nodded. "But now, I'd guess the prospectors will be heading downriver for their canoes. We should expect them to try to intercept us." He glanced at the bottom of his boat.

"What is it?" Susanne studied his face.

He looked up at her, scowling. "My canoe is taking on water."

The gunshots. Her voice was strident. "Were you hit?"

"Not me. But my canoe, I'm not so sure. A rock. A bullet. Something."

"Is it going to sink?"

"Nah."

She didn't believe him. She'd seen the look on his face. But the most important thing is that the bullet hadn't hit him.

The three of them caught up with Vera.

Pete called to her. "Dad found the girls. Bunny is all right, and she's on her way here."

Vera turned back to them, face ashen. It wasn't the reaction Susanne had expected from Vera when her sister-in-law learned Bunny was safe.

"Vera, what is it?" Susanne said.

"Perry." Vera gestured at the nose of the canoe, where only the top of Perry's head was visible. "He stood up to help paddle, and he slipped and hit his head on the edge of the canoe. He won't wake up."

CHAPTER FORTY-FOUR: DUCK

South of the Tukudika River, Bridger-Teton National
Forest, Wyoming
Saturday, June 25, 1977, 7:00 a.m.

Patrick

As Patrick rushed over to Vera's canoe, his midsection felt like it was going two rounds with Muhammed Ali. He grabbed the side of her canoe with one hand, walked himself to the front, and jostled Perry. "Son, wake up. No sleeping. You need to hang on in the whitewater, and we've got to get going."

Perry didn't respond. Patrick's fears swirled through his head. A brain hemorrhage. Subdural hematoma. Epidural hematoma. A rebleed, after he'd been holding his own. The medical jargon for the conditions ran through Patrick's mind, the symptoms typed below the words like they were instructional slides in a projector, with Perry's image front and center on each. He checked his son's pulse and his breathing. Both were normal. But he'd been knocked unconscious again. And he hadn't been himself that morning. Clumsy. A little confused. Patrick tilted Perry's head to the side and gently lifted an eyelid. His pupils reacted when the sunlight hit them, but did one look different than the other? A little sluggish? He couldn't tell. Patrick closed his own eyes for a split second. *Dear God, help us get him to the hospital and please let him be all right.*

He turned to Susanne. He tried not to look as devastated as he felt. "He's unconscious again. I'm worried about another concussion." He left out everything else he was worried about.

"No." Susanne's face was stricken. "Patrick, no."

He wished he could offer her reassurance, but he couldn't. "We have to hurry."

"Then let's go!"

To Pete he said, "I think I remember from the map that after this set of rapids we're pretty close to town. Unfortunately, there's a waterfall first. We're going to have to get Perry out and carry him around the falls. When we get to the bottom there, it's smooth sailing the rest of the way, and I'm sure we'll find someone who can help us. But first we have to cross this last stretch of whitewater." It hadn't gone well for him last time. He faced the other canoes and raised his voice. "Has everybody got their life jackets on?"

Annie's voice trembled. "I'm scared."

Pete gave his kids a smile, although it was a somber one. "These rapids aren't bad ones. Uncle Patrick and I went through them last night, no problem."

Patrick wasn't about to disagree with him. The kids needed confidence. But his stomach churned.

"Are you sure, Pete?" Vera sounded as scared as Annie.

"Absolutely."

"When you get through the first chute, it'll ease up for a little ways. Get out of the middle toward the left. It's calmer over there," Patrick said.

Pete gave everyone a thumbs up. "If we hurry, we'll be off the water at the falls before Les and Winthropp even get to their canoes. Patrick, I'll bring up the rear."

"Then I'll lead. Let's move it, everyone. Kids, stay low."

Susanne pulled his revolver from her waistband. "Patrick, take this back."

He reached for it. They fumbled the hand off, and it nearly landed in the water, but he managed to catch it, only getting the back of his hand wet.

He stuck it in its holster. "Thanks."

He sucked in a deep breath and gave Perry one last long, hard look before he moved off. No change. He dug his paddle in. Soon, he heard the splashes of paddles and canoes behind him. The calm water picked up speed and rumbled. He was worried about Susanne. He was even more concerned about Vera, and about Perry in her canoe, vulnerable. He prayed out loud the whole way, never stopping as his canoe rocked, dipped, and ricocheted between boulders. When the strainer tree was in sight, he started paddling hard left far earlier, his lips still moving.

This time, Patrick made it through with no issue. In fact, he couldn't believe he'd nearly ended up in the water the night before. The two sides of the river were different beasts. But the level of water inside his canoe was becoming a real problem. He held his canoe steady and turned around to watch the others take their turn on the rapids, ready to break into rescue mode if necessary. Vera looked terrified, but she did fine. Susanne pumped a fist in the air as her own canoe exited the rough patch. Pete looked like he'd been whitewater canoeing his whole life.

Vera shouted, "He's awake. Perry's awake!"

Her canoe was too far behind him. Patrick couldn't get to his son. "Perry?"

Vera said, "He hears you. He just gave me an okay sign."

"Hang in there. We're going to get you out of here, Perry." Patrick didn't care what Perry'd given her, the plan didn't change. He moved back into paddling position. Water was up to his ankles now. He feared the hole was getting bigger. He dug in and pulled against the water, but his canoe barely moved forward. Vera passed him. Perry was sitting up on the seat with his head cradled in his hands .

Susanne went by.

"Perry's awake, honey."

"Thank God."

"No change in plans. Getting him out of here is more important than ever."

"Okay. I'm just glad he woke up." Then she gave him a funny look. "Why aren't you moving?"

Patrick didn't want to panic her. "Waiting to talk to Pete."

She nodded, but she didn't look convinced. Her canoe left his behind. Patrick tried with all his might to make significant forward progress. It didn't go well. His brother caught up with him.

Pete said, "Are you all right?"

"I'm taking on a lot of water. It's slow going. But Perry woke up."

"Oh, man. That's great."

"We still need to carry him out. He can't hit his head again, Pete. We just can't take a chance."

"I understand."

"You take the lead. Get the women and kids to the far shore. Beach it before the waterfall."

Pete angled his path toward the far shore and paddled to overtake the women. He turned back and shouted Patrick. "How much further do you think?"

"It didn't look far on the map. I'd say another hundred yards or so. Unless the water speeds up, then get off the river immediately."

Pete raised his paddle in acknowledgement. He signaled the women to the right side of the river as he passed them. Patrick snuck a glance at the left shore.

CRACK.

THUD.

Patrick felt an impact but no pain. His brow furrowed. Was adrenaline masking the pain of a gunshot wound? He didn't think so. But he did think his canoe had taken a hit. *Another hole. Great.* He couldn't paddle away quickly, so his body was going to be an easy target. He stared back into the trees and rock formations on the riverbank, looking for the shooter. *Movement.* He saw Les was running with a rifle under his arm. Winthropp was just ahead of him. Two canoes were near the shore, and each man grabbed one.

"They're shooting. Keep moving. Pete, do you have your gun?" Patrick patted his own hip. Gun. *Check.* Knife in scabbard. *Check.*

"Yes," Pete shouted back.

"Take Perry and get to town. I'll meet you there."

Susanne turned. Her voice was near hysteria. "I'm not leaving without you."

"My canoe won't make it. But I'm armed."

"No!" she screamed. "Pete, go back for him."

He dialed his voice down to the tone he used on scared families before whisking their mortally ill and injured loved ones away from them. *Calm. Convey confidence.* "Pete, go on. Susanne, it's going to be all right." He blew her a kiss, keeping the prospectors in his peripheral vision. He was ready to duck if Les started shooting again. "Paddle, Susanne. Perry needs you."

The expression on her face gouged at his heart, but then she turned and started paddling hard and fast. *Good.* The group would take Perry and go for help. Now it was up to him to slow the prospectors down, or stop them altogether, to give the Flints a chance to get to safety.

And he knew that it would be far easier to do that without his family there.

CRACK. CRACK.

He ducked into the belly of the canoe. His focus had wandered, and he hadn't been watching. Hadn't ducked early enough. Not that it would do much good, other than make him a harder target to locate. The bullets would punch right through the sides of the canoe, if Les's aim was good. But these shots had gone wild. Patrick peeked over the edge toward the shore. Les was paddling and trying to fire at the same time. He wasn't reloading. If the rifle magazine held four shots, then it would be empty now. If it held more, then there was no telling how many bullets he had left. Patrick wished he knew.

CRACK. CRACK.

Wild again. *Good. Waste your ammo.* Six shots now. Patrick's mind raced. The prospectors were gaining on his sinking canoe rapidly. He needed a plan, but all he could come up with was to move. He sat up, low, and started paddling again. It was like running through sand with hundred-pound weights on each ankle.

In the distance, his family was dragging their canoes to the shore. Pete lifted Perry and eased him over his shoulder. Vera, Susanne, and Lana were gathering the rest of the kids. Susanne turned toward him one last time, her hand tenting her eyes. He didn't dare stop paddling. He tried to send her a message with the power of his intention. *Go. Go and take care of our boy and be safe.*

The family disappeared behind a tall rock face, Susanne last in line.

His family, safely away. His dad with the girls, safely upriver. He was relieved, but he also felt a strange energy course through him. He was free now to fight the prospectors without holding back. Like a man unafraid his family would be caught in the crossfire. To fight without a care for what anyone he loved would think of him. To fight them the way they deserved for what they'd done to his brother. His daughter. His niece. To all of them. Even, if his suspicions were correct, to the Hilliards. Because he didn't believe for one second that that grizzly would or could have killed three men with wilderness experience, although he knew the big bears wouldn't pass up the chance for a meal if one was left for them. *Left by Les and his gang.*

He stole a look back at the other canoes. Winthropp was closing in on him. The big man had twice the muscle mass of the much smaller Les. A lot more than Patrick, too. And Winthropp didn't have a canoe full of water. Patrick lifted his feet. There had to be six inches in it now. He eyed the waterline. Dangerously high, close to swamping.

He didn't have much time.

CRACK.

Seven. He saw a tiny splash about ten yards to his left. Was it still Les shooting? Patrick needed to be sure Winthropp wasn't firing now, too, and he risked another look back. No signs of a weapon on the bigger man. Both of his meaty hands on the paddle.

Patrick had an idea. If he could lure Winthropp close enough, he could put his paddle down and take Winthropp out with a shot from his own gun. He winced. Could he shoot another man at point blank range? Maybe he could just shoot to incapacitate him. But he knew that was always a bad idea. A wounded Winthropp was still a formidable foe. And he was much more likely to miss and waste ammo if he didn't shoot for the man's thick torso.

If Patrick shot, he had to shoot for keeps. He thought of his family. All of them. He knew he could do it, that he would do it, because he had to, to keep them safe.

He headed back toward the north side of the river, away from where the Flints had beached and hiked away. His canoe was barely wallowing along now, but he dug in and pulled like his life depended on it. Like Perry's, Trish's, and Susanne's did. Like those of his parents and his brother's family did.

He got the sensation that his canoe was speeding up. For a moment, he believed thoughts of his family had energized him. He'd gotten a second wind.

But then he realized what it was, and it wasn't a good thing. The *water* was moving faster. The falls were near. He had to make his next move quickly and get off the river before he was swept over. He aimed for a stretch of shore with a pebbly bank. It was next to a tumble of boulders. He didn't dare look back into the river at the prospectors.

He put his paddle down, got out his .357 Magnum, and raised his voice. "Winthropp, do you ever do what you want to do, or just what Les tells you to do?"

Winthropp answered with a growl. His voice sounded closer than Patrick had imagined it would be.

"What about you, Les? Are you a man, or do you just let Winthropp fight your battles?"

Silence. Patrick had hoped Les would answer. That way he could get a fix on the man's location.

CRACK.

The bullet pinged off a boulder, winging a chip of rock into the air. Eight shots. Patrick didn't know of any rifles with more than ten shots in the magazine, but that still left as many as two. More if Les had another loaded mag with him.

It was time to act. With a last mighty pull, he beached the canoe and stepped out. The ground under the water was rocky. Carefully, he scrambled to shore through them, barely noticing his ankle anymore. *No better painkiller than adrenaline.*

CRACK.

Nine. He sprinted the few yards to the boulders. Right before he reached them, he heard one last CRACK. Ten.

Something stung his hip. Pressure. A stinging, burning sensation. He'd been hit. Panting, he dove behind the giant rocks. He rolled, protecting his gun, then came to a stop and checked his hip. A patch of red was growing, spreading. He tested his weight on it by rising to his knees. It hurt less than he'd expected, was surprisingly stable. *Just a flesh wound.*

"Get out of that canoe and go after him," Les screamed.

Exactly what I wanted to hear. Patrick positioned himself behind the rocks for optimal cover. He cocked the revolver and peered around the edges of the boulders.

Winthropp must have taken Les literally. He jumped out before he reached the shore, then disappeared underneath the water. *Deeper than I would have thought.*

"No, you idiot, what are you doing?" Les screamed.

Blindly following your instructions.

Patrick took aim over the water, waiting for Winthropp to come up for air. He frowned. Why was the big man still under? Then, a hand broke the plane of the water. The fingers opened and closed, then it sank again.

"Winthropp?" Les yelled. His voice sounded more uncertain than angry now. "Come on out of there, now."

But Winthropp didn't surface. And after a minute, Patrick knew he never would. He slumped to the ground, stunned. Whether Winthropp had impaled himself on something or caught his foot under a rock, the man was drowning before their eyes. The doctor inside Patrick raged that he should do something. Save him somehow—the same man he'd been prepared to kill only moments before. But Patrick couldn't risk it. Not within easy range of Les and his gun. *But he's fired ten shots already,* one part of him said. Another part of him argued back. *He could have another magazine and ten more bullets in it.*

No. He was not going to try to rescue Winthropp. He still had to deal with Les, the man who most wanted to do his family harm. The man behind all of this.

"Winthropp!" the little man shouted. Then, softer, "Son of a bitch. Why'd you have to go and drown yourself, you idjit?"

Patrick snuck another look around the rocks. He heard splashing. Les, paddling. At first, Patrick thought he was headed for the bank. *That will work.* Patrick felt confident he could best the man one-on-one. But with a jolt, his eyes processed the scene. Les was turning his canoe. Turning and heading to cross the river toward where Patrick's family had gone.

With a roar, Patrick sprang to his feet and ran, the pain in his bad ankle and gunshot wound not registering at all. He launched himself at his own canoe, then, remembering it was filled with water, he stopped. Winthropp's had floated downriver and was headed for the falls. He tucked his gun in the back of his pants and dumped his own canoe out, then pushed it into the current and leapt in. It rocked, and he held on to both edges, helping it regain stability. Water started seeping in immediately. He reached for the paddle and started his strokes while still on his knees. He had to catch the bastard.

Les's head swiveled. He caught sight of Patrick and grinned at him. "You're going to make this easy by getting close enough to shoot before I go after your family?"

Patrick growled. He eased himself up to the seat and paddled harder, closing the gap between his canoe and Les's quickly with the help of the current.

Les laughed. He lifted his gun and took aim. Were there any bullets left? Patrick wasn't going to wait around to find out the hard way.

Patrick rose and, just as he dove into the water, he saw Les fumble for balance. As the icy river wrapped him in a shocking embrace, he heard the CRACK. *Damn. New magazine.* His boots, jeans, and long-sleeved flannel shirt became instant liabilities. He'd been a breaststroker on his high school swim team, but he struggled to execute the stroke underwater weighted down with his loose clothing. His hands struck his canoe. He grabbed hold of its side. The current was sucking him downstream at the same speed as his canoe now. Even with the cover of his canoe, he didn't dare raise his head out of the water for a breath. Instead, he opened his eyes. The water was shockingly clear. He saw explosions of white foam as the water collided with underwater rock formations. But he had one nice surprise. He was within a body's length of Les's canoe. His lungs were burning with lack of oxygen. Patrick didn't care. He released his canoe and pulled his arms through the water as he kicked. Then he sent himself with all his strength straight at the belly of the other man's canoe. His hands found its aluminum shell. He walked them up it and grasped the side rail. He kicked upward, then pulled down as his body descended back into the water. The water worked against him and kept the craft upright. He kicked again, drew a breath, and pulled like he was doing a chin up. The craft stayed upright for what felt like an eternity to him, then it tumped sideways. Under the water, he saw the bubbles and disturbance as Les fell into the river.

Patrick broke above the surface and gasped for breath. The sound of cascading water was deafening and close. He reached for the gun in his waistband. It was gone. He fumbled for his knife, but his fingers were so cold that he couldn't work the snap. He was running out of time, pulled along by the power of water moving at fifteen hundred cubic feet per second. He walked his hands around Les's sinking canoe. When he got to the other side, he saw Les attempting to swim for shore. The man was clearly not much of a swimmer, and his progress against the current was slow.

And then something hit Patrick's elbow. A paddle. He grabbed it. *A weapon.* With one arm, Patrick swam freestyle after Les. The prospector was only a few yards away. Patrick kicked. He pulled with one arm, using the paddle in the other for flotation. It kept his hips and legs from sinking which helped his kicks produce more power and speed, even without his other arm pulling. He was gaining on Les. Within seconds, he was close enough to grasp the man's shirt. He yanked him back toward him.

For a few agonizing seconds, the river pulled them downstream as one. Les squirmed in Patrick's grasp. He lifted something out of the water. A rifle barrel. He still had the rifle. How could that be possible? He aimed it at Patrick's face.

Could it fire after being submerged? Patrick wasn't taking a chance. He raised the paddle and slammed it down on Les's head.

THUD.

CRACK.

The rifle fired. *That answers one question.* Patrick closed his eyes, certain he was breathing his last, but he hadn't felt the sting of a bullet. He opened his eyes again and brought the paddle down on Les's head once more. He raised it for another blow, but he didn't get the chance.

Because he was falling. And Les was falling. Patrick saw spraying water. Rocks. Trees. Blue sky. And then nothing as he plunged down the face of the waterfall.

CHAPTER FORTY-FIVE: PAY

Jackson, Wyoming
Wednesday, June 29, 1977, Noon

Patrick

"Nice doing business with you," Brock said.

He stuffed a piece of paper into the cash register along with Patrick's money and a check, slightly hampered by the enormous bandage on his hand, the result of the marmot bite from a few days before. He'd informed Patrick that he didn't normally take out of town checks, but, due to Patrick's recent celebrity status in the Jackson news, and the fact that Patrick couldn't scrounge up enough cash to cover the total for the damaged canoes and lost paddles and life jackets, he'd made an exception. After he'd cleaned Patrick out of every last cent he had, of course.

Patrick stuffed his depleted wallet and checkbook back in his pocket. "And with you. Although I wish we'd picked a different week for our trip."

"Or a different river. We've got some nice ones you can check out on your next visit. The Snake. The Gros Ventre."

Susanne snorted. "That's not happening."

Patrick tried to catch her eye and smile at her, but she crossed her arms and studied a blank space on the wall.

Brock shrugged. "At least you all made it out alive."

Patrick nodded. "My son nearly didn't."

But he had. It had been four days since the Flints had escaped the Gros Ventre Wilderness with the help of none other than Klaus and Sylvie, who had been heading back up to the Yellowjacket Guard Station after a health scare of their own. Sylvie had been stricken with angina and stayed in the hospital overnight for observation. They'd rushed Perry, Susanne, and Patrick to the hospital, then alerted Wyoming Whitewater to the plight of the rest of the Flints. Brock and company had canoed down the river until they found Joe and the girls, then ferried them and the rest of the Flints to town, along with what was left of their equipment —including the canoe Patrick had ditched riverside when he went to check on the Hilliards. Joe and Pete had arranged for new tires and brought the vehicles down—even stopping to pick up the packs they'd ditched by the river. Of course, this meant yet another bill for Patrick. And Lana had set the group up in a motor court outside of Jackson, where they'd all enjoyed a low-key couple of days at the pool and playground.

Everyone except for Patrick, Susanne, and Perry. Perry had spent the time in a hospital bed with his parents by his side. His doctor had asked him if he remembered how he'd hurt his head. "My dad tripped me," he'd said, serious as could be. Patrick hadn't known whether to laugh or get a lawyer. "Um, no, son. You fell off a waterfall," he'd explained. Fortunately, the doctor hadn't thought Patrick had actually hurt Perry, and, instead of calling Child Protective Services, he said that people often didn't remember how their head injuries had occurred.

Perry's condition had improved rapidly from then on. He'd been lucky. The swelling and bleeding in his brain had already been going down on its own by the time they got him to the hospital. A few days of rest and hydration had been all he needed. Now, he was mostly recovered from the nausea and massive headache and had been released.

Patrick sympathized with Perry's ordeal, but he'd never had a severe concussion himself. Once he'd drank too much and been sick for days with a violent hangover. It was the closest he'd come, but even that fell far short.

"We were lucky. Perry was lucky," Susanne said. Her mouth was set in a firm, straight line.

Brock's eyes lit up. "Lucky you were with Mr. Flint. I read about you nearly bashing that dude's head in with our paddle. Like, I bet you're glad you sprung for that extra one now, aren't you?"

Patrick shifted before he answered, sending fresh pain through his sprained ankle and wounded hip. The bullet had only grazed him. He'd been fine after a few stitches. He'd refused treatment for the ankle, but he had bought an Ace bandage and kept it wrapped. His mom hadn't allowed herself to be taken to the emergency room either. She'd finally relented to an x-ray the next day. It hadn't shown a break, but she'd consented to a real sling afterwards.

"It depends. How much did it cost me again?"

Patrick didn't think it was worth mentioning that he'd actually used one of the Hilliards' paddles on Les's head. Les had survived the bashing and going over the waterfall while unconscious. Patrick cursed the thing in him that drove him to rescue bad guys. He'd done it again with Les when he'd seen him face down in the pool below the falls. Patrick had dragged him to the shore and stared at his blue-tinged face. He'd wrestled with what to do, but, ultimately, he'd given in to his moral code and administered CPR. It had sickened him when Les had spit up water and started breathing on his own. Thinking about hospitals and medical ethics, he remembered he needed to check in with the hospital in Buffalo. He was going to be a few days late getting back to work.

Brock roared with laughter.

"Well, as much as I spent, would you be willing to let me make a call on your phone?"

"Local or long distance?"

"Long distance." Patrick took out his wallet and opened it to show Brock it was completely empty inside.

"Keep it short." Brock handed him the phone.

Susanne was browsing the t-shirts, so Patrick went ahead and dialed the number, one of the few he knew by heart. He never memorized phone numbers on purpose. Why waste gray matter on something you could look up in the phone book?

The man that answered sounded cheerful.

"Wes? This is Patrick."

Wes Braten guffawed. "If it isn't the hero doctor. Are you back in town, Doc?"

"Gonna be late. That's why I was calling. I was hoping to talk to Dr. John."

"He's not here, but I'll leave him a message. I think things will survive without you. But you missed some excitement here."

"What's that?"

"Lamkin had her baby in our ER. A little boy."

He put his hand over the mouthpiece. "Susanne, Barb Lamkin had her baby."

Susanne dashed over to him, leaving the t-shirts swinging on their hangers. "In prison?"

"No. At the ER." He held the phone so she could hear through the ear piece, too. "Poor kid," Patrick said to Wes.

"Not poor kid. He's already got a foster family."

Susanne's eyebrows shot sky high.

"Who?"

"Deputy Ronnie Harcourt and her husband."

"Ronnie and Jeff?"

"Yep. Hey, Doc, an ambulance just pulled up. Gotta go. I'll leave that note for Dr. John."

"Thanks, Wes."

The connection was replaced with a dial tone. Patrick hung up and handed the phone back to Brock. With the close friendship between Susanne and Ronnie, he knew this baby—and a piece of Barb Lamkin—would remain in the Flints' lives for a very long time.

"Ronnie and Jeff will be great parents," Susanne said.

"Yes, they will."

"But this means the trial will be soon."

Out of the frying pan and into the fire. He hoped someday soon things around their house would be placid and boring. Murder and mayhem wasn't all it was cracked up to be. "I'm sorry," Patrick said. "Let's get out of here. Catch up with the rest of the group for lunch."

She nodded, her face grim. He put his hand on her back and headed toward the door. He could still feel her resistance to him in the stiffness of her posture.

"Thanks for letting me use the phone. Take care," he said over his shoulder to Brock.

Brock called after them, "I feel sorry for that other family, though. The ones they killed." He couldn't seem to drop the subject of their ordeal.

Patrick had stopped short at that, hand still on Susanne's back. The Hilliards. He couldn't get the memory of the grizzly gorging on their murdered bodies out of his mind. A recovery team had brought them back—what was left of them, anyway. It was enough, Patrick was told, to confirm they each had been shot. Patrick wanted Les, Hector, and Booger to pay for their crimes. Not just the murders of the Hilliards, kidnapping of Pete, Bunny, and Trish, and assaults against the rest of the Flints, but also the killing of Jimbo. Patrick had learned that, indeed, the dead body that had floated down the river a few days earlier was the prospectors' partner.

Diego and Winthropp had gotten off easy, dying in the wilderness, compared to the life in prison they deserved. Of course, both he and Pete had borne witness to Les's control over the men. Les should be held responsible for Diego's and Winthropp's deaths, too, in Patrick's opinion. Thank goodness, he and Pete would not be. They'd been honest with the sheriff and the FBI about the actions they'd taken to try to escape the men and their efforts to fight back against them. Law enforcement had assured them it would all be classified as self-defense, to Patrick's immense relief.

The door opened. Joe and Lana walked in. Joe was sporting butterfly bandages on his banged-up forehead. Lana—still wearing her safari outfit, but this time with a wide, bright yellow scarf or belt thing around her waist—was holding onto her husband's arm with the hand not in a sling. Patrick felt a pang of guilt. The entire family had been giving him the cold shoulder since they got back, Susanne most of all. He couldn't help but feel he was being cast as a scapegoat. It wasn't like he'd known Les and his men would be out on Trout Creek. And in the end, he'd fought Les in hand-to-hand combat and then survived going over a waterfall, which he thought ought to have been enough that they'd cut him some slack.

But, on the other hand, the family had been up there because of his choices. And he had pushed, he guessed. Well, he knew. He felt guilty about that. Even a little bit responsible. But not completely. And it didn't feel good having everyone hate him. Especially his wife.

Patrick waved to his parents, then said to Brock, "I feel bad for the Hilliards, too. Very bad." The words didn't begin to cover how he felt about them, but they were all he had. "They were good people. And all of it over gold nuggets in a cave."

Joe shook a copy of the *Jackson Hole News*. "It wasn't even gold. The fools kidnapped my granddaughters and went on a killing spree over pyrite."

Patrick's jaw dropped. "Iron disulfide."

"It was *fool's gold*?" Brock said.

Joe brandished a fist. "Those 'nuggets' were nothing but rocks with veins of pyrite. The paper said they were worthless. Like those lowlifes were."

"That's not all it said." Lana gently pushed her husband's arm down. "The cave is a treasure trove of Mountain Shoshone antiquities."

"The Tukudika." Patrick focused his complete attention on his mother. "And this was a new find?"

"Apparently so. Hand me the paper, Joe." She took it from him. "The article said the prospectors uncovered the entrance when they found a vein of what they thought was gold." She started reading. "The find included Sheep Eater soapstone pots, tri-notched arrow points, and an intact bow made from the horns of a bighorn sheep." She looked up. "And a lot more. They're calling it the most significant find in this area in the last fifty years."

Brock said, "I'll bet that's worth a fortune. Collectors line up for that stuff."

"Hopefully it will go to a museum." Patrick bowed his head. The beveled, bifacial knife he'd found on Booger. He was going to have to turn it over to whatever government agency took custody of the artifacts. That made him a little sad, but he knew it was right that it be studied and shared with the public.

Joe said, "The fellow I took the girls back from. Diega. He had some, too."

Lana's forehead crinkled. "Diego, dear."

"Same thing."

"Not exactly. In Spanish, the feminine ends in 'a' and the masculine in 'o.' If you call him Diega, you're sort of calling him a girl.'"

"Diega, Diego. Whoever he was."

"Actually, it was Hector, Dad." Patrick almost laughed. When Patrick had told Trish and Bunny that their "Mr. Smith" was actually named Hector, Bunny had said, "Whatever his name is, he's *not nice*." Patrick couldn't have said it better himself.

Joe glowered at his son. "This *Hector* had a pocket full of Injun relics."

Lana's face spasmed. "Indian, Joe."

"Injun, Indian. Same thing."

She sighed and shook her head. Patrick wanted to tell her not to bother, that no one could make his father more attuned to the feelings of other people, but that he loved her for continuing to try. And his father had other redeeming qualities. A lot could be forgiven of a man who ventured alone into a wilderness to rescue his granddaughters from killers.

Lana said, "The paper says the other two are singing like canaries. They say it was all that ringleader fellow."

"Les." Patrick nodded. That wasn't surprising.

"Apparently, he promised to split the gold with them if they'd help him get it out before July when the tourists and rangers overrun the whole area. They're also saying they didn't kill anybody. That it was all him."

"I hate to back up their stories, given that Hector took the girls and Booger tried to trap the rest of us, but Pete and I did hear them talking about Les forcing them to do things, and I believe that Hector at least didn't kill anyone. But he did plenty of other rotten things. Like kidnapping."

"Should have taken him out when I had the chance," Joe muttered. "I felt safer behind enemy lines in World War II than I did on this trip. Next time, you're visiting us in Texas."

The door opened again. Four blond kids walked in. Bunny, pulling Trish by the hand, and Perry, followed by Brian, whose big eyes were fixed on his older cousin.

"What are you kids doing here?" Susanne gave them the smile she'd withheld from Patrick.

Perry grinned under a big white bandage around his head. His face had regained some color and his buzz cut had grown out to the bushy stage. "Uncle Pete sent us. The pizza is ready. He said he's willing to let Dad have some if he pays for it." The greater Flint clan was next door, celebrating Perry's release from the hospital with a pizza party before Pete, Vera and their kids got on the road back to Texas with Patrick's parents.

Susanne put a hand over her mouth. *Is she hiding a smile?* Patrick sucked in a deep breath. Everyone was taking a chunk of his hide. *You have it coming.* But it sounded like this was meant as a way to earn his way back into their good graces.

"Fine," he said.

The kids all grinned.

To Brock, he added, "Anyway, thanks again."

Brock waved to them and disappeared into the back of his shop.

Trish stepped in front of Patrick. "Dad, I have something to ask you."

"What's that?" She looked beatific, so he braced himself. *She wants something.*

"Since I was so helpful and babysat the kids—well, Bunny—basically the whole trip, I was hoping you'd consider paying me. So I can use it for a down payment on a car." She batted her long, thick lashes.

"Uhh . . ." He looked to Susanne but again her eyes found something more interesting to gaze at, this time the wood floor.

"That reminds me." Joe pulled something from his pocket. It was a piece of paper. He handed it to Patrick

"What's this?" Patrick studied it. *A receipt?*

"The bill for repair of the station wagon."

"Repair? You mean for the tires? I already gave you a check for those."

"No. For the cracked windshield and dents you put in my car with the canoe you didn't tie well enough onto the Suburban."

Patrick frowned. He'd forgotten about that. The hits just kept coming. He wondered if he could find a second job in Buffalo, but he wasn't sure when he'd find the time to work one since his hours as a doctor were so demanding.

Susanne took the bill from his hand, her eyes widening at the number. He tried to take it back from her. He hadn't even seen the total yet. But she smiled and put it in her pocket.

"There are some things you're better off not knowing, Patrick." She turned to her father-in-law. "But it's a small price to pay for you bringing Trish back to us, you old softie, and your son would be *delighted* to cover it. He is the one, after all, who dragged us all the way up the Tukudika River where your car got beat up, Lana hurt her wrist, Perry nearly died, Pete was almost murdered, Trish and Bunny were kidnapped, you had to risk your life to find them, and the rest of us had to survive a grizzly, whitewater, and a group of deranged murderers." She smiled sweetly at Patrick, then winked.

His heart somersaulted. She might be enumerating everything that he'd pushed the family into, however well-intentioned he'd been, but that wink said she forgave him, and that was all that mattered to him now.

She turned back to her father-in-law. "I don't suppose you'd take a check, Joe? Patrick doesn't carry this much cash with him."

Joe frowned. "As long as you think he's good for it."

Patrick groaned.

"He may not be, but I am."

Brian was suddenly standing in front of his aunt. "Hey, Aunt Susanne, I almost forgot. Who was that guy you said was helping you, you know, right before we got in the canoes and the bad guys were shooting at us?"

Her face went pale.

Patrick touched her elbow. "What's wrong? Are you okay?"

She rolled her lips in, then released them. "I'm fine now. Then, maybe I was a little stressed out and imagining things. I, um, I thought I saw someone out there. An Indian man." She gave a nervous laugh. "Although he seemed pretty real at the time. Without him, I don't know if I would have found my way back to the group without the prospectors finding me first."

Perry came over to them. "I saw him, too. Right before Dad whacked Booger over the head."

Trish raised her hand. "Me, too. When Grandpa Joe rescued Bunny and me."

A huge grin spread across Patrick's face. "And me, too. Right before Perry fell off the waterfall on Trout Creek."

The four of them stared at each other.

Susanne shook her head. "What do you think it means?"

"That we've all come down with a case of Dad's Indian obsession," Perry said.

"Hardee har har." Patrick rubbed his forehead.

"Why would a Sheep Eater help us? White people like us drove them off their land and onto reservations." Trish looked perplexed.

Patrick couldn't explain how they'd all four seen someone who'd probably been dead for two hundred years, but even as a doctor, he'd seen plenty of things that science couldn't account for, and he was okay with that. "Good people are good people, I guess."

Grandpa Joe said, "This nonsense doesn't get you out of paying for the damage to my car."

Patrick laughed and put his hand on his mother's shoulder. "Come on, Mom. Kids. We can figure all this out over pizza. Let's leave Dad and Susanne alone with the repair bill so I don't lose my appetite."

He felt his mother's shoulder moving. She was pulling something from her wallet. Her back was turned to him, but he caught a glimpse of the one-hundred-dollar bill she slipped Trish, and the finger she put to her lips. But he kept his mouth shut and pretended he didn't see a thing.

Before he could exit the shop, his brother walked in.

"Hey, Pete. We were just on our way down," Patrick said.

"Can I have a word with you first?" Pete said.

Uh oh. "Sure."

The two brothers walked underneath "Snake Charmer," the rugged old boat Patrick had noticed during his first visit.

Pete took a deep breath. "I just wanted a chance to tell you that, in retrospect, I know I put you in a tough position, bringing the kids along for this trip. I'm sorry. I should have warned you ahead of time. Vera feels exactly the same way."

Patrick was so stunned he only nodded.

"We would have all been lost out there without you, even if I didn't always agree with you. I know things got really messed up. And we all were scared and frustrated. But you're the best, man." Pete clapped him on the shoulder. "I know it's not your fault things turned out like they did. Thank you for trying to give us the best vacation ever. It certainly turned out to be the most memorable one."

A strange heat built up behind Patrick's eyes. He opened his mouth, but no words came out. So, instead of speaking, he threw his arms around his brother. Suddenly, he wished Pete and his family weren't leaving. That he had more time with them all, but especially with his best buddy since they'd both been in diapers. He held back tears, but it was tough.

When he finally let go, Pete socked him in the arm. Patrick socked him back.

Patrick turned to the kids and his mother and said, "Are you guys coming or what?"

"Waiting on you, Dad," Trish sniffed.

Together, they walked out of Wyoming Whitewater, with Patrick trying very hard not to think about the number Susanne was writing on a check to his father at that very moment.

***

*For my grandmother, Lura—an amazing woman (ahead of her time in
many ways), who put up with a lot of B.S. in the name of love.
And for my husband Eric, who some might say does the same.*

OTHER BOOKS BY THE AUTHOR

Fiction from SkipJack Publishing

The *What Doesn't Kill You* Series

Act One (Prequel, Ensemble Novella)

Saving Grace (Katie #1)

Leaving Annalise (Katie #2)

Finding Harmony (Katie #3)

Heaven to Betsy (Emily #1)

Earth to Emily (Emily #2)

Hell to Pay (Emily #3)

Going for Kona (Michele #1)

Fighting for Anna (Michele #2)

Searching for Dime Box (Michele #3)

Buckle Bunny (Maggie Prequel Novella)

Shock Jock (Maggie Prequel Short Story)

Live Wire (Maggie #1)

Sick Puppy (Maggie #2)

Dead Pile (Maggie #3)

The Essential Guide to the What Doesn't Kill You Series

The *Ava Butler Trilogy*: A Sexy Spin-off From *What Doesn't Kill You*

Bombshell (Ava #1)

Stunner (Ava #2)

Knockout (Ava #3)

The *Patrick Flint Trilogy*: A Spin-off From *What Doesn't*

Kill You

Switchback (*Patrick Flint #1*)

Snake Oil (*Patrick Flint #2*)

Sawbones (*Patrick Flint #3*)

Scapegoat (*Patrick Flint #4*)

Snaggle Tooth (*Patrick Flint #5*): 2021

Stag Party (*Patrick Flint #6*): 2021

The What Doesn't Kill You Box Sets Series (50% off individual title retail)

The Complete Katie Connell Trilogy

The Complete Emily Bernal Trilogy

The Complete Michele Lopez Hanson Trilogy

The Complete Maggie Killian Trilogy

The Complete Ava Butler Trilogy

The Complete Patrick Flint Trilogy #1 (coming in late 2020)

Nonfiction from SkipJack Publishing

The Clark Kent Chronicles

Hot Flashes and Half Ironmans

How to Screw Up Your Kids

How to Screw Up Your Marriage

Puppalicious and Beyond

What Kind of Loser Indie Publishes,
and How Can I Be One, Too?

Audio, e-book, and paperback versions of most titles available.

ACKNOWLEDGMENTS

When I got the call from my father that he had metastatic prostate cancer spread into his bones in nine locations, I was with a houseful of retreat guests in Wyoming while my parents (who normally summer in Wyoming) were in Texas. The guests were so kind and comforting to me, as was Eric, but there was only one place I wanted to be, and that was home. Not home where I grew up, because I lived in twelve places by the time I was twelve, and many thereafter. No, home is truly where the heart is. And that meant home for Eric and me would be with my parents.

I was in the middle of writing two novels at the time: *Blue Streak*, the first Laura mystery in the What Doesn't Kill You series, and *Polarity*, a series spin-off contemporary romance based on my love story with Eric. I put them both down. I needed to write, but not those books. They could wait. I needed to write through my emotions—because that's what writers do—with books spelling out the ending we were seeking for my dad's story. Allegorically and biographically, while fictionally.

So that is what I did, and Dr. Patrick Flint (aka Dr. Peter Fagan—my pops—in real life) and family were hatched, using actual stories from our lives in late 1970s Buffalo, Wyoming as the depth and backdrop to a new series of mysteries, starting with *Switchback* and moving on to *Snake Oil*, *Sawbones*, and *Scapegoat*. I hope the real life versions of Patrick, Susanne, and Perry will forgive me for taking liberties in creating their fictional alter egos. I took care to make Trish the most annoying character since she's based on me, to soften the blow for the others. I am so hopeful that my loyal readers will enjoy them, too, even though in some ways the novels are a departure from my usual stories. But in many ways they are the same. Character-driven, edge-of-your-seat mysteries steeped in setting/culture, with a strong nod to the everyday magic around us, and filled with complex, authentic characters (including some AWESOME females).

I had a wonderful time writing these books, and it kept me going when it was tempting to fold in on myself and let stress eat me alive. For more stories behind the actual stories, visit my blog on my website: http://pamelafaganhutchins.com. And let me know if you liked the novels.

Thanks to my dad for advice on all things medical, wilderness, hunting, 1970s, and animal. I hope you had fun using your medical knowledge for murder!

Thanks to my mom for printing the manuscripts (over and over, in its entirety) as she and dad followed along daily on the progress.

Thanks to my husband, Eric, for brainstorming with and encouraging me and beta reading the *Patrick Flint* stories despite his busy work, travel, and workout schedule. And for moving in to my parents's barn apartment with me so I could be closer to them during this time.

Thanks to our five offspring. I love you guys more than anything, and each time I write a parent/child (birth, adopted, foster, or step), I channel you. I am so touched by how supportive you have been with Poppy, Gigi, Eric, and me.

To each and every blessed reader, I appreciate you more than I can say. It is the readers who move mountains for me, and for other authors, and I humbly ask for the honor of your honest reviews and recommendations.

Thanks mucho to Bobbye Marrs for the fantastic *Patrick Flint* covers.

Patrick Flint editing credits go to Rhonda Erb, Whitney Cox, and Karen Goodwin. The proofreaders who enthusiastically devote their time—gratis—to help us rid my books of flaws blow me away. Thank you all!

SkipJack Publishing now includes fantastic books by a cherry-picked bushel basket of mystery/thriller/suspense writers. If you write in this genre, visit http://SkipJackPublishing.com for submission guidelines. To check out our other authors and snag a bargain at the same time, download *Murder, They Wrote: Four SkipJack Mysteries*.

p.s. My dad is defying his diagnosis and doing fantastic now. Next up, *Snaggle Tooth* and *Stag Party* in 2021. It's my prayer we'll be collaborating on this series for many years to come.

ABOUT THE AUTHOR

Pamela Fagan Hutchins is a *USA Today* best seller. She writes award-winning romantic mysteries from deep in the heart of Nowheresville, Texas and way up in the frozen north of Snowheresville, Wyoming. She is passionate about long hikes with her hunky husband and pack of rescue dogs and riding her gigantic horses.

If you'd like Pamela to speak to your book club, women's club, class, or writers group, by Skype or in person, shoot her an email. She's very likely to say yes.

You can connect with Pamela via her website
(http://pamelafaganhutchins.com)
or email (pamela@pamelafaganhutchins.com).

PRAISE FOR PAMELA FAGAN HUTCHINS

2018 USA Today Best Seller
2017 Silver Falchion Award, Best Mystery
2016 USA Best Book Award, Cross-Genre Fiction
2015 USA Best Book Award, Cross-Genre Fiction
2014 Amazon Breakthrough Novel Award Quarter-finalist, Romance

The Patrick Flint Mysteries

"Best book I've read in a long time!" — Kiersten Marquet, author of *Reluctant Promises*

"*Switchback* transports the reader deep into the mountains of Wyoming for a thriller that has it all--wild animals, criminals, and one family willing to do whatever is necessary to protect its own. Pamela Fagan Hutchins writes with the authority of a woman who knows this world. She weaves the story with both nail-biting suspense and a healthy dose of humor. You won't want to miss *Switchback*." -- Danielle Girard, *Wall Street Journal*-bestselling author of White Out.

"*Switchback* by Pamela Fagan Hutchins has as many twists and turns as a high-country trail. Every parent's nightmare is the loss or injury of a child, and this powerful novel taps into that primal fear." -- Reavis Z. Wortham, two time winner of The Spur and author of *Hawke's Prey*

"*Switchback* starts at a gallop and had me holding on with both hands until the riveting finish. This book is highly atmospheric and nearly crackling with suspense. Highly recommend!" -- Libby Kirsch, Emmy awardwinning reporter and author of the *Janet Black Mystery Series*

"A Bob Ross painting with Alfred Hitchcock hidden among the trees."

"Edge-of-your seat nail biter."

"Unexpected twists!"

"Wow! Wow! Highly entertaining!"

"A very exciting book (um... actually a nail-biter), soooo beautifully descriptive, with an underlying story of human connection and family.

It's full of action. I was so scared and so mad and so relieved... sometimes all at once!"

"Well drawn characters, great scenery, and a kept-me-on-the-edge-of-my-seat story!"

"Absolutely unputdownable wonder of a story."

"Must read!"

"Gripping story. Looking for book two!"

"Intense!"

"Amazing and well-written read."

"Read it in one fell swoop. I could not put it down."

What Doesn't Kill You: Katie Romantic Mysteries

"An exciting tale . . . twisting investigative and legal subplots . . . a character seeking redemption . . . an exhilarating mystery with a touch of voodoo." — *Midwest Book Review Bookwatch*

"A lively romantic mystery." — *Kirkus Reviews*

"A riveting drama . . . exciting read, highly recommended." — *Small Press Bookwatch*

"Katie is the first character I have absolutely fallen in love with since Stephanie Plum!" — *Stephanie Swindell, Bookstore Owner*

"Engaging storyline . . . taut suspense." — *MBR Bookwatch*

What Doesn't Kill You: Emily Romantic Mysteries

"Fair warning: clear your calendar before you pick it up because you won't be able to put it down." — *Ken Oder, author of* Old Wounds to the Heart

"Full of heart, humor, vivid characters, and suspense. Hutchins has done it again!" — *Gay Yellen, author of* The Body Business

"Hutchins is a master of tension." — *R.L. Nolen, author of* Deadly Thyme

"Intriguing mystery . . . captivating romance." — *Patricia Flaherty Pagan, author of* Trail Ways Pilgrims

"Everything about it shines: the plot, the characters and the writing. Readers are in for a real treat with this story." — *Marcy McKay, author of* Pennies from Burger Heaven

What Doesn't Kill You: Michele Romantic Mysteries

"Immediately hooked." — *Terry Sykes-Bradshaw, author of* Sibling Revelry
"Spellbinding." — *Jo Bryan, Dry Creek Book Club*
"Fast-paced mystery." — *Deb Krenzer, Book Reviewer*
"Can't put it down." — *Cathy Bader, Reader*

What Doesn't Kill You: Ava Romantic Mysteries

"Just when I think I couldn't love another Pamela Fagan Hutchins novel more, along comes Ava." — *Marcy McKay, author of* Stars Among the Dead
"Ava personifies bombshell in every sense of word. — *Tara Scheyer, Grammy-nominated musician, Long-Distance Sisters Book Club*
"Entertaining, complex, and thought-provoking." — *Ginger Copeland, power reader*

What Doesn't Kill You: Maggie Romantic Mysteries

"Maggie's gonna break your heart—one way or another." *Tara Scheyer, Grammy-nominated musician, Long-Distance Sisters Book Club*
"Pamela Fagan Hutchins nails that Wyoming scenery and captures the atmosphere of the people there." — *Ken Oder, author of* Old Wounds to the Heart
"I thought I had it all figured out a time or two, but she kept me wondering right to the end." — *Ginger Copeland, power reader*

OTHER BOOKS FROM SKIPJACK PUBLISHING

Murder, They Wrote: Four SkipJack Mysteries,
by Pamela Fagan Hutchins,
Ken Oder, R.L. Nolen, and Marcy Mason

The Closing, by Ken Oder
Old Wounds to the Heart, by Ken Oder
The Judas Murders, by Ken Oder
The Princess of Sugar Valley, by Ken Oder

Pennies from Burger Heaven, by Marcy McKay
Stars Among the Dead, by Marcy McKay
The Moon Rises at Dawn, by Marcy McKay
Bones and Lies Between Us, by Marcy McKay

Deadly Thyme, by R. L. Nolen
The Dry, by Rebecca Nolen

The Body Business, by Gay Yellen
The Body Next Door, by Gay Yellen

Tides of Possibility, edited by K.J. Russell
Tides of Impossibility, edited by K.J. Russell and C. Stuart Hardwick

My Dream of Freedom: From Holocaust to My Beloved America,
by Helen Colin

FOREWORD

Scapegoat is a work of fiction. Period. Any resemblance to actual persons, places, things, or events is just a lucky coincidence. And I reserve the right to forego accuracy in favor of a good story, any time I get the chance.

Made in the USA
Columbia, SC
15 December 2020